Crystalle Valentino writes erotic fiction. She is the author of *After Hours*, *Personal Services* and *A Private View*, all available from Black Lace.

CRYSTALLE VALENTINO

A Private View

BLACK LACE

1 3 5 7 9 10 8 6 4 2

First published in 1998 by Black Lace, an imprint of Virgin Books
This edition published in 2013 by Black Lace, an imprint of Ebury Publishing
A Random House Group Company

The Random House Group L

Addresses   found at:

A CIP ca   Library

The R   rdship
C   on
org   on
FSC   eme
sup   ling
G   t:

Paper from
responsible sources
FSC FSC® C016897
www.fsc.org

ISBN 9780352347565

To buy books by your favourite authors and register for offers visit
www.blacklace.co.uk
Printed and bound by Clays Ltd, St Ives plc

Chapter One

'You think it's beneath you?' Phyllida said archly, her blue eyes glittering with catlike challenge.

'Of course I don't.' Jemma's own eyes, golden and starred with brown flecks, and thickly edged with dense black lashes, as black as her tumbling mane of gleaming hair, answered with a flat, obstinate glance. The tall, blonde woman was always taunting her, calling her too cautious, too reserved.

'Then do it. You might even enjoy it,' purred Phyllida.

Despite her dislike of the woman, Jemma considered the offer. Like Phyllida, she was a catwalk model, well paid and happy in her work which took her all over the world.

She was not a supermodel – her curvy white-skinned body held too much lushness, too great a promise of ripening pleasures to suit the current vogue for emaciated waifs, and it was the skinny waifs who usually made it to the top of the tree. However, Jemma was not one to waste time and effort in pointless envy. She was content with her progress. She was a modest success. So why bother to try something totally different, as Phyllida was suggesting?

The two very different-looking women were changing back into their own clothes after the London showing of the spring collection by a world-famous and flagrantly gay designer. Jemma endeavoured to consider Phyllida's words more carefully. It was hard to think in the sweaty bustle of the overcrowded changing room, packed as it was with semi-nude models and chattering dressers.

Behind-the-scenes was so different from front-of-house. Front-of-house was opulent chandeliers, huge ruched pink curtains, the gleaming white runway edged with now-empty spindly gold chairs on which fashion editors had sat throughout the last two hours of the show, jotting furiously on their notepads about this dress or that jacket.

Back here, there was only sweaty, noisy chaos.

Jemma knew only too well that a model's life was not particularly glamorous. Sometimes it could be downright tedious. And because of that knowledge, she felt a pang of interest in Phyllida's challenge; she had a hunger for new experience. She was sorely tempted to pick up the gauntlet that Phyllida had flung at her feet.

She was, after all, accustomed to displaying her body. And what was so different between displaying it only lightly and tantalisingly clad, as she often did, and revealing it nearly or even totally naked? She had a good body – not as tall as Phyllida's but firm, well-fleshed, and provocatively female. So why not?

Jemma found the idea a little daunting, but also erotic enough to start moisture dewing the warm, plump cleft between her legs. Embarrassingly, even though she was seated, clothed only in her unbuttoned sheer white silk blouse and about to pull on her knickers, her little pink bud was hardening in response to her thoughts and she found herself wriggling on her chair. Her nipples also stiffened and showed through the material of her blouse.

Phyllida giggled, her eyes shining with excitement as they beheld this stimulating sight. 'You see? You like the idea. Modelling that way for a photographer excites you. Particularly one of Dominic Vane's calibre. And he's so handsome too.'

Jemma put a protective hand over her mound in case anyone could see her getting wet. Some of the other girls and even a couple of remaining press photographers had started to look. Sometimes she wished her body were not so swift to rouse, even if her current live-in lover Steven found this a bonus: even when she was tired or angry, or annoyed with him for some reason, her wetness enabled him to enter her easily. Even now, thinking about Steven's hard, blond-furred body and straining upright cock had this effect, flooding her with welcoming lubrication, causing her pale-pink and perfect nipples to strain against the thin concealing fabric of her blouse, the soft touch of which only aroused them more. She shivered deliciously.

And, if she were honest, it was not only Steven's body

that stirred her. In fact she was beginning to get a little bored with Steven, who was an accountant and who had an accountant's penny-pinching mentality. No, what so perturbed her was the thought of that other body – Dominic Vane's.

She had seen his face in the gossip columns time and again; he was justifiably famous for his deeply erotic portraits of the women he so clearly adored. That cavalier's smile, the glinting green eyes, the hair that was thick, straight, nearly as dark as her own and even longer, and usually tied back in a tail. He was tall, she knew that. He was lightly muscled and lean.

Of course she had only ever seen him clothed, which was a pity. Jemma felt certain that Dominic Vane could rival Michaelangelo's *David* for beauty of body. She had already found him attractive, devastatingly so. But she had never supposed for one moment that she would have the opportunity to meet him, or work with him. The idea did excite her. Even more exciting was Phyllida's claim that he had specifically asked for her through the model agency because he so badly wanted to photograph her. She looked up at Phyllida, her hand falling away from between her legs.

A camera clicked and a flash fired, recording her readiness to face the challenge presented to her. Half annoyed and half amused, Jemma thought that there was no way a shot like that could get into the tabloids; it would be too sexy, even for them. The loitering male photographer, red-haired and clad in tight denim jeans that did nothing to hide a hard bulge of arousal, grinned at her. She smiled back. Clearly the shot would be for his own private viewing.

'Well?' demanded Phyllida, wiggling her naked bottom into the tight confines of her plush, burgundy lycra body. Her breasts, which were surprisingly heavy, swayed luxuriously as she pulled up the straps, and her pale-pink nipples vanished beneath the clinging material.

Jemma lazily stretched her arms above her head. She had observed Phyllida's jiggling breasts and wriggling buttocks with quiet appreciation, but now her eyes wandered back to the photographer. Poor man. He too had witnessed Phyllida's dressing and was soon, from the look of the hard outline rearing inside his jeans, going to have to find relief, or burst.

And so was she.

'I'll do it,' she said, and sighed a little because she had such urgent needs and, although she was growing dissatisfied with Steven, Steven would, for the moment, have to do.

Hurrying now in eager anticipation, Jemma demurely closed the sides of her blouse, sending a regretful glance to the handsome young photographer. She pulled her panties up over the provocative black triangle between her legs, and rose to slip into her tight black lycra skirt. It was too hot for tights or stockings and, with her slender legs naked, she squirmed her feet into high-heeled pumps.

Half-hoping he was still watching her, since she found his observation of her so stimulating, she raised her eyes, but he was gone. Ah well, she would go home now to Steven, and perhaps he too would be in the mood for pleasure.

Phyllida was smirking at her as she, too, dressed ready to depart for her chic London flat. It was across the teeming city from Jemma's own snug basement apartment.

'You see? You're a born exhibitionist, Jemma,' she said in an almost congratulatory tone. 'You love showing your body, so why not do it and get paid at the same time?'

'I do enjoy it,' Jemma had to wistfully agree, her mind and the frantic pulse of her sex still focused on the photographer. She imagined him developing the shots he had taken of her, and of how wanton she must appear in them, completely without shame: her legs open, everything exposed to him, her nipples as hard and tempting as ripe cherries.

Considering how he might react to such a sight was a delicious titillation for her. She pictured him in the red-stained light of the darkroom, his wide shoulders tense, his eyes gleaming with concentration as they beheld her voluptuous display. He would of course be intensely aroused. He might even have to unzip those ferociously tight jeans, for how could that huge rearing cock bear to be so cruelly stifled?

Lasciviously Jemma wondered about his penis, which would feel like silk-clad iron to the touch. Would the pubic hair that cushioned his impressive cock be the same vivid red as the hair on his head? He would have to free his balls, too, for they would be terribly hard and uncomfortable in clinging jeans, and his thighs would be rock-hard and covered with downy hair.

Jemma came back to herself to find that Phyllida was sniggering unkindly; she had been watching her vacantly staring face, rendered soft and flushed by lust.

'He went through there,' said Phyllida. She pointed to a door at the back of the room. 'I heard the dresser talking to him earlier. He's using a small room there as a temporary darkroom. He's shooting in black and white, he said, for atmosphere.' She gave a smile and shook her head. 'I can't blame you. He is rather gorgeous. Good hunting then, Jemma. See you.'

With Phyllida gone and the place emptying fast, Jemma wondered what she could be getting herself into. Packing up her bag, the thought struck her that Steve was not going to be pleased about her agreeing to model nude for Dominic Vane. Although they had a fairly open relationship, Jemma being exposed to a world-famous and quite notoriously womanising man was sure to annoy him.

She thought about the tedious journey home by taxi, the greetings, the inevitable argument and, far better, the endless lovemaking that would follow as they made up. Jemma went and tapped on the door Phyllida had indicated.

'Just a minute!' He had a deep voice, slightly gruff. She liked it; it was sexy.

When the door opened, the photographer stood there looking at her in wonder, as if her appearance had been a wish that had, against the wildest odds, come true. Behind him she glimpsed a bench topped by trays awash with chemicals, a small portable enlarger, a timer, a stool – all lit by a red globe that he had hung on to the wall. He had made the room into a cosy little lab all of his own. The handsome red-haired young man stepped to one side as their eyes met in silent communication, and Jemma stepped into the hot scarlet half-light with him.

'You were taking shots of me,' she managed rather breathlessly, turning to face him.

'I hope you didn't mind,' he said, his eyes prowling hungrily over her thinly clad body.

'No.' Jemma put her bag on the floor. His eyes were making her feel hopelessly, recklessly wet all over again. Her panties were moist and felt too tight, too restrictive. 'In fact I enjoyed it. And you helped me make up my mind about something.'

'Oh?' He looked surprised. 'What?'

'Modelling nude for a photographer who specialises in the erotic. I didn't think I could do it, pose naked in front of a man, but I really liked posing for you. And I want to reward you, for making me see that I was just being silly, that it would work out fine.'

'Reward me? How?' He was still; his hands at his sides. He was spare and muscular, just the type of man she admired, although her sexual tastes were varied. Looking down, Jemma could see that he too had become aroused again.

'By giving you a private, an *exclusive* view,' said Jemma archly. 'Right here and now.'

Her hands went to the front of her blouse, unbuttoning it slowly for his delectation. His tongue licked briefly at his lips, but otherwise he remained still, watching, waiting in the red dark of the little room which stained her pale skin to a warm and vibrant pink.

Jemma's nipples, when she uncovered them, were the colour of dark wine, and he gasped anew at their beauty as she dropped the silk blouse to the floor. Her breasts were round, high and gloriously full. She slid her hands up over her waist, over her ribcage, to cup them and lift them proudly. Each index finger stroked the rapidly hardening nipples with languorous delight, and his stifled groan of desire made her smile in satisfaction.

Then her hands released the big dark-tipped globes and meandered down. Sliding beneath her tight, short black skirt, they pulled down her panties while she bent at the waist. Her breasts swayed gently, arousingly, as she did so. Slowly she stepped out of the flimsy lace panties, wet now from her juices, then she straightened, hooked her fingers into the waistband of the skirt, and pushed that down too.

Jemma stepped free, wearing nothing now except her high heels. She was consumed by a ferment of joyous lust so intense that she just had to touch herself. As he looked on, she parted her long legs a little, took the first two fingers of her right hand and, pushing the thick, black hair of her pubes aside, she parted her labia, so that her clitoris, her inner sex, everything, was exposed to his eager eyes. Jemma held herself open for him, letting him see and share her joy.

'Do you like what you see?' Jemma asked him teasingly.

In fact there was no need to ask. His cock was a hard line beneath his jeans, his breathing coming fast. But it was all part of the game she was so enjoying, a delicious, delirious game, and her play aroused them both and enhanced their mutual pleasure.

'Oh yes,' he said throatily.

'Because if you don't,' she went on, her hand trailing lightly from her crotch up to her burgeoning nipples, stroking first one and then the other, moistening them with her own sweet juices, 'I shall simply dress and go away, instead of . . .' She deliberately let her voice trail away.

'Instead of what?' he asked in a strangled voice, his eyes glued to her lightly questing hand.

'Instead of letting you have me.'

He swallowed. 'You're beautiful,' he said, and reached out and doused the darkroom safe-light, replacing it with the dimly muted overhead one. Jemma blinked and glanced in concern at the trays of fluid on the bench beside the stool.

'Your prints,' she warned.

But he was taking up his camera. 'They don't matter. I'd rather shoot you like this,' he said huskily, raising the lens to his eye. 'Totally naked and ready for a man to take you. Look, your inner thighs are wet. And your sex looks moist and puffy, just like it did for me out there.'

He focused, and fired. The flash dazzled her. Jemma blinked, but soon recovered happily. It was warm in the room, comforting as a womb. She sighed, content, as he snapped again and again, directing her to lean back on the stool, open her legs wider, lift her breasts, lick her lips. It was all very enjoyable, but suddenly he groaned in distress and put a hand to his penis.

'I'll have to . . .' he said apologetically, trailing off his words to avoid saying something crude.

'What?' Jemma's dark eyes gleamed in anticipation of a treat. 'Take it out?'

'Yes.'

One hand still holding the small camera, he unbuckled his woven, tan leather belt and unbuttoned his fly. Now it was the man's turn to tease. His blue Chambray shirt was long enough to completely cover his upright cock. In disappointment Jemma watched as he hooked his fingers into the jeans and pushed them down so that they were crumpled around mid-thigh. The side-slit tails of the shirt allowed her to see that he wore no pants to restrain his obviously splendid organ, and revealed a patch of paler skin on each side of his hips, where he modestly wore trunks while sunbathing. She gave a little pout of displeasure as his cock remained concealed, although it pushed energetically at the shirt like a pole holding up a tent. Even his balls were hidden from her.

The photographer chuckled at her momentarily frosty expression, and took a photograph of her like that.

'Let me see it,' she pleaded.

'What? My arse?' He put the camera aside, grinning

rakishly, and turned around, flipping up the tails of the shirt. He had a glorious arse – taut and small and full of muscle, the skin on each globe fine and white in contrast to his lightly tanned thighs.

'It is lovely,' sighed Jemma, her emotions beginning to freefall into a veritable ferment of desire. Soon she would need him inside her; very soon. 'But I meant your cock.'

'My cock?' He looked at her jauntily over his broad shoulder. He dropped the backflap on his shirt and fiddled with the front of it. She fervently hoped he was unbuttoning it.

Presently, and much to her delight, he pulled the shirt off and it drifted to the floor amid her own clothes. 'There, you can see my back now. Women love backs. Broad backs, well-muscled. I work out, you know. And they love male buttocks.' He clenched his buttocks teasingly, and laughed at her groan of pure wanting. He turned, but again she was thwarted. His right arm and hand now concealed the glory of his penis from her. His chest was lightly furred and he had the obligatory 'six-pack' of abdominal muscles on show. His navel dipped sweetly, and his stomach was tightly toned. A bundle of ginger curls escaped the grip of his hand between his legs. But his balls were still hidden.

'Ask me,' he challenged, his eyes upon her freely displayed sex. Still perched upon the stool, Jemma leant back louchely against the bench, propping her still-shod feet upon the steel footrest, her knees spread invitingly wide. If Steven could see her now, she thought in faint amusement. He wouldn't be jealous though – or at least not much. Steven would be entertained by this little scene and, if he were here, he would certainly want to join in, watching the photographer have her and then having her himself; or perhaps even taking the photographer from behind while the photographer pleasured himself inside her. Steven could, when the mood took him, be remarkably inventive.

This arousing thought made her press herself urgently upon the sticky plastic cover of the stool. 'Show me,' she moaned.

He removed his arm and Jemma's dearest wish was at last granted. His fine full penis lunged from hiding to seek fulfilment. The shaft was lined with veins; the head, meaty and full and sporting a dewy droplet of pre-come in its eagerness to proceed. His balls, furred with thick ginger curls, were taut with readiness.

'Oh, lovely,' murmured Jemma appreciatively. 'And now come here.'

He came obediently and stood with suggestive close-ness between her parted legs. Slowly, savouring the moment, his hands rose and each one claimed a breast, kneading it, caressing the aching nipples. Whispering his pleasure in them, his ginger head dipped and, as his hands lifted the soft flesh of her, his tongue took first one hard bud and then the other into his mouth to be kissed and sucked.

Jemma arched her back in response, relishing his attention, her hands finding enjoyable work to do with his cock. Satiny to touch, it thrummed with energy as she gently stroked it. Then, becoming bolder, she slipped her index finger over the wet opening of his glans and rubbed it. His murmurs of delight fell upon her ears, soaking into her consciousness like the sweetest, rarest honey. Encouraged by her passion, his mouth took her nipple more firmly, his teeth grazing lightly then his lips sucking urgently. Jemma's small inarticulate cries at this extremity of pleasure made his hands go to the hot, wet cave between her legs. Clasping her engorged clitoris between thumb and forefinger, he parted her labia and, with his long middle finger, sought her centre of pleasure.

Easily his finger entered her to the hilt. He massaged her tender clitoris, and then eased another finger inside her, then a third, pushing and retreating, pushing and retreating, in a teasing parody of copulation. Although his fingers were long, and his hands pleasingly big, Jemma felt a desperate need now for even deeper fulfilment, and was glad when he withdrew his fingers, drying them roughly on her pubic hair, then clasped his penis and brought the trembling head to her wet sex.

'Oh yes,' muttered Jemma, as his glans shouldered its way inside her, followed by the whole width and deeply satisfying length of his full, young cock.

Moaning, he thrust hard into her after that first tentative entry, so that his balls slapped against her. Then he withdrew almost totally; then he was in again, entering her now each time with a harshness and need that would almost have been painful, had she not been so completely aroused. The sensations he engendered were exquisite; her orgasm was hovering deliciously close. Out again, almost; then in – in so hard, so brutal. Then out and gone from her, so that she gasped, bereft and amazed – and then the door came open suddenly, and a man's tall outline filled the frame.

Jemma almost yelped with shock, but the young photographer's glance over his shoulder was far from embarrassed at the state they were in, naked and hungrily seeking satisfaction like wild young animals. His look was cursory and accompanied by an easy smile.

'She's perfect for you, Dom,' he said, and Jemma saw that, far from being deflated by this intrusion, his penis, gleaming slickly from her own juices, was waving lustily between her legs like a divining-rod over water, so keen was he to continue.

The man – 'Dom' – stepped into the room and closed the door behind him; he sauntered closer to the busy couple. Torn between feeling half-mad with unsated desire and at the same time desperately embarrassed, Jemma automatically covered her breasts, attempting uselessly to conceal them, creating an unconscious picture of such guilty excitement that her eager young lover groaned at the sight. She tried to close her legs, but could not, and succeeded only in clamping her thighs more firmly about her lover's hips.

'Put it back in her,' instructed the intruder with obvious amusement. 'Or you'll come all over her belly instead of taking full measure. She's nearly there, too. I'll watch.'

To Jemma's amazement the man stationed himself

slightly to the side of them so that he could view the proceedings more clearly. Jemma looked at him in amazement as he stood there with his arms folded across his chest, as detached as if watching two animals mating in a wildlife programme.

Distracted though she was, Jemma noted that he was in his mid-thirties, and was lean and sparely muscled, like a hunting cat. He looked somehow familiar. His face was sculpted, strong and with stupendous cheekbones, and his hair was as thick and straight and black as her own, but even longer and worn loose. His brows almost met in the middle, an indicator of a stormy temper, and his eyes were chillingly, piercingly green, like pale jade, as they stared at her nakedness.

'Ahhhh!' squealed Jemma as the quivering, heated cock once again drove deep into her. She hadn't been expecting it, she had been too busy looking at Dom; but as her eyes met his it was suddenly as if *he* was between her legs, fucking her. Dazedly her gaze dropped to his open-necked black silk shirt and down the front of the soft black cord trousers he wore. The material bulged hugely at his crotch. His eyes might be cool, but he definitely found the sight of their lovemaking a turn-on.

'Uncover your tits,' Dom ordered, and Jemma found her hands dropping to clutch the stool and steady herself against the photographer's heavy thrusts. She was hotly aware of her breasts bouncing enticingly as the young man so thoroughly fucked her; and of Dom's eyes on her nipples, which were hard as peachpits. She was panting now with each thrust, and so was the photographer. Dom's eyes drifted down to her sex, where she and the red-haired young man were joined in a medley of black and gold, and suddenly the sweet sensations of climax gripped her, arching her back like a bow, making her clasp wildly at the young man and, by so doing, sending him too hurtling over the precipice of desire into a long, throbbing orgasm.

When at last they were spent, and the photographer withdrew from her, Dom said: 'You're right, Neil, she's perfect.' To her, he added: 'I'm Dominic Vane. How do you do?'

Chapter Two

'And did he proposition you?' asked Steven when she tentatively broached the subject of Dominic Vane at home that evening.

'No.' Well, he hadn't. The truth was, she rather wished he had. Dominic Vane exuded a powerful allure, as did all famous men. Even now, a little tired though she was after the day's exertions, the thought of his eyes feasting coolly upon her body while the red-haired photographer fucked her, was enough to bring a hectic flush back to her cheeks.

Steven looked at her shrewdly. Not for nothing was he a top-flight accountant; he rarely took things on face value, and was always prepared to delve deeper; to explore every avenue until he had all the facts.

'But you wanted him to,' he breathed, emptying the last dregs of chilled Sauvignon Blanc into his glass and placing the empty bottle on the floor beside the sofa. They had enjoyed a leisurely dinner, and were both feeling relaxed. After her experience in the darkroom,

Jemma was feeling particularly mellow, sipping her wine, inclined to confide.

'He's very attractive,' she said in massive understatement.

'I thought I read in one of the arts reviews that he hadn't even had an exhibition in over a year. The critics were saying he'd lost it.'

'Lost it?'

'His talent. His muse, if you like, had apparently deserted him.' Steven smiled wryly. 'Perhaps he wants you to fulfil that function.' His mouth twisted. 'And a few others, I don't doubt.'

Jemma considered this. Having introduced himself to her in such strange and stimulating circumstances, Dominic had then pressed a card bearing the address of his London studio into her hand, saying curtly: 'Tuesday at eight, then.'

After which, he had departed with disappointing speed, even before the two young lovers had time to dress. Thinking of fulfilling the function Steven had so clearly alluded to was by no means distasteful to her. It was even enough to make her feel inclined to make love again, right there and then. And Steven was good-looking, too, she reminded herself. She had always admired his rather austere looks, even if he did sometimes break their unwritten first rule as a free-loving couple by displaying a boringly possessive streak.

'So, who have you been fucking then?' asked Steven crudely, his hazel eyes glittering with lust, his own rough talk arousing him. 'If not Dominic Vane? I can smell sex on you.'

Jemma shrugged lightly, holding the chilly glass against the hot skin of her throat. Her eyes grew dreamy. 'It was another photographer,' she admitted with a rueful smile. 'In fact, it was a set-up – almost a conspiracy.'

'What was? You mean someone tricked you into spreading your legs for this other guy?'

'Not exactly.' The whole thing had been master-minded by Dominic, she didn't doubt that. But what he had hoped to prove or achieve by it, she as yet had no idea. A frown furrowed her pale brow briefly. 'Phyllida was keen I should take the job with Dominic, and he'd already checked I was free with the agency. Then Phyllida pointed me in the direction of this other photographer, who had been taking an interest in me all day.'

'Watching you strip off backstage,' guessed Steven.

'Yes.' Jemma's eyes lowered thoughtfully. As she had suspected, Steven was quite turned on. He shifted a little on the sofa, his hand going to the crotch of his light-tan-coloured trousers to ease the obvious discomfort there. 'And then,' she went on, 'when we were, well –'

'Conjoined? In the act of copulation?' suggested Steven a bit breathlessly.

'Yes.'

'Naked?'

'Yes, we were both naked. Then Dominic came in

unexpectedly, and the photographer told Dominic that I'd be perfect for him.'

'What, the guy had his cock stuck inside you, and he's making conversation with this other guy who's just charged in unannounced?'

'Yes.'

'And you're perfect why? Because you enjoy getting laid?'

'Because I like to pose, I think. I didn't realise it until today, but I do.' She put her empty glass aside and gazed into the flames that leapt hypnotically in the fireplace. 'I liked the photographer looking at me, taking shots of me. And I liked Dominic seeing me that way, too. It was exciting.'

Steven smiled. 'I like seeing you that way myself,' he said, and took her hand and placed it upon the urgent bulge between his legs, squeezing her flesh to his cock through the thin material of his trousers.

Jemma smiled too, eager to please. She rubbed his sex gently so that it jerked and strained beneath her hand. She hadn't even had time to bathe yet; she had time only to strip off her dayclothes and slip into her Janet Reger peach silk teddy to relax in, when Steven had called out that the dinner was ready. No wonder he could smell sex on her; she must reek of it – of another man's penis and skin and caresses – but, luckily, Steven was finding all this arousing rather than an annoyance. Or so she thought, until he spoke again.

'I suppose I really should punish you for your infidelity,' he said, eyeing her beadily.

'Oh?' Jemma's mouth opened and her tongue slowly travelled over her lower lip. 'Punishment' was a favourite game of Steven's – one she always joined in with relish.

'Yes.' He leant back upon the sofa. 'Come here.'

Jemma moved closer so that she was kneeling on the sofa beside him. She leant over and placed her glass upon the floor and, as she straightened, Steven slid one spaghetti-thin strap of the teddy down her arm, sending the silken cup of the shimmering garment slithering away to uncover one breast.

'Like an Amazon,' murmured Steven, his palm now lubriciously rubbing her hardening nipple. 'One breast naked, the other covered.' He slid the other strap down, too, and the insubstantial material descended further, settling about her hips. Steven lounged back and beheld with a connoisseur's delight the splendour of the two fully exposed globes, their skin so milky-pale, their nipples so dark and so enticingly erect.

'Unzip me,' he breathed, and Jemma, her breath coming in gasps of impending excitement, gladly complied, her fingers swiftly delving into his fly to push down his boxer shorts and release his eager penis. It sprang out like a jack-in-the-box from its hiding place, long and slim like Steven himself, and Jemma stroked it lovingly with her cool fingers until it twitched with desire, seeking greater pleasures.

Jemma leant over his lap, kissing the hot, wavering head of his cock. When Steven groaned his acquiescence to her attentions, she poked her tongue into his cock's little slit, salty with love-juice, and flicked at its most sensitive core. Then, with butterfly-like movements of her tongue, she worked her way down the long stem of his penis, before returning with a promising suck to its tip, before slipping it fully into her mouth.

'No, not yet,' muttered Steven through gritted teeth, grasping a handful of her hair to bring her head up and away from his already wild state of arousal. Desperately he clasped the base of his cock, holding off the orgasm that threatened to shower her breasts with his come. 'Lie down across my lap,' he ordered, his voice harsh with the effort of such restraint.

Accepting her punishment, Jemma positioned herself across him as he asked, so that she was face down on the sofa. Her crotch was separated from his mighty stem only by the thin material of her underwear.

'That's it. Now spread your thighs a little,' Steven prompted. 'Like you did for that photographer, remember?'

Jemma willingly did so, bringing her rigid and aching clitoris into even closer proximity to his cock. She moaned her need of him, and he laughed. His hand, which had rested upon the plump curve of one scarcely concealed buttock, moved between her legs and pulled at the skimpy material covering her secret place, so that the two little poppers sprang apart and the fabric fell loose. With deliberate slowness Steven rolled the teddy up, uncovering her flaring hips and pale buttocks and the deep valley between them, until the garment was nothing but a broad belt of silk about her small waist.

'I love your arse,' mused Steven, stroking the fleshy mounds lightly. 'You naughty girl.'

The first smack across her backside tore a small shriek of surprise and consternation from Jemma, but Steven continued anyway. He was spanking her bare-arsed, like a licentious headmaster taking liberties with a naughty schoolgirl. Jerking up on to her elbows, her breasts swinging free and naked, she shot him a look of protest over her shoulder. Another blow fell, and another, stinging and sensitising her soft flesh until she felt her backside must be glowing pink. It felt like a radiator giving off heat.

Unfortunately not only her buttocks were getting hot. When Steven stopped administering her punishment, he eagerly pushed the twin hillocks of her arse wide apart, admiring the tight magenta rosebud of her anus, her wet pink lips, and her hungry swollen clitoris – all so alluringly fringed with curling black hair. His fingers probed lightly at her, and Jemma stiffened in ecstasy, her fingernails driving deep into the sofa's soft velvet moquette.

'Steady,' he soothed her, and one questing finger slipped easily into her well-lubricated vagina while his thumb made delicious circles around her clit.

Jemma almost sobbed aloud in anguish when his hand left her. She could feel his penis, hard as rock and trapped beneath her, and she wanted it desperately to be inside her where it belonged. When she felt his cock again she leant into it, arching her back gladly, eager to receive him but the intruder was cold! Not hot like his cock, not warm like his fingers, but cold!

She froze in surprise and glanced back to find that he was fucking her with a candle while she ground her clit into his lap. Sighing in acceptance because it felt so good, she bent her head and allowed the punishment to proceed. It was curiously arousing, this thing that was as thick as a man's cock but without a cock's hot responses. Her breath was becoming ragged – she only wanted him to continue, never to stop – and her sex dragged at the inert thing, making sucking sounds as Steven drew it in and out of her more and more swiftly until, finally, she sighed in relief as her orgasm crashed her on to a far, peaceful shore and left her there, shipwrecked.

Moaning deliriously, Jemma was aware of Steven lifting her hips, of him coming out from beneath her so that he now knelt behind her on the springy sofa. Over her shoulder she watched dreamily as he placed a cushion under her to lift her, then she watched him push down his trousers and underpants to free his penis, which she could see was so hard and ready that it was pressed up tight against his stomach. His balls, clouded in brown hair, bobbed beneath it like chestnuts. Steven had to almost force his cock down by clasping it in his hand. Presently, in satisfaction, Jemma felt his maleness nosing at her opening, then pressing inside.

Oh, so much better than the fat chilly candle! she thought, and murmured her appreciation of his fleshy heat, his size, his strength, as he pumped energetically into her, at last delivering his spurting tribute with a cry of pleasure which sent Jemma spiralling dizzily into ecstasy.

Later, in bed, Steven took her again and, afterwards, while they lay in a haze of satiation, he said: 'You really want to do this thing with Dominic Vane?'

Jemma shrugged with studied nonchalance, but inside she was seething with eager curiosity about the mysterious photographer.

'It'll be a change from catwalk work,' she said, stifling a yawn of feigned boredom and sleepiness. 'That's all.'

'I'm away next week.' Steven yawned too. 'Munich. Business.'

So much the better, Jemma thought happily. That way, if anything exciting developed, Steven would not be around to cramp her style.

'I'll miss you,' she said with a smile, but his answering smile was cynical. They both knew where they stood in the relationship, and next week might be the opportunity both had been secretly seeking for some time – to look elsewhere, to spread their erotic wings, to break free.

'What, with Dominic Vane snapping you in the nude?' Steven laughed and switched off the light, plunging the bedroom into darkness. 'I shouldn't think so.'

Jemma stared into the peaceful dark, thinking about what Steven had just said: Dominic Vane, photographing her in the nude. But in her imagination it was Dominic who was naked, broad-chested and narrow-hipped, dark hair arrowing down the front of his body and thickening around a fine cock that was prodigious in its dimensions and erect above a pair of very full balls. She pictured him that way, glowering at her in concentration through the lens.

Admit it, Jemma, she mused to herself. You want him like crazy.

It was true, she did.

And I'll have him, she thought in determination before she fell into a deep and untroubled sleep. No matter how hard he tries to fight it. I'll have him.

Chapter Three

On Tuesday evening, Jemma took a taxi to the swish address in the high-class residential area of Kensington that was on Dominic's card. She had prepared carefully for this assignment, wearing only loose-fitting clothes so as not to mark her delicate skin. Elasticated or over-tight items were out. She carried her beauty case containing her make-up and all sorts of equipment to restyle her hair if necessary. For the moment, not sure of Dominic's requirements, she had left it hanging loose. She wished to impress Dominic with her professionalism, even while her heart pounded frantically in her breast and her palms were clammy with the onset of very unprofessional nerves.

At the door she was admitted by a startlingly good-looking young man, whom she guessed was not yet twenty, with dark, liquid-brown eyes, a curly mop of dark hair and a struggling goatee beard. She wondered what he was doing here. Perhaps he rented a room there. It seemed unlikely; the place was too palatial to indicate a need to take in lodgers. Well, perhaps he was a relative of Dominic's, or a pupil. She mused upon this little puzzle while the youngster led her up flight after flight of stairs.

'Dom has the attic for his studio,' he explained over his shoulder, blushing a little as he looked back at her.

Jemma smiled at the boy. Just as well I'm fit, she thought. She worked out at the gym twice a week, and swam as often as she could. Nevertheless the stairs seemed endless, winding ever upwards, until finally they came to a crooked little azure-blue door and she was led into Dominic's studio.

The studio was vast, and stretched the whole length and width of the grand old house. The floor was sanded and varnished warm pale pine, with no carpets; and the ceiling was supported by massive exposed beams studded with glaring spotlights. The windows were completely covered in a rich, plain cream fabric which was neatly drawn against the night. All around the perimeter of the big room, monochrome prints of varying sizes were hung. Jemma instantly recognised Dominic's distinctively sensual style in the work. Everyone knew Dominic Vane's style. His work was instantly recognisable – much copied, slickly publicised and often hotly debated. What Jemma saw next startled her somewhat.

Dominic was there, wearing tight thigh-hugging jeans and an open-necked white shirt. A tripod and large-format camera was set up and ready. But there was another man set up to shoot, too. A man in his fifties with a fine figure, sparkling blue eyes, and a sweep of distinguished silver hair offset by a deep healthy tan. As Jemma watched, the youngster who had shown her to the studio took his place behind a third tripod and camera, and smiled shyly back at her.

Jemma looked at Dominic in confusion. Then she saw that behind him, tacked to a cork noticeboard, were the shots the photographer had taken of her in the darkroom at the fashion show last week. Shots of such extreme sexual abandon that she felt herself begin to colour every bit as much as the young man had when he looked at her.

'Shall we get on?' Dominic prompted her coolly.

'But I understood that I would be posing for you alone,' objected Jemma, finding her voice at last.

'Did I say that?' He raised an eyebrow.

'Well, no, I suppose not.'

'Well then.'

Jemma considered the situation. What did it matter, really? The presence of the two other men was a little disappointing, delaying the moment when she would have Dominic to herself, but she could wait. 'Is there a room where I can get changed?' she asked.

'Changed?' Dominic grinned at that, and looked at the two other men – the elegant older one, and the shy, handsome youth, both of whom smiled back, amused at her folly.

'My dear girl,' said Dominic, 'portrait photographers are like doctors. To a doctor your body is just blood, bone and tissue. To us it is merely angles, planes and curves. Undress in here.'

Which was all very well, Jemma thought a little crossly, but she had yet to have a doctor examine her while sporting a thundering great erection such as Dominic had right now! By no means ashamed of her body – and sensing he was testing her in some way – she shrugged, put her small case on the floor, and slipped off her raincoat. Without fuss or demur, she pulled her red shift dress over her head.

There!

But suddenly she lost her nerve as she glanced around at the eagerly staring men. Even the handsome youngster was erect, although he was trying in embarrassment to conceal the fact beneath his baggy sweater. The older man too was displaying a fine hard outline beneath his trousers. As Jemma's eyes rested on it, it surged needfully. Her eyes rose to the twinkling blue eyes, the hawklike face, and she couldn't suppress an answering smile.

She still wore her red mini-slip, cut low on the breast and with a tiny frill around the hips. It was so short that if she moved suddenly, her pubes peeped from beneath the hemline and her buttocks were partially uncovered. Trying not to think too much about what she was showing – after all, very soon she was going to show far more – she walked over to the gold, velvet-covered chaise longue Dominic indicated to her. It had been placed in front of a large, plain canvas background screen amid a forest of gold-tinted flash umbrellas. Tentatively Jemma sat down, trying to keep her legs together. She knew very well that they could see beneath the little skirt of her slip to where her dark bush was exposed, and the thought of that heated her cheeks and made her nipples pout.

'We can't start with you wearing that thing,' Dominic pointed out, distractedly checking the focus.

'I thought you were going to photograph me,' retorted Jemma, still a bit miffed at his omission.

'I might. First, I am also seeing how you react under more difficult conditions. This sort of modelling's tough, you know. It takes patience, and strength.' His hungry green eyes dropped to the provocative red slip. 'And guts.'

'Like taking photographs?' snapped Jemma, growing hotter from the hard sweep of his eyes.

'A bit.' He smiled and looked straight at her. 'You weren't this timid last week. Alastair and James have already seen the photographs of you; they know all about your glorious tits and that your crotch is covered in hair as black as midnight. They can see your crotch now, as you very well know, and it's exciting them, which must be obvious. Just look at the staff on young James – he's bursting.'

Jemma looked, and realised that Dominic did not exaggerate. The young man was trying to conceal his arousal, but without much success. She smiled at him in sympathy and relented, grasping the hem of the mini-slip and tugging it off over her head, then tossing it to the floor. The three men were silent. Dominic's expression was triumphant.

'You see?' he said to his fellow workers. 'Alastair?' he queried.

'Magnificent,' agreed Alastair, his cock tenting his trousers outrageously.

'No need to ask James's opinion,' said Dominic slyly, and young James half-smiled, squirming and blushing as he beheld Jemma's nudity.

Jemma sat there eyeing the three of them, her legs placed primly together, her arms held loosely at her sides. Really, this was all very strange and extremely stimulating! She had come here expecting Dominic to be alone. Actually, she had banked on it, and had hoped to seduce him that night. But no; he was playing out one of his curious games again, and she was highly entertained by this one. So entertained that her nipples were already very hard, and the feel of the soft, nubby velvet of the chaise longue beneath her swollen sex was very pleasing.

'We'll have her hair up, don't you think, Dom?' asked Alastair.

Dominic shrugged. 'Just as you like,' he said, and looked at her expectantly.

Jemma could have kicked herself. She had left her beauty case, with her grips and brushes in, by the door. Now she was going to have to walk over there without a stitch on and fetch it.

Rising, she sent a smile to James and to Alastair – but not to Dominic; she was still a little piqued by his duplicity – and walked with apparent calm over to her case. In fact she felt anything but calm, being all too aware of the picture she must be presenting to her three avid watchers. Try as she might to tense her muscles and so restrain them, her breasts jiggled freely as she walked, and her pearly-white buttocks wiggled too. Embarrassingly, the feel of the warm air of the studio on her naked skin, the sheer eroticism of strolling about naked, and the sensation of their admiring eyes upon her, all combined to awaken her sex almost unbearably, so that as she stooped to collect her case, she was obliged to press her thighs together quite firmly to muster some restraint.

Straightening self-consciously, she turned and walked back to the chaise and sat down, this time crossing her legs to conceal the fact that her arousal was causing her a problem. If they looked closely, they would be able to see her slick wetness and the swollen lips of her labia. Looking up, her eyes caught Dominic's, and his knowledge of her arousal was written plainly on his face.

Jemma put the case upon the chaise, unfastened it, and removed her brush and two large hairclips. Slowly she brushed the long dark hair up from her nape, her belly tautening with each stroke, her breasts swaying heavily from side to side as she moved. Young James groaned aloud as she lifted her arms to fasten the hair up on top of her head with the clips, then she placed the case on the floor and straightened in readiness.

'Very nice,' said Dominic dryly. 'But unfortunately, your display has aroused our young friend too much for him to be able to concentrate on his work, so perhaps, instead, we should include him in the pose. Don't you think, Alastair?' he asked his elegant older companion.

'That would be good,' agreed Alastair.

'Over by Jemma, then,' Dominic instructed James, and the young man rose nervously and approached the chaise. Jemma smiled up at him encouragingly. 'Clothes off, I think, James,' said Dominic.

Feeling the young man's embarrassment, Jemma discreetly looked aside while he peeled off his clothes. When she looked back, he was naked, his pale well-muscled body sparsely furred with fine dark hair, and his very lively young cock pointing to the ceiling in its enthusiasm for this exercise. As James approached the chaise awkwardly, his penis bobbed about and, feeling it doing so, his blush deepened, but Jemma's smile reassured him.

'Something like Rodin's Kiss, James,' prompted Dominic.

Alastair was already focusing and snapping busily, but Dominic was simply watching the little tableau before him with arms folded across his chest and a thoughtful expression on his face. Jemma felt a stab of annoyance at him. What was he playing at? He had claimed to want to shoot her, and so far he had shown absolutely no inclination to do so. Well, she thought impishly, if he could play games, so could she!

Admiring James's sweet, taut little arse as he sat down beside her, she laid a friendly hand on his thigh, stroking it lightly. His cock jumped as if pulled by a wire. She winked at him covertly and reached over to her case to take a small screwtop jar from among her face creams and body paints. Sensing she now had the complete attention of all three men, she unscrewed the jar. In the lid was a small, soft, stubby brush, which she loaded with the caramel-coloured stuff in the jar. Leaning over James's lap, she dabbed a little on to the swaying tip of his cock. She smiled into the boy's delighted eyes, then looked challengingly over at Dominic.

'What is that stuff?' asked James with a gasp of excitement as Alastair laughed aloud.

Jemma smeared more of the goo on to his penis, working in long, lusty strokes that caused the young man to lean back in complete surrender, bracing himself on his hands and submitting his cock totally to her ministrations.

'Chocolate body paint,' said Jemma, having made certain that every straining inch of his surprisingly big cock was covered. Satisfied it was, she carefully refastened the jar, then stood up and bent over James, giving the two men behind her an entirely intentional view of her peach-like behind and the deep split in it, from which her anus winked at them coyly from above her visibly wet lips.

Looking deep into the young man's lust-filled eyes, Jemma lightly kissed his full, well-formed lips then drew back. James's eyes fell hungrily to her unfettered breasts that hovered so tantalisingly close to his face. Jemma indicated by gentle pressure that he should open his legs for her, and he eagerly did so, leaning back, the flesh of his thighs bulging handsomely as they were pushed up by the thickly padded chaise. His balls too benefited from this pressure from beneath, standing up proudly in their enclosing sac of skin. His big phallus looked for all the world as if it were covered in a thick brown sheath.

Jemma knelt between his legs and proceeded to slowly touch his chocolate-coated cock with her tongue, licking the sweet substance from its base, then up over its proud stem, then feasting most thoroughly upon his sensitive glans.

Enjoying her work, Jemma relished James's feverish moaning and hoped that the exciting tableau the two of them were creating would have the desired effect. With every morsel of the chocolate she lapped, she attended the excited boy, using her hands to fully bare his glans by pushing the skin firmly down the stem of his cock. Then she concentrated on his tip, burrowing into his moist little slit with her tongue, rubbing and licking. At last, to the straining James's undying delight, Jemma took his penis fully inside her mouth and sucked him lustily until he grabbed her hair and shouted out. She felt his juices, tasting like the delicious salty tang of the plumpest, freshest oysters, spurting rhythmically into her mouth.

Panting and swallowing, she released his upright member from its hot, wet prison and, smiling, pressed a kiss upon the swooning boy's inner thigh. Then Jemma heard what she had hoped for – the firm tread of a man's step behind her. Yes, she thought, as a hot, clothed body moved close behind her. Oh yes! Dominic was pushing her legs roughly apart, and she heard him unbuckling his belt and unzipping his jeans and pushing them impatiently down. She braced her hands upon James's knees as Dominic's full cock slid urgently between her legs. His thick bush of wiry pubic hair teased and tickled at her anus as he sought her more-than-ready opening. His glans nosed at her, then it pushed inside, then his stem followed. He rammed himself in hard, and Jemma called out his name in ecstasy, her eyes closing in pleasure, as Dominic pounded her willing sex.

His hands enclosed her breasts, pressing the hot cushiony flesh and the erect nipples almost flat to her chest in the grip of his passion for her. Steadily and mightily his throbbing organ worked inside her. His orgasm, when it came, was explosive, marvellous, but altogether too soon to allow her the full measure of her own satisfaction. A little deflated, Jemma opened her eyes and, gasping for breath, looked down at the big tanned hands that clasped her breasts.

Suddenly she stiffened. The hair upon the backs of the hands was grey. She glanced swiftly back, to see Alastair there, and not Dominic at all. Alastair smiled into her eyes and dropped a kiss on to her heaving shoulder. She felt him beginning to diminish inside her.

'But I thought –' she panted.

'You thought I was Dominic,' purred Alastair. 'I know, darling girl. You called out his name.'

'I'm sorry.' Jemma didn't want to offend him. He had, after all, conducted himself quite well throughout their brief coupling.

'Think nothing of it. I enjoyed the experience very much.' With remarkable equanimity Alastair released her and slid himself gently from inside her. His cock was drooping a little, but was still more than worthy of her appreciative glance. He dried it thoroughly with a handkerchief, then tucked the satisfied member back inside his trousers.

James, despite a cock that in the enthusiasm of youth seemed never to subside, and even now trembled upright as if questing for more female delights, was also reaching for his clothes. Jemma sagged against the leg of the chaise, hot with undimmed desire, her eyes searching the room in confusion. Dominic was gone. James and Alastair had both obliged her very pleasingly, but she had come here determined to have Dominic, not them. Alastair extended a gentlemanly hand to her, his eyes watching her with sympathy.

'He'll be waiting for you through there,' said Alastair, indicating a door she hadn't noticed at the far end of the big room.

At last!

Her body humming with unfulfilled lust, uncaring now of her nakedness, Jemma ran to the door, opened it eagerly, and stepped through into a bedroom. It was wood-panelled, and dimly lit by two rainbow-coloured Tiffany lamps on either side of the bed, which was queen-sized, with a mulberry-red brocade coverlet. Above it was draped a modest canopy of sheer, star-spangled muslin. The coverlet was turned back to reveal crisp, soft white linen sheets and plump pillows.

To her delight and relief she saw Dominic standing by the bed, the low lights lending his finely planed face a saturnine and mysterious quality, his hair hanging loose and dark about his broad shoulders. Jemma was a little disappointed to see that he was still fully dressed. Nevertheless she approached him ready to remedy that situation, revelling in her proud nudity now, and more than ready to attain her own pleasure and grant him his. Her hands slid up over the thinly-covered firm muscles of his chest, then would have linked behind his neck to claim a kiss, but Dominic caught her hands in his, and pushed them back to her sides.

'Slip into bed,' he urged. 'You'll stay tonight?'

Jemma nodded, and obediently slipped beneath the sheets, not bothering to pull them over her, so that her full breasts and puckered nipples peeped above the covers to please his keen artist's eye and stimulate his desire. She lay there, looking up at him expectantly.

Dominic stood there watching her; he looked at the dark fan of her hair spread out on the pillows like a bolt of black silk; at her sparkling eyes and her delectable mouth; and at her breasts so carelessly revealed to him.

'I'm going down to my villa at Cap Ferrat in a couple of days. Will you come?' he asked.

At that moment she would have said yes to anything he cared to suggest. And the south of France. She loved that coast, with stately Monaco close by and the idyllic lazy villages like Menton, and ritzy Cannes, and flashily vulgar St Tropez.

'I'll come,' she agreed breathlessly, and pushed the covers back further, revealing her furry bush of black hair and her long, slender legs. Urgently she opened them to him and saw his eyes feast upon her. 'Come to bed,' she whispered. 'Come and have some fun.'

'No, I've work to do,' said Dominic and, to Jemma's disbelief, he turned and left the room. 'Sleep well,' he said, glancing back from the doorway. Quietly he closed the door behind him, leaving Jemma in a maelstrom of unsatisfied desire, intense puzzlement, and acute curiosity.

Chapter Four

Jemma was beginning to feel, in the most pleasurable way imaginable, that she had been swept into another world by her professional association with a photographer as famous and talented as Dominic Vane. Within the week the arrangements had been made and now, here she was, on a private plane flying out of chilly Heathrow and bound for sunny, exclusive Nice in the south of France.

Usually plane travel bored her, but this journey promised to be more interesting than the norm. For one thing, Dominic was lounging beside her on one of the six spacious seats, making her pulse quicken by his mere presence. And, for another, the crew were extremely attractive and attentive. There was a blonde stewardess with a wide, obliging smile discreetly fussing over them, offering champagne and fresh fruit juice. There was also a steward whom Jemma found particularly alluring, his short-sleeved uniform shirt revealing strong tanned arms, his smile punctiliously polite but his blue eyes very bold whenever they locked on to hers.

Dominic had taken her up into the cockpit before take-off, and introduced her to the pilot and co-pilot, who were both wearing epauletted short-sleeved shirts and navy-blue uniform trousers. They were both big, burly men of the quiet and capable variety so frequently found flying planes, and they eyed Jemma with great interest, which she found flattering and also quite arousing.

'It's Max's plane,' Dominic explained to her as they sipped champagne from fluted crystal glasses and the craft soared over the English Channel, skimming the clouds and giving only tantalising glimpses of the blue sea far below.

'Max?' queried Jemma, feeling the deliciously sparkling liquid working its warming, soothing magic on her limbs.

'He's my main dealer, and my agent.'

Jemma thought this over. 'Perhaps you pay him too much.' She smiled.

'Max says I pay him too little.' Dominic returned her smile warmly. 'You'll meet him when we get there. You'll like him.'

It sounded almost like a command. Well, thought Jemma, easing back in her seat and feeling as pampered and lovingly cosseted as a favourite pet, perhaps she would like Max. She was willing to go along with whatever Dominic had in mind. Perhaps Max would like her, too. And perhaps they would indulge their mutual appreciation by going to bed together. Perhaps.

Recognising her sexual curiosity about Max to

be a result of her frustration over Dominic, Jemma considered the situation more seriously. It was possible that what Steven had intimated was true. Perhaps Dominic had lost his creative drive, and with it his ability to perform the sexual act. She let out a small sigh at that thought. And yet, he did become aroused at the sight of her being taken by other men, so why didn't he take her himself? She had invited him to. She sighed again and closed her eyes. Well, if she and Max made love, Dominic would just have to watch. She knew he liked that very much: liked seeing her open wide for another man, wrap her legs around him, take a hard and urgently aroused cock deep inside her – even while his own cock seemed to be bursting with stifled need of the same release.

She wriggled a little in her seat at the thought of Dominic watching her with that red-haired photographer, watching the sway of her naked breasts as the man energetically plunged his penis into her.

A little moan escaped her lips. She couldn't stop it. Deep inside her was a fear that Dominic would never relent; would never give them both the exquisite pleasure of the shared sexual joy she knew they were capable of. Her own needs were too urgent for her to bear a long, barren wait with perhaps only disappointment at the end of it. No, she needed to be touched, held, enjoyed; and if Dominic was not prepared to do that, then there was only one other course open to her.

'Jemma? What is it?' Dominic's voice was concerned. She felt his warm breath on her neck as he leant closer, and her nerve-endings seemed to catch fire with longing.

She opened her eyes and found herself gazing into his, so vividly green and clearly worried. She blinked, colouring slightly because she could see that he had thought she must be ill, possibly airsick, and now that her eyes were open, her pupils wildly dilated, a light blush staining her neck, it was obvious to him that her small sound of distress had been one of pure animal need.

'Poor little Jemma,' he murmured huskily, understanding at once. His eyes lowered to follow the small movement of his hand. She was wearing a thin, silk, powder-blue suit, the jacket open over a silky white top. No tights, because she had found that, since encountering Dominic, any restriction around her sex was almost unbearably titillating. Anyway, her legs were good enough to do without them. She could just endure the light little G-string she wore; in fact she found that wearing such a flimsy undergarment kept her in a permanent state of mild but not unpleasant arousal. An arousal so sweet that it was almost – but not quite – pain. Anticipating the heat of Nice, she had decided against a bra, and Dominic's hand was now parting the folds of her jacket, revealing the white top and revealing also the twin hard buds of her nipples, their darkness clearly visible against the pale and almost semi-transparent top.

'Poor Jemma, I know what you need,' he went on, deliberately brushing the back of his hand against one nipple. Jemma strained toward that hand, wanting it to cup her breast, aching for his mouth to take her nipple through the fabric.

'Then give me what I need,' she pleaded breathlessly.

Dominic drew back. They could fuck now, this instant, she thought; the steward and stewardess were busy behind the curtain at the back of the plane, preparing their lunch. No one would see. And, even if they did, she hardly cared. No man had ever made her feel such abandon before. She was already putting down her glass on the small magazine-strewn table. Eagerly she moved closer to him, easing him back into his seat with one hand on his hard-muscled shoulder; she flipped one knee across his lap, hitching up her skirt, her fingers trembling as they went to his belt. Her eyes beheld the twitching bulge of his penis trapped beneath it, and her heart soared.

'Oh, Dominic,' she groaned, but his hand suddenly caught her own, and stilled it.

'Wait,' he said, and pressed the button beside his seat.

Presently the steward emerged from the curtained alcove at the back of the plane. Jemma saw him pause before he drew the curtain closed behind him, arrested by the sight that had greeted him. She was still on Dominic's lap, and what they were about to do must be obvious to anyone. Hurriedly she pulled back, regaining her own seat, every pulse in her body rioting with desire and anger. So Dominic was still determined to merely play with her, teasing her beyond the limits of her endurance. The frustration was immense!

Jemma sat back trying to compose herself as the

steward moved forward and stood beside the empty seat to her right. Dominic was in the window seat, and she was sitting in the middle one; such space, such comfort, could never be achieved on a commercial airline, but Jemma suddenly wished that they were on an ordinary passenger flight. If they were then Dominic would have to restrain his playful urges and spare her frustration.

'Yes, what can I do for you?' The steward smiled, and Jemma was struck anew by his boyish handsomeness, his clean, floppy blond hair, his healthy tan, and the sparkling boldness of his blue eyes. When his eyes met hers it was very clear what he wanted to do for her. And right at this moment, Jemma almost wished he would. But his gaze skipped past her to Dominic.

'My companion requires your services,' Dominic said casually, and reached over while Jemma was distracted by her own thoughts, to push up her flimsy top. Jemma gasped in surprise as the cabin's cool air hit her stomach and then her breasts. Looking down, she saw that the fat buds of her revealed nipples were still taut from Dominic's caress. Flustered, she looked up at the steward and saw the lustful gleam in his eyes as he admired this unexpected bounty.

'You see the state she is in?' Dominic went on. 'It would be cruel of you to leave her in such frustration, don't you agree?'

The steward nodded understandingly. 'Well, yes. Although I have to say that I cannot fully appreciate your companion's distress, because the top . . .' He shrugged, indicating the problem.

'Ah yes, I do see,' said Dominic, looking thoughtfully down at Jemma's naked breasts and at the top which drooped irritatingly above them, obscuring them rather too much for any man's tastes. 'Slip your jacket off, Jemma,' he said, and dazedly Jemma did so, her thoughts spiralling into frenzy, her nerve-endings warming at this most stimulating game. 'And now the top. Take it off,' said Dominic.

Jemma moved happily to obey. Whatever he had in mind, surely it would at least provide some release from this tortuous longing! Straining a little – and by doing so causing her breasts to poke forward enticingly, much to the delight of the two watching men – she undid the six small mother-of-pearl buttons at the back of the top, and shrugged it off on to her lap. The gesture caused another little ripple of pleasure for Dominic and the steward as Jemma's unfettered breasts swung like bells when she moved.

'Is that better?' Dominic asked the steward.

The steward cleared his throat, his eyes glued to Jemma's breasts. 'Much better,' he said a trifle hoarsely. 'Although the skirt . . .' he said hopefully, trailing off.

'You're right. Jemma, slip it off.'

With no thought of refusal, Jemma unzipped the skirt and placed it, and the jacket and top, over the little table before them. All she wore now were her high-heeled shoes and the dainty, tantalising little side-tied G-string, upon which the steward's blue eyes were now riveted. The black G-string barely covered the dark triangle of pubic hair beneath it. Jemma's flat belly, the erotic dip of her navel into which the steward now felt an almost overwhelming urge to slip his tongue, the full and naked twin temptations of her breasts, and her delicate arms and shapely white thighs were all desperately alluring to the tumescent young man.

Dominic put out a hand and ran one long finger under the waist-string of the tiny, tempting thong she was wearing. 'And this thing – how does it come off?' he asked her, his voice husky, his eyes playing games with hers.

'It unties at the sides or just pushes down,' Jemma sighed, utterly abandoned to whatever fate he chose to deal out to her now.

'Push it down. Just there, on to your thighs,' he instructed.

Breathlessly Jemma complied, revealing her dark bush to their eager stares and increasing her own desire a hundredfold by doing so. Her own eyes were locked on to the urgent swelling at the steward's crotch as she wished that he would reveal himself to her, just as she had revealed herself, at Dominic's instruction, to him.

But no!

'Turn this way a little, Jemma,' Dominic said, and so she did, swivelling sideways so that she faced him and had her back to the aisle seat. She waited there impatiently, wanting only to continue the game with all speed. Dominic reached down and, almost as if hypnotised by her beauty, trailed a long finger down the soft fur of her pubis and into the even softer cleft beneath, encountering the tiny wet nub of her clitoris. Jemma's head went back and her hips tilted forward. A purring moan escaped her lips. This was what she wanted. For Dominic to touch her; to make her come to the ultimate point of ecstasy just as she knew he could. But all too soon his hand was gone again and, as her eyes flickered open and looked deep into his, she saw there something that surprised her – something that was almost like fear. Their eyes stayed that way for what seemed like an eternity but was in fact no more than seconds. His tortured emotions had been revealed to her and her aching need had been shown all too clearly to him.

Then his gaze became shrouded in the concealment of blank sophistication, and the inner Dominic, so briefly revealed, was gone. His eyes left hers and met the steward's in silent command. Jemma glanced back over her shoulder and saw that the steward was eagerly loosening his belt. Transfixed, she continued to watch as he unzipped his trousers and hastily pushed down his brief undershorts to uncover first a hard, flat stomach and then, much to her appreciation, a lustily twitching upright penis nestling against a bed of blond hair.

The steward sat in the aisle seat, twisted round at an angle behind her, and slipped both hands around her middle, reaching them up and clasping her breasts. Jemma, pleased, wriggled her naked buttocks back into the steward's lap, delighting in the feel of his hard, hot cock. Growing bolder, she reached behind her with one hand and, forcing its very lively head down, slipped his cock between her open legs so that it could stimulate her more thoroughly.

The eager young man groaned as she did this, his engorged cock receiving the full benefit of her warm, wet cleft and the promise of even deeper pleasures yet to come. As Dominic watched with extreme interest, his own erection painfully obvious to Jemma, the steward rubbed his palms back and forth over her sensitised nipples, then lifted her breasts teasingly for Dominic's inspection.

'They're gorgeous,' Dominic said throatily, and seemed about to lean forward and kiss her hard dark buds. But he didn't, and the moment passed.

Meanwhile, the steward was pumping his cock happily between Jemma's legs, arousing her almost beyond bearing. When she looked down, she could see her own dark thatch of hair and, every so often, the wet, engorged glans of the steward's penis would poke out like a tongue as he thrust forward.

Enjoying this display, Dominic reached forward and, with deft fingers, unfastened one set of ribbons on Jemma's flimsy undergarment. As the steward paused in his labours, intrigued, Dominic worked between Jemma's legs, catching hold of the ebullient young cock and tying it securely with the ribbons. The steward and Jemma were now locked together by this silky tether, and the situation was made even more delightful by the fact that the stricture of the ribbon about the steward's cock served to slow his ultimate moment and make it last longer for them both.

It was a delightful and educational experience, but not one that either of them could tolerate indefinitely. At last the steward's hands left her breasts. One clasped her hip to ensure that she kept her thighs spread despite the slight constriction caused by the fetters of the G-string, and the other took hold of his beribboned penis and searched diligently for the opening it craved. Jemma felt the hot tip of the big organ pushing at the opening of her vagina and assisted it joyfully, wriggling her hips down on to the column of flesh so that their conjoining was effected smoothly. She felt his glans slip into her, and then, inch by inch, the whole hot throbbing length of his cock was engaged; even the soft ribbons of her G-string were inside her. Aware that he could not move freely because of the position he was in, and because his tether disallowed it, Jemma kindly accommodated the steward by lifting and dropping her hips in a steady rhythm. Feeling other eyes upon her, Jemma glanced around and saw that not only was Dominic admiring this arousing sight, but so was the co-pilot! She hadn't realised that the door into the flight deck was slightly ajar, but now she could clearly see the man looking back from the plane's complex control-panel and enjoying the sight of her in the throes of naked ecstasy.

Even further stimulated by this unexpected audience, Jemma's hips pumped faster and faster. She felt the cock lodged deep inside her growing harder still, and the balls that rubbed teasingly against her became like little rocks in the instant before the steward cried out and clasped her tighter as his orgasm erupted.

'Good?' Dominic asked him with a grin, after a moment's pause to let the young man regain his composure.

The steward nodded breathlessly. 'Wonderful,' he assured Dominic, as Dominic set about freeing him from his silken bonds. Jemma felt she could have shrieked with disappointment. It was all very well for the steward; he had come – she had not!

As the steward rose, rearranging his clothing, Jemma looked hopefully at Dominic. He shook his head briefly.

'I don't understand,' Jemma complained.

'Does it matter? Haven't I seen to your pleasure?'

'But I haven't . . .' Her voice trailed away in embarrassment but her hands went to the achingly sensitive mound between her legs, massaging it desperately.

'Then come with me, and watch.' Dominic stood up. His erection was still enormous, and Jemma felt as cheated as a small child denied a treat. Mulishly she watched as he went to the back of the plane with the steward. The curtain was pulled aside, and Jemma gasped. The stewardess was there, but her uniform blouse was gaping open to reveal her breasts. As Jemma watched, Dominic started to kiss the girl while the steward looked on. And very soon she found she could bear to watch no longer. Only the stewardess's wild cries of pleasure as Dominic made love to her told Jemma exactly what was going on. She refused to look. She didn't want to listen, but could hardly avoid it. Feeling chilly and no longer concerned with the pleasure she so desperately had wished to claim as her own, she stiffly pulled her disordered clothes back on. Seeing the co-pilot still watching her, she tossed her head and pointedly looked out of the window, wondering what on earth she had got herself into with this strange, devastatingly attractive man who had bought her services as a model. Gazing at the fluffy white clouds below, she thought about the expression she had surprised in his eyes just now. He had looked afraid, but afraid of what, though? Of losing control, perhaps? Of succumbing to the passion he so obviously felt for her?

She didn't know. She tried to convince herself that she didn't care, either. But she knew that was a lie.

Chapter Five

At Nice airport there was all the usual rigmarole of customs and collecting baggage to get through, but it was certainly made easier and faster by travelling in such first-class style. Jemma was grateful for the speed at which their arrival was processed. It was hot, almost sultry, outside the air-conditioned cocoon of the Gulf Stream jet. Over the tarmac shimmered a dense haze of heat. She felt she needed a bath and someone to talk this strange situation over with, in precisely that order. As the busy hum of the airport went on all around her, she felt locked in a prison of most unusual self-doubt and extreme curiosity about Dominic Vane.

Her eyes were drawn to him constantly, as he checked over his camera gear, making sure all the silver cases, the tripods, and the lighting equipment had arrived unscathed. She watched the Chambray fabric of his shirt tighten across his powerful shoulders. Watched as he smiled at the girl on passport control, and the visible knee-weakening effect his smile produced. Watched as he knelt with an athlete's ease, opened one of the cases, and then resealed it, satisfied.

Well, she was glad he was satisfied. At least one of them was.

Finally it seemed everything was completed, and they walked out to the waiting limo. The chauffeur who had been leaning against the driver's door, waiting patiently, straightened as they approached. Jemma noted how tall he was. She was glad she was wearing sunglasses, because her, sudden interest would certainly have shown in her eyes.

And yet, what was she worrying about hurting Dominic's feelings for? If she was interested in other men, he appeared not to mind in the slightest. Maybe he was interested in men, too. That could be the problem.

If that was the problem, she thought ruefully, then she had better seek her pleasures elsewhere more whole-heartedly, or risk dying of frustration! And the driver was frankly delicious: tall and slim but gratifyingly wide across the shoulders. From beneath the gleaming patent peak of his cap she saw wings of neatly-styled straight dark hair protruding slightly. His nose was curved, classically Roman; his mouth was firm but wide; and his chin was strong, with a delectable little cleft in its centre. The black uniform, with its knee-high well-polished leather boots, tight trousers and double-breasted gold-buttoned jacket, suited him perfectly, and Jemma was curious to know what he might look like without it.

Not that she was likely to get the time or the opportunity to find out, she thought, watching wistfully as he stored their bags in the huge boot of the car. He was obviously just a hire-car chauffeur, and she would never see him again. She was issuing a heartfelt sigh over this sad realisation when Dominic said to the man: 'How are you, Armand? Well, I hope?'

Armand slammed the boot closed and turned with a grin. Jemma couldn't see his eyes behind the sunglasses, and she found that irritating. He looked a bit sinister, in fact.

'I am well, M'sieur Vane. And you, I trust?' he enquired in heavily accented English. Nothing, thought Jemma, sounded sexier than a Frenchman speaking English. Even the most incongruous statement sounded like an invitation to climb into bed.

'Oh, fine.' The men shook hands warmly, like old and comfortable acquaintances.

Jemma watched them, intrigued. Not a hire-car driver, then? They did look very at ease with each other, Dominic and this beautiful Armand. Hmm, she thought. Perhaps even a touch more than friendly. Yet Dominic did enjoy women. He had proved that on the plane, with the stewardess, although not with me, Jemma remembered with a tightening of the lips. Not even when he could easily have done so. And, as a result, the hot cave between her thighs was still soaking wet, still aching for release from its needs. She could feel her engorged lips pushing lustily against the little black G-string, and the damp ribbons of the garment were a reminder of the all-too-brief delights she had shared with the handsome young steward.

Dominic took her arm. 'Jemma, this is Armand, who looks after my villa for me and sees to all my needs when I am here,' he explained. 'Armand my friend, this is Jemma – my muse.'

His *muse*? Jemma looked enquiringly at Dominic, but was distracted when Armand reverently took her hand in both of his. He was wearing black leather gloves. She could smell the expensive scent of the well-used hide, and the fresh lemon cologne he wore filled her nostrils. Despite the impediment of the reflective sunglasses, she could feel his acute interest as he looked her over. Embarrassed suddenly, she wondered if his sense of smell was as sharp as hers; perhaps he could smell how hot she was, how steeped in sex. The cap lowered as he bent from the waist, clicking his heels together punctiliously. His lips dryly touched the back of her hand, which was enclosed like a small nestling animal in his large, leathery grip. His mouth was open a little and, to her pleasure, she felt the slight rasp of his close-shaven skin. In surprise she felt his tongue flick briefly across her hand. She almost let out a gasp, but stifled it quickly, not wishing to appear gauche.

Jemma felt, irritably, that these two were playing some private game, and that she was a part of that game. But she was certainly not a party to whatever rules they might have chosen to play by. So she was his muse, was she? Did he mean that, or was he subtly sending her up? Giving her an artistically important title, while intending to make fun of her hopeless lust for him? Stringing her along and enjoying her bewilderment, then laughing with his sophisticated French friends behind her back?

Jemma decided there and then that she would not allow him, or any of his friends, to needle her. She would play along with their game, enjoy it where she could, tolerate it where she could not.

'Charmed,' murmured Armand, straightening. Jemma smiled into the sunglasses, but all she could see above the tight curve of his lips was her own reflection, looking back at her. Like a hall of mirrors, she thought, with a little shiver despite the intense heat of the day.

'Hello,' she said blandly, concealing her interest in him as best she could.

Turning, Armand opened the door for them, and Jemma and Dominic slipped inside its luxurious interior. Jemma was quite startled by the limo. It was incredibly spacious inside, with long side seats, and what appeared to be a cocktail cabinet. There was even a television. It could easily seat eight people, and its coolness meant that it was obviously air-conditioned. One of those long side seats, she thought unbidden, could even serve as a bed – in an emergency.

Jemma looked sideways at Dominic, wondering if he too was considering the possibilities of those long, softly upholstered seats. But his face was blank. She sighed in annoyance. Blank faces and riddles. That was all she was going to get out of these two men. Or maybe not.

Maybe, if she were patient, she might fathom the reason behind Dominic's restraint. She had time enough, and she could wait.

The big engine throbbed into life, and the car began to move – taking her to what, she had no idea. But for the moment she felt excited by the prospect of adventure, of new situations and faces. For too long, she now realised, she had stuck with predictable, reliable Steven, using their life together as an excuse for not pursuing a more hedonistic, sensual lifestyle that she could truly embrace and enjoy. Hiding, she thought, as the coast road opened up before them and the limo purred powerfully on. That's what I've been doing. Hiding away from new possibilities. Sinking, inch by inch, into the stultifying quicksand of mediocrity and boredom.

'You're quiet,' said Dominic, who had removed his own shades to reveal those intense lime-green eyes. They watched her probingly, wanting to see inside her head, she knew, to find out what she was thinking.

Jemma looked at him and could not suppress a smile. God, he was so handsome, so sexy. She frowned. He was also remote. A challenge. He had said she was his muse. A joke, or fact? 'I was just thinking,' she said.

'About what?'

Beyond his noble profile she could see the sea, and the sunlight glittering on tiny white waves far out on the water. Seabirds dipped and wheeled above them, riding the thermals, dicing with death on the cliffs that towered to their left. The cliffside road was precarious, she realised, but something about Armand's smooth, careful handling of the car inspired confidence in his driving abilities.

'About being your muse, if you must know.' Jemma's smile broadened to a teasing grin. 'It's very flattering.'

'I'm glad you're pleased,' he said cautiously, after a moment's thought.

Jemma glanced forward to where a dense sheet of smoky glass separated the driver from their luxurious enclosure. She could see the back of Armand's capped head, and wondered if he could hear what they were saying. There must be an intercom somewhere, but was it switched on? 'It came as a bit of a surprise,' she said, her eyes returning to Dominic's.

'Oh?' He still sounded suspicious of where this conversation might be taking him.

'Well, you haven't mentioned it before.'

Dominic shrugged and stretched out his legs. It was almost a gesture of relief, she thought. As if her comment had been less threatening than he had expected it to be. It was only her own composure that seemed under threat now, as his movement called her attention to the denim stretching tight over the bulge of his crotch. In a moment she was back on the plane, listening to the stewardess's cries of delight as Dominic had her. The curtain had been left slightly open, and she had seen the threesome quite clearly. The steward who had so recently pleasured Jemma had been watching avidly and had become aroused all over again by the entertainment. The stewardess had had her buttocks braced against a work-surface, and her small but very bouncy pale-nippled young breasts had been fully revealed by the gaping front of her uniform blouse. Her

skirt was pulled up around her waist, and her pants had
been cast to the floor. Jemma recalled the sight of the
girl's naked thighs around Dominic's neck and, in the
moment before Dominic unbuttoned himself, Jemma
had seen the stewardess's pink, dewy, blonde-furred
cleft, and the eager, open mouth of her sex as it had
strained toward him.

Excited almost beyond bearing, Jemma had
watched in total thrall as Dominic had unbuttoned
his straining jeans with one hand. She had wanted to
call out, 'No! Give it to me, not her!' But pride had
stopped her. He obviously desired blondes more than
brunettes. Some men did. Who was she to dictate his
sexual preferences?

All she could do was watch as the last button came
undone, and then gasp at the glimpse she'd had of his
penis. It was no more than that, just a glimpse, but it
seemed to have been burned into her brain like a fresh
brand. He was big. No, more than big, he was huge.
A woman would have to be very aroused indeed – as
the stewardess had been – to be able to take him fully
inside herself. Jemma had moistened her lips as she
watched him couple with the stewardess. She had been
dry-mouthed with excitement. Almost as if she had
changed places with the girl, she had relished the jolt of
her hips as the tip of Dominic's cock effected its lusty
entry; relished too the sight of him sinking it quickly,
urgently, into her ready sex; and the sight of Dominic
pushing down his jeans, revealing the hard, pale globes
of his muscular buttocks, freeing his hips as he began to

pump vigorously inside the gasping, ecstatic woman. It had been almost too much for Jemma to bear.

Just imagine, she thought now, as the car slid swiftly on to their destination, imagine how it must have felt. All that length, that power, that incredible heat, first easing into her and then moving, faster and faster, until she exploded with desire.

Jemma fidgeted, having to stifle a moan of frustration. That was all she had seen of his naked cock, a glimpse – as it entered another woman!

She wanted more than that. A hell of a lot more. And she would get it; she was quite determined on that score.

She looked at Dominic. He was clearly thinking her words through; censoring his reply, Jemma guessed.

'There seemed no need to tell you before. Does it matter that I didn't mention you were my muse? Are you offended?' he asked.

'No . . .' Jemma paused, seeking the right word. 'Just bewildered.'

'Bewildered?'

Jemma felt her temper start to escalate despite all her best efforts to remain cool. 'Yes, bewildered. Because you so obviously prefer blondes.'

'Do I?' His tone was teasing now.

'The *stewardess*, Dominic,' she burst out angrily. 'You you –'

'I fucked her.'

'Yes, and . . .'

'And you watched me fucking her.'

Jemma swallowed. How had he known she would be unable to look away, despite her own torment? 'Yes,' she admitted.

'And enjoyed watching.'

'Well, of course I did. Oh damn you, Dominic, you know precisely what I mean!'

Dominic's teasing smile faded in the face of her obvious distress. He reached out a soothing hand, but Jemma twitched angrily away. His lips tightened, and the hand caught quickly at the nape of her neck. Jemma struggled and lashed out at him, but she was pulled inexorably forward until they stared into each other's eyes, inches apart. His hands caught both of hers to his chest, so that she was unable to land the furious blows she wanted to inflict on her tormentor.

'Bastard!' she panted.

'Bastard or not, you want me,' he said coolly.

'No, I don't,' Jemma lied, enraged.

'No?' Her right hand was forced down by his until it lay in his lap. Without wanting to, Jemma felt the rigid outline of his erection, its heat touching her flesh even through the covering of his jeans. She could smell the musky male scent of it and inhaled hopelessly, adoring that scent, wanting to bury her face in his crotch, to free that mighty organ and claim it for her own.

'See?' Dominic's voice was a throaty purr against her neck, making her shiver as if with fever. 'I could have you now, right now, and you'd love it.'

Jemma's eyes flashed as her head spun round. Her eyes locked with his. 'What, and have you use me while you fantasise I'm that blonde stewardess? I don't think so,' she said scornfully.

'Oh you don't?' he challenged.

'No. I don't.'

For a moment it seemed that her words might provoke him into making love to her, but the answering flash of anger in his eyes was gone in an instant. An expression almost of regret replaced it. Slowly, he released her, and Jemma sank back on to the leather upholstery, feeling that she had somehow fought and lost a major battle. She felt drained.

'Forget it, Jemma,' said Dominic, and his voice had lost its caressing edge. Now it sounded hard, unyielding. 'However much you want me, forget it. Satisfy yourself with other men or women, whichever you please. You'll want for nothing here. Everyone seems to drip sex. It must be the climate.'

Jemma looked at him mulishly. 'Oh, thank you. So I can make do with any available hard cock that takes my fancy, just so long as the cock in question is not yours.'

Dominic laughed out loud at that. He gazed at her admiringly. 'That is what makes you such a spectacular muse,' he said when his laughter had died away.

'What?' snapped Jemma.

'Your spirit,' Dominic said calmly. 'That is what I want to capture with my camera. Your sensual nature, which constantly threatens to take you over. Well, while we are here it will take you over. You'll see.'

Jemma sat back, mulling over his words. They sounded almost like a threat to her; like an invasion of her deepest, most personal psyche. Did she really want that? When she strolled down a catwalk, she was just a clothes horse. But what Dominic was saying was that he wanted to get much deeper than that. Past the thin protection of clothing, past her inhibitions, and into her very soul. She looked ahead, feeling a tremor of misgiving raise goosebumps along her arms as a massive pair of wrought-iron gates loomed up before them.

'Oh look,' Dominic said casually, 'we're here.'

Chapter Six

Jemma knew that many millionaires had their private retreats on Cap Ferrat; they had passed one or two on the way here, and she had noted their beauty, their wooded seclusion, but only vaguely, being too engrossed in her unsatisfactory conversation with Dominic to pay them much heed. But those places were mansions; this place, she saw with some relief, was more like a villa. Yes, there were gates and an entry-phone system, but there were no security guards, no feeling of forboding induced by being among the rich and under threat.

As the limo cruised up a winding drive between hedges of lush vegetation, the villa came slowly into view. It was large, but not intimidating. It had a friendly, relaxed look to its pretty shuttered facade, and huge vines climbed over the front of the villa to lend it a cool, inviting feel. The limo glided to a halt and Armand swiftly came to open the door for her. As Jemma stepped from the car, she felt his eyes on her legs, even though the mirrored sunglasses concealed his appreciation. She felt hot and sticky, and the afterglow of her pleasing session with the young steward had long since vanished.

'Armand will see that your things are unpacked,' said Dominic as they mounted the steps and entered the blissfully cool villa. 'Would you like me to show you around the place?'

Jemma turned to him with a tired smile. 'What I would like is a bath. Can Armand see to that, too?'

Dominic's mouth twisted into an answering smile. 'Armand can see to anything you like,' he said, and it was all there in his eyes, and implicit in his words.

To her irritation, Jemma felt a blush colouring her cheeks. Armand was standing right beside them at that moment, impassively carrying their cases. He must have heard what Dominic said, but he simply placed the cases inside the hallway and returned to the car to get the rest.

'What if Armand likes blondes too?' hissed Jemma, furious that she had displayed her weakness to Dominic.

'Armand likes brunettes,' Dominic assured her. 'He likes you.'

Jemma sighed angrily. She was exhausted suddenly, and far too tired for all these verbal parries and ripostes. 'And I like him. I suppose.'

'There you are, then.'

'This isn't funny,' Jemma said flatly.

'Haven't you ever been turned down before?' Dominic asked callously. Jemma stepped away from him deliberately as Armand deposited another load of cases behind the door.

'Armand,' she said firmly, 'Mr Vane says that you see to everything around here. Could you show me to my room, please? And run my bath? Or is there a maid to do that?'

Armand removed his cap and tucked it beneath his arm. He gave a slight, very correct bow. 'There is a maid. She's called Celestine. But today she is not here, so I will be happy to help you,' he said. 'If you will follow me . . .?'

'Gladly,' said Jemma, snatching her attaché case and pointedly turning her back on Dominic.

'See you later,' he said casually to her retreating back.

Jemma didn't bother to answer. If she had, she would probably have told him to go to hell.

Armand, easily carrying her two heavy cases, led her along a cool, turquoise-painted passageway. It was almost like being underwater, it was so deeply shaded, so soothing, and yet, somehow, so vibrant. There were seven doors, and Armand led her along the passage to the very last one. Jemma found herself unable to suppress an exclamation of pleasure as Armand opened the door and allowed her to precede him into the room.

The first thing that filled her vision was the sunny vista of the sea and sky, fully revealed by the long line of huge floor-to-ceiling windows and patio door that ran the length of the opposite wall. The carpet was incredibly thick and comfy beneath her tired feet. It was a deep cream colour, as was the coverlet on the big bed. Long swathes of diaphanous, softly stirring muslin fell from the ceiling to drape the bed in mystery. As she walked further into the room, she felt a stimulating sweep of air from the slowly turning ceiling fan above her head. The silk drapes beside the windows moved gently in the salty breeze from the half-open sliding glass door, which led on to a long balcony.

Jemma looked outside and could see fine, white wrought-iron seats around a circular table under a big cream parasol; and flowers. Many, many flowers in all the vibrant, lusty shades of nature: crimson and purple, orange and yellow. Almost imperceptibly, she began to relax.

'You like it?' Armand's voice by her shoulder startled her, she was so lost in the beauty of her surroundings. A huge gilt-framed mirror filled the wall beside the door, reflecting all the room's beauty, and doubling its impact. And yet . . . wasn't the room a bit bland?

Yes, it was.

And then she realised why. There were no photo-graphs in there – no paintings, and nothing in any way personal to Dominic or to whoever else had stayed here.

'I love it,' she politely assured Armand, turning with a smile. The reflective sunglasses were gone, and she looked into a pair of deep blue, black-fringed eyes. He smiled too, and they looked at each other with frank interest for a moment before Armand said in that charmingly accented English of his: 'I will run your bath. The journey was tiring, eh?'

'Exhausting,' Jemma admitted, still feeling the faint

pleasurable wetness of her encounter with the steward between her thighs.

Armand clicked his heels together, bowed slightly from the waist, and went to a door in the far corner of the room, then vanished inside. Jemma heard the gush of the water as he filled the bath. Wearily she sank on to the bed and looked at the view. It was her view for however long she stopped here. How long would that be? Her fighting spirit and determination arose. For as long as it took to seduce that cool bastard Dominic Vane; to have him on a bed, or a floor, or anywhere, come to that; just to have him begging to fuck her, begging for the sort of release only she could give him.

After all, she was his muse. And that was something special, wasn't it?

'It's ready,' called Armand. She rose and, after kicking off her shoes, trudged through the deep-pile carpet to the bathroom, which was a revelation in itself. Armand was testing the water in the deep circular bath with its heavy old brass fittings, his uniform sleeves pushed back. Steam rose in clouds as he straightened and looked at her. Jemma was transfixed by the patterns and images presented by the mosaic tiles all around the small room. They formed what looked like a Roman frieze, of the kind found in ancient bath-houses; but there all similarity ended. These images were frankly sexual, documenting in astonishing detail all the myriad positions available to a copulating couple.

'There are twenty-six,' said Armand, as she stood frozen in shock and delight.

'What?' Jemma's eyes swung back to meet his.

'Positions documented here. I have counted. But I believe there are many, many more.' He gave her a grin. 'At least the *Kama Sutra* says so.'

And I'll bet you've tried a few out, thought Jemma.

'Here, let me.' Armand gently turned her around and unbuttoned the back of her blouse. A protest rose immediately to Jemma's lips, an instinctive reaction against unexpected advances. But then she stopped herself. If Armand wanted to help her undress for her bath, then why not? He was gorgeously attractive, after all, and she was by no means ashamed of her body. Let him look, if he wanted to, and they would both enjoy the experience.

With surprisingly deft movements Armand pushed the silky material up. Obligingly Jemma lifted her arms so that he could slip it over her head. She could feel her breasts swaying and her nipples beginning to pucker as they were exposed to the air. Armand placed the blouse on a spindly little chair with an ivory velvet padded seat and turned back to her. His smoky blue eyes were fastened for long moments to her deliciously heavy, naked breasts. Amused, Jemma ran her hands up over the luscious curve of her hips, over the smooth flatness of her stomach, and cupped each silky white globe with its perky dark nipple in her hands, lifting each one to a jaunty and enticing angle for his inspection. Gratifyingly, Armand's eyes narrowed and an appreciative hiss of breath escaped him.

The front of his uniform trousers bulged, but he

was a man of some restraint, she saw, and he diligently continued in the task of undressing her, stepping behind her and unfastening her skirt with intense concentration while she smiled and let her hands fall to her sides. She stepped out of the skirt as he lowered it to the floor, and this too he placed on the little chair.

'And now for this little piece of nonsense,' said Armand, returning to his task and hooking two fingers under the black G-string's insubstantial fastenings so that he could ease it down over her hips, her thighs, her calves, her ankles. Jemma stepped out of the little scrap of silk, and Armand tossed it on to the chair. They faced each other, and Jemma felt a bone-deep thrill of excitement. It was intensely erotic to have this fully uniformed handsome young man look her over as she stood there in the nude before him. Wetness seeped afresh between her thighs, but she kept her expression teasing, enjoying this game of restraint and wondering what new avenue Armand would choose to take them down next.

'Stand in the bath,' he said at last, and held out one brown, strong hand to her.

Willingly Jemma took his hand and stepped into the bath. Still teasing, she said in her most haughty manner: 'I can manage now, thank you, Armand. You may go.'

Armand shook his head. 'But I have not yet seen to your bath properly.' He seemed scandalised by the idea of leaving her now. His eyes were lingering on the triangle of black hair on her pubis. Jemma could feel her unruly clitoris swelling as if to let her know it wanted attention.

'As you wish,' sighed Jemma, giving herself up to
the moment. As Armand busied himself with fetching
toiletries, she gazed in wonder at the carnal scenes
depicted in the mosaic: a man taking a woman from
behind; another from the front; a woman mounting
a reclining man; a man performing cunnilingus on
a woman with her legs spread wide and a rapturous
expression on her face. The permutations were all a
pleasure, it seemed.

As well as the mosaic's arousing content, the large
mirror on the far wall gave back a steam-draped image
of a naked and obviously excited Jemma waiting like a
lady of leisure for her uniformed slave to bathe her.

Was that what he intended to do? Just to bathe her?

She knew she hoped for more than that. The steward,
pleasing though he had been, had not truly sated her;
and her sight of Dominic in the throes of passion with
the stewardess had banked the fires of her own passion
almost to bursting point.

Almost.

It certainly looked as if almost was going to be a
feature of this time with Dominic. She could foresee
herself constantly teetering on the brink of fulfilment,
forever aroused and then denied. Oh, she could use her
own body for pleasure. She could use those handy little
sex-toys she always carried with her, when necessary.
But she wanted Dominic. And if she could not have
Dominic, with his sexily flowing long dark hair, hard
body and taunting green eyes, then Armand seemed
like a very good substitute.

He was dipping a large, soft sea-sponge into the water, rubbing it between his hands to form a thick, silky-looking lather. The appealing scent of sandalwood rose and flicked tantalisingly at Jemma's nostrils. Rivulets of warm water streamed over the backs of his hands, flattening the dark hairs there like an animal's fur when it plunges into a stream.

'You'll get your uniform wet,' she cautioned, hoping that this would persuade him to take it off. Together in this luxuriously capacious bath, they would form another couple to complement the ones enjoying themselves so flagrantly in the mosaic. She would soap his chest, then watch the foam dribble down over his stomach, flood his navel, then wet the hair at the root of his cock. The image seemed to loiter pleasurably in her brain, and she wanted that image to become reality.

But Armand only shook his head, and applied the deliciously foamy sponge to her stomach, moving it in soft circular motions that pulled gently and soothingly at the skin beneath it. Then he ordered her to turn round. Jemma lifted her hair out of his way, enjoying this sensual massage very much as Armand set to work on her neck, then her shoulders, then her back, kneading away the tensions of the day; then he progressed to her buttocks, deliberately working the hard muscles there to release all her stress.

Jemma had to brace herself quite firmly against the pressure of his diligent sponging, supporting herself with her hands pressed flat against one of the mosaics. In this mosaic, she saw with eyes half-closed in purring delight, there was one woman and two men; while the first man entered her cunt, the other was applying himself to her anus. Instantly Jemma's mind started running along delectable avenues of possibility. She could imagine herself in that big bed next door, with Armand and Dominic, all three of them together, swooning with the heady pleasures of sex.

The firm touch of Armand's hands and the soft caress of the sponge were testing her restraint sorely. As if sensing her building desire, Armand slipped the sponge deftly between the crack in her pert behind to massage her anus. Jemma moaned aloud with the erotic sensations he was invoking. She could still see herself in that steamy mirror; could see how her back was arched invitingly towards Armand's probing hand and the sponge. Her nipples were as dark and hard as walnuts. Unable to stop herself, she began to press back harder against him, inviting him to probe deeper, to explore the swollen lips of her sex, to touch her cunt, to manipulate her rigid clitoris and bring her to the peak of satisfaction.

Armand, responding like a true gentleman and a very satisfactory slave, accepted her invitation with alacrity. His soapy hand slipped in beside the sponge, and his finger explored the offered treasures at a leisurely pace. Jemma moaned loudly, impatiently, and spread her legs wider. Armand chuckled against Jemma's wet back, and the feel of his hot breath against her soaking, sensitised skin was enough to make her shudder and groan. 'Armand!' she pleaded breathlessly, and he kissed her back – tiny teasing little kisses over and over – and then her neck where she was even more sensitive. Her arms that were held above her trembled with the sensations he was stirring in her. His tongue slid up her neck to her ear, and he nibbled it gently. Jemma had never before realised how arousing a man's breath on wet, naked skin could be. Now she knew. He had taught her a new sex trick, one she would use to delight future lovers.

'What would you like me to do, hmm?' he whispered against her shuddering skin. 'This, perhaps?' Between her legs, the sponge pressed against her hard little bud causing ripples of pleasure, while his long finger intruded easily into her wide-open sex. Jemma gasped in delight and hastily pushed down on to the hard digit.

'So wet,' marvelled Armand, admiring the sweet curves of Jemma's straining back and the almost irresistible globes of her buttocks as she pumped eagerly at his finger. 'Wet enough to take even more, I think,' he said.

'Much more,' agreed Jemma hoarsely, letting her hair fall so that she could brace herself once more against the wall and apply herself more diligently to the welcome task he presented her with.

'What would you have me do, my lady Jemma?' he murmured, leaning closer, nuzzling her neck while she kept pushing herself mindlessly on to his finger, his hand, the sponge – a delicious trio of pleasure-givers all trapped between her legs. 'I am your willing slave, as you know. So direct me.'

'Your cock,' she gasped. 'I want your cock inside me.'

'Ah no.' She felt his head shaking gently against her skin. 'Not quite yet, my impatient lady.' Deftly he eased another finger into her liquid depths.

'Oh yes,' groaned Jemma, and Armand slid in another.

'These three fingers I have now inside you,' said Armand caressingly against her skin, pushing his fingers deeper to punctuate his words, 'they are as big as my cock. You feel that, my lady Jemma?' He pushed them right in, hard, then withdrew almost to the blushing lips of her sex, then pushed back in again. Out again, then in. Jemma rocked frantically against his movements, matching her pumping rhythm to his. Her breath was coming in pants, and Armand too was sounding quite breathless with the effort to maintain control.

'I don't believe they are as big as your cock,' said Jemma between gasps and thrusts. 'I saw it standing up just now under your uniform. It looked much bigger.'

'What a very naughty lady you are, to be looking,' Armand chastised her.

Jemma, bracing herself with one hand, reached back and grasped the front of his trousers. The bulge there was very impressive, and the hard little nuts of desire beneath his cock were not to be denied for very much longer, she could tell.

'And feeling, Armand,' she said, letting go of his penis to brace herself more firmly against the wall and continue with her eager assault on his hand.

'Now you have been extremely naughty, my lady Jemma,' Armand growled against her shoulder. His teeth nipped her playfully.

'So punish me, my slave,' encouraged Jemma. Steven had always loved punishment games, and so had she. She felt confident, riding Armand's hand most enjoyably, that she could take whatever he cared to dish out to her. But what he dished out was not what she had expected. He withdrew his hand.

She glared angrily over her shoulder at him as he put the sponge in the water and rinsed his hands. 'What . . .?' she began.

Armand straightened with a challenging smile and began to towel his hands dry. Jemma watched in disbelief and disappointment. Just moments ago those glorious hands had been on her, in her. 'So now you are furious with your slave, hmm?' he taunted her throatily.

'Yes,' snapped Jemma. She was still panting, her skin was still shivering, her muscles still trembling. Her nipples were hard, her clitoris was up and ready, her cunt completely open to him. And now he had stopped!

'You are clean now,' he said, tossing the towel aside and giving her an assessing look. 'We will continue next door, yes?'

Jemma gulped, trying to make rational conversation when she was in a state of such heightened sexual arousal. 'Yes,' she muttered. 'All right.'

'Come then.' He leant closer and slipped an arm behind her legs to lift her into his arms.

'Now you really will get that uniform wet,' said

Jemma with a shaky laugh as he carried her through to the bedroom.

Her second shock was that they had company. Dominic was standing beside the bed, a Hasselblad camera set up there on a heavy-duty tripod. He was holding a light meter over the bed and checking the reading. Jemma took in what he was doing in a daze of disbelief. His very presence there was surprise enough. He looked freshly washed, and those were clean button-fly jeans, she saw, and the shirt he wore was spotless and lime-green, the colour of his eyes, with the sleeves rolled up to his elbows. His dark hair was tied back in a tail. He looked invigorated, and ready to go to work.

Armand laid a very damp and increasingly angry Jemma down on the bed. Despite her annoyance she was terribly stimulated by the situation. She knew that Dominic could clearly see the state Armand had got her into. Her legs were slightly open, her slit was very wet, and her pupils were dilated. She refused to pull her legs together like some Victorian damsel. Let him damned well look, if he wanted to. He intended to take pictures of her just like this, naked and aroused. But so what? She was his muse, his inspiration. She wasn't ashamed of her body, so who cared if he wanted to shoot her like this? She knew she looked good – flushed and rosy from the bath, her skin gleaming wet, her eyes sparkling with anger and desire, and good health and great muscle-tone very much in evidence in every line of her body.

'Come on then, Armand, I'm ready,' said Dominic

with an edge of impatience to his voice. He shot his muse an ironic look. 'And Jemma certainly is.'

'Of course,' said Armand, and stepped forward, replacing his chauffeur's cap on his head.

'That's it,' said Dominic, putting his eye to the view-finder and adjusting the focus. 'Now the shades. Then give her what she wants.'

Jemma could see the picture already in her mind's eye. The naked, spread-eagled woman on the bed, still wet and gleaming from her bath, the fully clad chauffeur looming over her. The fan turned lazily above them, casting moody shadows into the brightness of the room. Armand put his sunglasses back on. He looked suddenly remote, even sinister. He still, Jemma thought with a faint feeling of outrage, had his boots on!

She had no time to protest, however, because in a second Armand had unzipped his fly and she immediately became engrossed in trying to glimpse his cock beneath the long tunic of the uniform's well-fitted gold-buttoned jacket. Obligingly, Armand unbuttoned the bottom fastening and pulled it back. His penis came into view, startlingly pale against the black of the uniform, but as hard and upright as a relay-runner's baton. Jemma admired it thoughtfully, from its swollen tip to its root, where it was enclosed in dense black curls.

'You see,' Jemma said idly with a voluptuous smile, 'I told you it was bigger than your three fingers.'

Armand looked down proudly at his cock and grasped it with one hand while he moved on to the bed to kneel between Jemma's parted legs. Jemma's eyes were riveted to it, and to what he was doing: pumping his treasure luxuriously with his hand to increase the stimulation.

'Give it to her, Armand,' said Dominic, and he reached over and briefly touched her hot sex, as a breeder might, to ascertain a mare's readiness to accept a stallion. Jemma gasped at the touch, and it inflamed her all over again. But the casual nature of it was infuriating when she wanted his touch to be that of a lover – not of a detached artist, or a livestock breeder!

'She's so ready,' murmured Dominic, retreating behind the camera.

'You cold bastard,' Jemma spat at him furiously.

Dominic merely smiled. All right, thought Jemma. So she could play games, too. Let him watch, let him do whatever he wanted, but she would put on such an act of passion that he would be churning with jealousy before she was through with him. He would want to be in Armand's place between her thighs, and she determined to make sure that he would continue to want her, burn for her, every second she was here.

She was distracted by Armand pulling her hips toward him, so that the peachy skin of her naked bottom came into delicious contact with the slightly scratchy material that covered his thighs. Oh yes, Jemma could see that there was something terribly erotic about a fully-clad man and a naked woman together in bed. Perhaps, she thought, and the thought made her bite her lip against a tremor of pleasure, perhaps it would work in reverse, too.

She thought of wearing a uniform rather like Armand's, one that fitted tight at the waist to emphasise the lush curves of her figure, and with that austere peaked cap on but with her hair hanging loose. And, beneath her on the bed, she would have Dominic, preferably tethered so that he could not get free to resist her advances. His muscles would be straining in protest as he tried futilely to effect an escape, but his upright penis would betray his arousal. She fantasised about unzipping her fly and lowering her trousers, squatting over her prisoner, and then slowly, inch by sensual inch, lowering her hot, juicy cunt on to that big, eager cock.

She writhed against Armand, groaning a little with the desire that her session in the bath with Armand and her daydreams about Dominic had jointly caused. Now, she really wanted Armand to proceed. Jemma grasped the cold, polished brass rails of the headboard with her hands, her back arching with invitation. Her breasts rolled heavily with her movements. Lasciviously she rubbed her dewy slit against Armand's exposed member before lifting her hips in open invitation.

Armand willingly accepted. Pushing the lively head of his penis down, he lodged its tip neatly into her and pushed eagerly, effecting a very smooth, rapid and stimulating entry. Waves of delight poured over Jemma as Armand began to thrust energetically inside her. Her mouth was open in a soundless 'O' of pleasure, her lips pouting with arousal. She licked them with her tongue to moisten them a little, maintaining her grip on the brass bedstead. Her breasts bounced lustily with every thrust from Armand. Dominic's motor-drive started to whirr, and the sound attracted her attention.

Jemma looked at him there, behind the camera. Slowly her gaze fell and there it was, tenting the front of his jeans – his erection. Panting now, she reached out and touched it briefly. To her annoyance, Dominic moved back a little, placing that big treasure of his beyond her reach.

'Bastard,' she moaned, but Armand's thrusts were reaching fever pitch, and Jemma could deny the pleasures of her own sex no longer. Armand kept pulling out and rubbing the head of his cock over her clit, increasing her excitement a hundredfold. Orgasm broke over her like a tidal wave, sweeping her away in a timeless moment of sheer sensuality. Only dimly did she hear the camera still firing, but Armand's own orgasm was very strong, and deeply felt by both of them. Her rhythmic contractions had pushed him over the edge. Finally they lay, gasping and entangled, Armand still very much the gentleman in that he was careful to keep his weight off her by leaning on his elbows. The peak of his cap touched her brow for an instant before he pushed himself back from her, sinking back on to his heels. His subsiding penis slid free of her, and neatly he tucked it back into his uniform trousers. With a brief caress of her thigh, he rose from the bed, nodded to Dominic, and left the room.

'That was good,' said Dominic into a silence that was

only counterpointed by the faint rushing of the waves far below on the sandy coves of the Cap.

Jemma turned lazily on to her side and stared at him. 'It could have been better,' she replied huskily.

Dominic's eyes met hers as he removed the film, licked the paper to seal it and slipped it into his jeans pocket. His erection had gone, she saw with disappointment. 'Forget it, Jemma,' he said firmly. 'It isn't going to happen.'

Jemma shrugged, determined not to let him see how much his resistance rattled her. 'But you want it to,' she pointed out.

'No,' he said, but his eyes were lingering on her heavy breasts, then skimming down over the gentle curve of her hips, and over her legs.

'Yes,' she said, and turned on to her back with a smile that was pure invitation. 'And why not? I'm here, and I want you. I want you now.'

His mouth twisted in a wry grin. 'I'll send Armand back in, if you wish.'

Jemma sprang up suddenly, her breasts swinging, her eyes alight with fury. She knelt up on the bed. 'You know it isn't Armand I want,' she hissed.

'Really? Then you gave a very convincing performance. Congratulations.'

Jemma shrugged. 'Don't be obtuse. You know that was just sex.'

'And this is just work,' retorted Dominic, gathering up his camera equipment. 'Dinner's at eight. You can rest until then.'

When the door had closed behind him, Jemma sank back on to the bed and frowned at the floor for a moment; then she closed her eyes and, for once, took his advice. She was tired, after all.

Chapter Seven

When Jemma awoke, the light was growing dusky but the air in the room was still very warm. Lying on her back on the big, comfortable bed, she stretched with a cat's lazy sensuality and decided that she was thirsty. She would ring for room service.

She sat up and had a look around. There seemed to be no bell. There were, however, two little cupboards on either side of the bed, each one topped with a substantial cream-shaded lamp. Jemma opened the first cupboard and was surprised to find some of her own bits and pieces in there. Interested, she had a look in the other one. There she found a small refrigerator compartment, and the longed-for pitcher of fresh orange juice, and a clean glass.

She rose cheerfully, then crossed to the sliding glass door and stepped outside on to the balcony, placing both pitcher and glass on the table. She sat down on one of the metal chairs, which was pleasantly warm from the day's sun beneath the skin of her bottom, and poured the juice into the glass. The light was fading, and a dusty-rose glow had settled on to the distant horizon where it kissed the glinting Mediterranean. Several expensive-looking motor-yachts moored at anchor were lit up now, and as Jemma sipped her juice she imagined the people on board in their cabins, dressing slowly for dinner on deck. It was a very romantic and terribly sexy image – dinner beneath the stars!

'Jemma.'

The voice startled her. Her head shot round and she saw Dominic standing further along the balcony with a small camera raised to his eye. The flash fired and she blinked, irritated. She had been enjoying this moment of sweet isolation, drinking juice, looking around, fantasising about the lives of the wealthy. Now she realised that her balcony was by no means private. In fact she now saw that it ran the length of the villa, and that Dominic was standing outside another set of sliding doors, which probably led into his room.

She wondered idly if he locked those doors at night, or if he left them open to admit the salty sea breeze. Well, one night more than a breeze would come to disturb him, she decided. That would teach him to intrude on her privacy. If muses were allowed privacy.

'Turn around in the seat a little bit,' instructed Dominic.

Jemma thought that obviously muses were not allowed privacy, but she was here to do a job and, ever the professional model, she turned, swivelling her legs toward the front of the balcony and resting her left arm along the back of the intricately-worked white metal chair. She looked at Dominic and took a lazy sip of the juice. The camera fired busily, and the flash half-blinded her again, but she was used to that. There were always photographers at the catwalk shows.

'Your nipples are very erect,' Dominic commented, then said, 'Put your head back a little, so the breeze catches your hair.'

Perplexed, Jemma complied with his instructions. 'Of course my nipples are erect,' she said while she posed. 'It's getting cooler.'

'And is that the only reason?' Dominic asked, coming closer and dropping down on to one knee, turning the camera and its flash attachment so that he could get an upright shot of her.

Jemma noticed how his muscles moved under the lime-green shirt as he got into position, and she felt her nipples tingle with the eroticism of the moment. Where his sleeves were rolled back, his arms looked very strong, muscle-corded and capable. Indulging for a brief while in a fantasy where those arms were around her, where those hands caressed her breasts, and even touched her bush and parted the hot lips of her sex, made her wriggle slightly upon the hard seat to relieve a sudden surge of lust.

'I think you say things like that to me because you know how they will affect me,' said Jemma, refusing to rise to the bait this time.

'You mean my talk arouses you.' He was still staring

up at her through the camera's lens, adjusting the focus. 'Put the glass between your breasts.'

Slowly Jemma slid the moisture-beaded glass down the long delicate arch of her throat and into the soft valley between her breasts, gasping slightly as she did so. Her flesh was so hot, and the glass so cold.

'Of course it arouses me,' she said with a delicious shiver, rubbing the glass against her skin. With a faint moan she moved the chilly vessel over the heavy curve of her right breast until it touched the turgid nipple there. Her eyes closed in rapture as she rubbed the glass back and forth against the hard bud.

'That's good,' Dominic said huskily as the motor-drive whirred.

'Mmm, it certainly is,' sighed Jemma, opening her eyes to see if he was as aroused as she was. And there was the evidence: his jeans were bulging again. She longed to lean forward and let his tortured penis out of its prison but, for the moment, direct action seemed like a bad idea. 'Just think how much better it would be, though, if you were naked too,' she suggested hopefully.

'You'd like that, would you? Look, put the glass down now, stand up and straddle the chair.'

'Straddle?' Jemma looked bewildered.

'As if there were a lover sitting there. As if he was ready for you, and you were going to mount him.'

'Mount him,' Jemma repeated vaguely. The air felt thick with their mutual longing now. Damn it, how long would he go on denying both her and himself? wondered Jemma. What was the point of it, when it was perfectly clear what they both wanted? 'I don't understand,' she said with deliberate obtuseness. This wordplay was torture, but it was torture of a most pleasurable sort, she found.

Dominic got to his feet, letting the camera fall loose on to the strap around his neck. 'Put the glass down and stand up,' he said, and his voice was even more husky now.

Jemma rose and placed the glass on the table. Whereas the lower part of her lovely body had been almost concealed from him before, now it was fully revealed. Her thick black bush gleamed silkily in the fading light, and the smooth, sexy flatness of her belly seemed to be drawing his artist's eye rather more than it should. As she moved, straightening to look at him, her breasts swayed voluptuously. Hoping to add to his discomfort and force a reaction from him, Jemma compounded the movement by reaching up and briefly raising her hair off the hot nape of her neck, which lifted her breasts to their most perky and provocative angle. Then she let her hair fall, and again her breasts swayed with the movement.

A half-strangled groan came from Dominic, but somehow he controlled himself. 'Straddle it. Like this.'

He demonstrated, throwing one leg over the chair and sitting so that he was facing the chair's back. Then he rose and stood aside so that she could get into the same position. Jemma gave him her sweetest and most innocent smile as she stood there, naked as Eve.

'If you could fetch a towel . . .' she said.

'The seat's not cold.'

'No, but I'm rather wet, and it would be uncomfortable, sitting on a metal seat and being wet, don't you agree? And it's entirely your fault I'm wet, as you well know.'

Dominic returned her smile with a slightly strained one of his own. 'I'll fetch a towel,' he said, and went into her room.

When he returned, he placed the towel on the chair. 'Better?' he asked solicitously.

Jemma nodded. Grasping the back of the chair and not hurrying over the procedure in the least, she positioned herself beside the chair and then opened her legs to their widest extent to straddle it. Easing herself down on to the seat, she wriggled to get comfortable, giving Dominic another tortuous look at her lushly soft breasts as they jiggled. Jemma's thighs fastened tight upon either side of the chair's back. Looking through the gaps in the delicate curling shoots and leaves of the wrought-iron back, Dominic was treated to a view of her delicious curves and of the inviting black thatch at the juncture of her thighs. Her inner thigh muscles were pulled tight, the skin there looking very silky and shadowy.

Jemma had crossed her arms along the back of the chair and was now resting her chin upon them and regarding him with a blankly innocent expression.

'Of course, if there *were* a man sitting beneath me now,' she began throatily but with a guileless smile, 'and if he were naked, like me, why then he could be inside me like a knife into butter, I'm so aroused right now.'

'I can see that,' said Dominic tightly, trying to get his wandering mind back to the job in hand. He put the camera to his eye and started to adjust the focus, but all he could see was naked skin, nipples he wanted to lick and suck upon, and a small waist he wanted to enclose with his hands so that he could lift her and do exactly what she had just called so vividly to his mind.

Jemma straightened, placing her hands on the chair's seat to support her. She leant back a little, letting her arms take her weight, and peered down at her open sex. 'I can feel it standing up,' she said. She put one finger lovingly upon the tip of her clitoris, enjoying the sudden stab of sensation this induced, then remembered that she was observed and suddenly felt shy. Blushing a little, she placed both hands over herself, hiding both her erect clitoris and her pubic hair from Dominic's view.

'Perhaps I should summon Armand?' suggested Dominic, firing busily now. 'That looks extremely sexy.'

Jemma pressed her hands more firmly into her lap. It felt sexy too. Would he be shocked if she caressed herself openly in front of him? She hardly knew him yet. Perhaps she should be a little more decorous, more restrained. Perhaps, like some other men she'd known, Dominic liked to set the pace and was digging his heels in just because she seemed willing to proceed.

Men, she thought irritably.

'Why bother to summon Armand?' She shrugged, worrying that she might be going too far but, at the same time, unwilling to back down now. 'You're here.'

Dominic put the camera to one side and looked at her. 'I am not going to sleep with you, Jemma. Get used to the idea.'

'You say that, but you want to. And "sleep" isn't what I have in mind.'

'Turn your head that way a little,' instructed Dominic, and carried on shooting.

'You know you want to,' she went on, her voice still softly seductive. 'You could be the lover on this chair, Dominic, and I could be mounted upon you right now. That lovely big cock of yours is straining to be released, just look at it. Imagine it, Dominic. Just imagine it. You could sit down on that chair and I could straddle you so that I was completely open for you, just like this.'

Jemma removed the shielding hands from her pussy and leant further back, lifting her thighs off the seat a little so that she was more fully exposed to him. Dominic looked shocked; his face went as red as a teenager's when confronted with his first glimpse of a woman's bush.

Jemma knew he could see the slick, pink flesh and was unable to tear his eyes from it. She slid a finger down the partly concealed slit beneath the little bud, revealing to him the pink folds of her labia. In an act so flagrantly sexual that it immobilised him as if he were a block of stone, she parted the folds with two fingers to display to him the dewy opening of her vagina.

'Look, Dominic,' Jemma encouraged him, shivering with her own sexual need now. 'I'm offering it to you, here and now. Have it. It's yours.'

But it was no good.

Jemma could see that Dominic was really angry now; she'd gone too far, too fast. The camera was hanging loose around his neck. His erection was still obvious, but fury had the upper hand now, not passion. The green eyes were suddenly very cold.

'Jemma, you are here to work, not to seduce me,' he pointed out.

'I hadn't realised that one would exclude the other,' Jemma replied defensively, feeling bitterly let down.

'Well, realise it now.'

Jemma tried to defuse the situation by replying lightly. 'OK. If that's what you want. But I thought that muses are usually mistresses to the people they inspire, aren't they?'

'Sometimes, yes,' Dominic admitted grudgingly, then he glanced down at his wristwatch. 'But not this time, all right? I'm going to dress for dinner.' Dominic's eyes avoided hers and the even greater lure of her body this time. 'You'd better be getting ready, too. We'll call it a wrap for today.'

With that, he turned and went back to his own room, shutting the sliding glass door very firmly behind him. Jemma sat in a state of unsatisfied, growing desire, straddling the damned chair when she ached to be straddling *him*. Why would he not see that and admit that he wanted it too? *Why?*

This was beginning to drive her insane. She rose and went back into her room, and rummaged in her bag for her mobile phone. Then she dug out her small electronic diary and found Steven's number in Munich. The receptionist at his hotel told her that there was no answer from his room right now, but that she would make sure he called her back at the earliest opportunity.

'Thank you,' said Jemma, and rang off, tapping the little instrument tetchily against her thigh as she sat on the bed with the open bag beside her. If she knew him – and she did – Steven was probably tongue-deep in some luscious German blonde right this instant, and the knowledge made Jemma feel even more bereft of sexual comfort.

Right now, even Steven would be a welcome diversion, even though their relationship had been getting a bit stale lately.

Armand had been very entertaining indeed; she wanted to see more, much more, of Armand during her time here.

But Dominic! What was wrong with that man?

Jemma reached into her bag and extracted a large pink, upright rubber penis. She looked at it regretfully, thinking of Dominic's real version that was so inaccessible to her, then pressed the button in the base so that the vibrator started to buzz softly. She lay back across the bed, pulling up her knees and guiding the softly moving tip of the vibrator into the hot, deep neediness between her thighs.

She murmured a sigh of satisfaction, pushing the warm rubber substitute for a man's hardness deep into her more-than-ready vagina, where it throbbed and shuddered most appealingly, making her gasp. With her free hand she caressed her nipples, then trailed her hand down to her bush, pressing upon her little mound to excite herself more.

Her gasps were growing faster, matching pace for pace the thrusts she was inflicting upon herself; hard, desperate thrusts like those a very ardent lover might give when finally allowed to enter a woman he has desired, pursued, feted, for far too long. This lover, Jemma thought to herself as her lips curved into a secret smile of pleasure, would not ejaculate and be finished too soon like an over-excited boy having his first screw. Her portable sex-machine was always reliable, always upright, always available. It would go on and on, until she had had enough.

Jemma's back arched as she met each welcome thrust. A light sheen of sweat broke out on her straining stomach and widespread thighs. Her breasts bounced with every move she made in the throes of sexual excitement. She alternated between thrusting the false cock in and out of herself and playing it over her swollen clit, sending shockwaves of rude pleasure through her body. Finally her orgasm struck and washed over her in a great, glorious welter of sensations, and she gave out a long, low series of satisfied cries.

Jemma would have been surprised to know that Dominic was watching her from the room next door. The two-way mirror gave him a clear view of the masturbating woman on the bed in the next room. He wanted to turn away, to stop tormenting himself with the sight of her, but he could not. Her slickly gleaming body, still moving in the last throes of her passion, attracted him like a magnet.

He had showered and shaved, and now he stood there wearing nothing but a brief white towel slung around his waist, his dark hair hanging loose upon his muscular brown shoulders. He was riveted by her unknowing performance.

He could not look away.

Jemma was arching her back, coming so hard. The toy penis was buried to the hilt between her dark-shadowed thighs. Dominic could not hear the sounds she made, but he could imagine them, and could almost feel her breath on his skin, her little white teeth nipping at his shoulders as *he* made her come to the pinnacle of desire.

Which he never could, he reminded himself. That was out of the question.

Finally Jemma's wild movements subsided and she lay quiet, her breasts rising and falling hectically as she regained her breath. He watched her withdraw the wet vibrator and toss it on to the coverlet, letting her arm fall limply back beside her head. She lay there, spread-eagled without the faintest idea that she was being observed. God, she was beautiful.

He wondered who she had been phoning. It was probably the guy she lived with in London; that lover of hers who could enjoy her body whenever he chose – the lucky bastard. Ruefully Dominic looked down at the towel. The evidence of Jemma's beauty and its effect upon him was there again. His penis was up. His penis was *always* up whenever she was near. But he had to resist. Aware of a small spot of dampness growing on the towel, he undid it and let it fall to the floor. His naked cock, hugely aroused, twitched lustily at him. His balls hung as heavy as a bull's beneath the big quavering staff, ready for action.

Groaning with lust, Dominic stared at Jemma in the aftermath of her self-administered pleasures, and gave in to the terrible temptation of her. He grasped his penis and roughly, almost punishingly, pumped the big organ with his hand until he came, crying out with the rapture of it, spattering the mirror-image of Jemma with the hot tribute of his come.

Chapter Eight

Dinner was served at eight in the long, dark-beamed dining room that stretched along the back of the villa. The room, Jemma saw as she entered on Dominic's arm, was of a pleasingly baroque Spanish style. It was dominated by several huge pieces of highly polished furniture, including a sideboard that would take four men to lift, and a cupboard those four men could easily stand inside. A truly massive table stretched the length of the room and reflected back in its lovingly buffed surface all the softly glittering pools of light cast by the four multi-branched candelabras placed equidistantly along its length.

Jemma took her time to look around while the others gathered at the sideboard to take the wine from the silver salver that Celestine, the maid, offered. It was a gorgeous room. A big fire burned in the hearth beyond the head of the table and, while the walls were stark white, in contrast there was also a lot of passionate red used as a highlight. The tapestries on the walls, the rugs on the polished floors, the flowers arranged so splendidly on the table and sideboard – all were predominantly red.

Red was very much one of Jemma's key colours. She loved its exuberance, and its sexiness. And it suited her, with her dark hair and creamy-pale skin – and that was why she had chosen to wear it tonight. The gown she wore was a deceptively simple silk Grecian design, one-shouldered and gracefully swathing down over her glorious body to fall in soft folds around her gold-sandalled feet. The gown had been a gift from an admiring couturier after several very satisfying sexual encounters in his small, fabric-strewn studio. She had gone there for fittings before shows, and had come away glowing and replete with good sex, and with this beautiful gown that looked so devilishly simple, but which caressed every inch of her as she moved, so that everything was covered but much revealed.

She had put her hair up in a loose knot, had applied scarlet lipstick and more mascara than she would usually bother with, and was carrying a little gold-sequinned purse to match her sandals. She knew how good she looked, and was gratified that she was drawing a lot of attention from the other guests.

But their attention seemed somehow off-key. They were staring at her too fixedly, as if she were some kind of unique event or unexplained happening. Stiffening her backbone, Jemma smiled sweetly back at them – at Max Klein, Dominic's agent and also his main dealer, and at Max's wife, Annalise. When she did so, they both smiled a little in return, then looked away, as if caught in a shameful act.

Inwardly shrugging off their weird behaviour, Jemma turned her attention to Armand, who was acting as waiter for the evening and who looked extremely handsome in his black trousers, crisp white shirt and black waistcoat as he brought in the soup. He at least behaved as if she were fairly normal, smiling back at her with mocking deference. Bearing in mind what they had been up to together this afternoon, Jemma thought his subservient manner very amusing indeed, but she went along with it, nodding graciously to him as he pulled out a chair for her.

She sat down as Armand snuggled the heavy brocade-seated chair under her bottom.

'That dress is ravishing, my lady Jemma,' he said, leaning close by her ear as he shook out her napkin. His breath tickled her skin in a way that was both disturbing and pleasurable.

'Thank you,' she said, then added teasingly, 'but should a waiter really comment upon a lady's dress?'

Armand shrugged lightly as he placed the napkin on her lap, cheekily taking the opportunity to press his hand against her warm crotch. 'I'd rather strip it off you, but what can I do? For tonight, I am your servant.'

'Armand!' called the maid, Celestine, and there was a faint glower of disapproval on her pretty face as she saw him laughing and whispering with Jemma.

'I have to go and attend to things,' Armand said regretfully.

'Like your jealous girlfriend?' taunted Jemma.

'Celestine?' Armand gave a very Gallic lift of the shoulders. 'She has nothing to be jealous about. We give each other pleasure, but so what?'

'She's very pretty,' said Jemma, eyeing the girl with some interest. Celestine was certainly an eyeful. She was dressed to be, in a perky French maid's outfit. The black bodice was cut very low, so that the tops of her breasts were revealed. The black skirt was daringly short, with a teasing glimpse of frilly white petticoat peeping from beneath its hem. Her maid's little white cap was properly starched, with two streamers of linen trailing down her back. The black seamed stockings she wore emphasised her very good legs. Watching the girl bending over the sideboard to reach a dish at the back, Jemma saw that they were indeed stockings and not tights; two plump, white slices of thigh were revealed as the girl stretched over.

'Yes she is, very pretty,' agreed Armand, leaving Jemma, to attend to the other guests.

Jemma was still eyeing Celestine with interest. The girl was of medium height, honey-blonde and green-eyed, and attractively flushed from preparing the meal. Yes, pretty. And a blonde like the stewardess Dominic had so plainly enjoyed. Jemma still harboured a suspicion that he had a real soft spot for blondes. If he employed this girl, and allowed her to clothe herself in so outrageously revealing a manner while she served at his table, perhaps he indulged in sex with her, too. Perhaps she crept into his room at night wearing this very same enticing uniform, and served him in a rather more intimate manner.

But the others were sitting down, Armand fussing around them, and she was momentarily distracted from her thoughts. Dominic sat down at the head of the table, his back to the warm glow of the fire. Jemma was on his right – like a consort, she thought wryly – and Annalise Klein was on his left. Max Klein sat down beside Jemma, giving her a broad and rather rapacious smile as he did so.

Jemma smiled back. She rather liked Max. He looked to be in his late thirties. His dark hair was wavy, but neatly cut and kept under strict control, unlike Dominic's sexy wild mane. Max seemed the soul of suave urbanity, expensively suited and wearing beneath the suit a crisp, white silk shirt and a dapper black bow-tie. He was the sort of man, Jemma thought, who would be perfectly comfortable in any social situation, and she liked such assurance, such confidence, in a man. He was much shorter than Dominic – a little shorter even than Jemma herself – and not fleshy, but broad and muscular. He was the sort of man, she considered, who would be very difficult to put down in a fight. He gave off an aura of having come from rough, dangerous streets to riches and comfort, but some tiny vestige of the alley-cat remained in his make-up.

She liked that little bit of alley-cat. It was slightly alarming, but exciting, too. She wondered if he might revert to type in bed, and be rough with his women. The thought gave her a little shiver of arousal, and she felt her nipples rise wantonly in response to his maleness.

'So you,' Max said in a deliciously throaty voice as he shook out his napkin, 'are the new muse, Jemma?'

'Yes.' Jemma was pleased that Celestine and Armand started serving the soup at that point, because she found Max's close presence at her side undeniably stimulating. She could feel herself becoming aroused once more, her sex getting dewy as her mind started to wander down pleasurable roads of imagination. Glad of the distraction from her erotic daydreams, she thanked Armand warmly as he placed the bowl in front of her, and received another proprietorial scowl from across the table where Celestine was serving Annalise.

The rosy candlelight painted Celestine's well-developed breasts with a gleam of ivory, and Jemma's eyes fell unconsciously to gaze at them. Turning, blushing slightly at her own wantonness, Jemma found that Max's eyes were similarly engaged. His eyes turned to meet hers, and they shared a moment of smiling complicity. They had both found Celestine's nubile breasts pleasing to look at. So what? Breasts were by their very nature alluring, drawing the attention of both men and women alike.

As she smiled at Max, his eyes dropped to her own pair of very fine breasts, which were only lightly concealed by the thin red silk of her gown. His bushy black brows rose slightly as he saw the urgent push of her engorged nipples against the flimsy material.

'Her breasts are lovely, but yours are even lovelier,'

Max said softly to her while Dominic and Annalise chatted of this and that. 'No wonder Dominic wants you.'

Jemma's smile faded; she turned her attention to tasting the soup. It was asparagus, and really delicious. Celestine's ill-temper didn't prevent her from being a good cook, evidently.

'He doesn't want me,' she replied lightly. 'Not in the way you mean, anyway. He wants to drive us both mad with lust by taking pictures of me in provocative ways, but he doesn't actually want to . . . you know.'

Jemma was amazed that she had said this to a total stranger; but then Max was the sort of man who invited confidences. He didn't have Dominic's potent allure, but he definitely had something. She was sure that women adored him.

'Fuck you?' Max supplied gently.

'Yes. That's it. He doesn't want to fuck me.'

Max chuckled, delighted by her sudden forthrightness. 'Jemma, my darling, don't be ridiculous. What man would not want to fuck you? I myself am already wondering what you look like naked.'

'Are you?' Jemma looked at Max in surprise.

'Certainly,' said Max, his dark-brown and rather hypnotic eyes meeting hers. He had beautiful eyes, made for seduction.

'Well, thank you,' Jemma said a little awkwardly.

She was thinking over what he had said before – that she was Dominic's 'new' muse. Which begged the obvious question. If she was the 'new' muse, then there had certainly been an 'old' one, so what had happened to her?

Jemma wished that Steven would hurry up and phone her back. What was keeping him, as if she didn't know? Steven knew more about the legendary Dominic Vane than she did. He had told her something, she remembered vaguely, about Dominic losing his inspiration for a while, and maybe even quitting photography altogether. She wished she had paid more attention to what Steven was saying, but then Steven had been busy seducing her at the time, which was likely to make a woman just a little distracted! When Steven called – if Steven called – she would ask for more details about Dominic's background.

A new muse. And, surely, an old muse. Who had she been? And why had she ceased to be the inspiration behind Dominic's allegedly brilliant and erotic work?

Jemma wished she knew more about the art world, but she had been so busy pursuing her modelling career – jetting from one country to the next – that such things had rarely impinged on her consciousness. Oh, she had glimpsed the gorgeous Dominic in the scandal sheets once or twice, and she had seen him in *Tatler*'s society pages at some glamorous thrash or other, but, beyond that, he was only a famous name to her. She knew next to nothing about him.

Now she wished she had taken the time to find out more before embarking on this strange assignment. However, her curiosity about Dominic's past liaisons and his present reticence did not preclude having a good time while she was here. And Max certainly looked like fun.

While Celestine and Armand cleared away the soup course and brought in the fish, Jemma took the opportunity to look over at Annalise Klein. Annalise had a distinctly queenly air, which was accentuated by the very upright bearing of her spare and quite muscular body. A dancer, Jemma thought. At some time she was certain that Annalise had danced for a living. When Annalise had been standing beside Dominic and Max, Jemma had noticed that she was at least six feet tall. Even when seated, she projected an aura of greyhound litheness and polished sophistication that was extremely attractive. Her dark-red hair was pulled almost punishingly back from her bony, beautiful face into a tight chignon. Her eyes were grey, and strikingly direct. The silvery grey panne velvet gown she wore, which modestly covered her from throat to wrist to ankle while at the same time appearing expensively and stylishly sexy, matched almost exactly the colour of her eyes.

Jemma looked at the woman with admiration. This sort of confidence only came with time. Annalise was surely in her late thirties or early forties, but she was truly stunning while appearing to be remote and untouchable.

Untouchable, Jemma thought, watching Annalise lay her long, thin hand with its perfect silver-grey, talon-like nails along the cloth of Dominic's jacket over his forearm. She gave his arm a squeeze as she talked to him.

Perhaps untouchable to all but Max and Dominic. The way Annalise's eyes sparred with Dominic's was by no means remote.

'Does it make you feel jealous?' Max asked, and the words startled her. It was as if he had read her mind.

'What?' Jemma felt herself beginning to blush, and this irritated her. She concentrated fiercely on eating her red mullet, annoyed with herself for being so transparent.

Max leant a little closer, and Jemma was enveloped in a sensually rich wave of Trumper's Lemon cologne that almost made her mouth water.

'Annalise and Dominic,' he said.

Jemma got a grip on herself. She was not a child, after all. That these people were very sophisticated in their tastes surely need not intimidate her. She gave Max a laughing glance. 'What, the fact that I think they've been lovers? No. Why? Should it?'

Max dabbed his mouth with his white damask napkin. Jemma saw that there was gold embroidery around the edge of the napkin, and looked down at her lap. Yes, on hers, too. Little cherubs, little *putti*, played flutes and lyres while they danced and sang around the napkin borders. What drew her eye and amused her so much was that these cherubs were extremely well endowed. Looking up, she suddenly saw that the *putti* on the gold-painted candelabra nearby were each similarly blessed with huge phalluses. Upon each sturdy member was hung a pear-shaped crystal droplet which sparkled in the alluring candlelight.

Max was watching her eyes, smiling at her obvious enjoyment of this spectacle.

'Some women would find it disturbing. And yes, they would be jealous.'

Jemma turned her head and their eyes met. 'Truthfully, Max, I'm not jealous if they have been to bed together. I should have thought that you, as Annalise's husband, might be, though.'

Max put down his knife and fork, turning his palms up in a 'so-what' gesture. 'Why hoard all the delights in life for oneself? That would be selfish.'

'But how would you feel if you didn't have access to those delights, and he did?' Jemma queried thoughtfully.

'Ah. I see.' Max sipped his wine from a silver goblet. Even the goblet, Jemma saw, was embossed with rampantly sexual cherubs. If Dominic was hedonistic enough to indulge his tastes in this way, to see Celestine dressed in such a provocative manner, to enjoy other women quite obviously, then surely he should be enjoying her?

'The artistic temperament is a strange thing,' said Max. 'So Dominic has not . . .' His voice trailed off politely.

'Fucked me?' Jemma said with blunt anger. 'No, he hasn't.'

Max's attention returned to the meal. 'Then I would advise you not to make waves, my beautiful one,' he said dismissively. 'Be his muse, his inspiration, and no more, if that is what he wants.'

'And what about what I want?' Jemma challenged.

Max gave her a smile. 'My lovely Jemma, other men can adequately fulfil all your needs. Why, I myself could oblige you, if you wish.'

Jemma was for a moment taken aback. Then she rallied. 'Well, you are very attractive,' she admitted.

'Thank you.'

'Annalise would not mind?'

'She would not.'

Jemma paused to consider this tempting offer, her eyes drifting over to Annalise and Dominic. Celestine was clearing their plates away. Standing opposite Jemma, she was bending over between Dominic and Annalise when what Jemma had guessed might happen suddenly did happen. One of the girl's very exposed breasts popped free of the maid's uniform, revealing a pert, pale-brown nipple of surprisingly large dimensions.

'Monsieur, I do apologise,' she said hastily to Dominic, but Dominic seemed not at all offended. Rather, he seemed quite entranced by this vision of loveliness before him.

'Not at all, Celestine,' said Dominic, his eyes fixed to her bountiful charms. 'Your breasts are so pretty, it's a shame to keep them hidden.'

'Thank you, monsieur,' said Celestine. A little flustered, she moved to tuck her breast back beneath the straining black material, but Dominic stayed the movement with a hand on her wrist.

'No, leave it. It's lovely.' His hand smoothed up over the back of hers until his fingers touched the hard protruberance of her nipple. Idly he rubbed the sensitive bud. Celestine's eyes closed in pleasure, a flush rising delicately from her throat to her cheeks. A small gasp escaped her lips, and her hands caught Dominic's wrist to prolong the delightful moment.

'That certainly is a beautiful tit, Dom, but why only one?' Max said jovially from across the table.

'See how greedy my guests are, Celestine,' said Dominic to the girl, sending a chiding glance to Max. Jemma found herself riveted by Dominic's darkly tanned hand working on the soft, pale flesh of the girl's breast. He was tugging the aroused nipple between thumb and forefinger, tugging gently and slowly as a lover's mouth might suck at it. Jemma's own nipples began to prickle and rise at this entertaining sight, and she saw that Annalise's too were standing up proudly beneath the silvery velvet.

'I don't mind, monsieur,' sighed Celestine, almost drowsy with pleasure under his massaging hand.

Agreeably she slipped her hand into the valley between her breasts and extracted the other one from its confines. She looked around at the diners with pride; Celestine knew how pretty her breasts were, and how unusually large and pale were her nipples, set upon their fat, well-rounded cushions of soft flesh. Even Armand, leaning against the sideboard, paused in his duties to enjoy the sight. Jemma's eyes slipped down his body to where the front of his trousers bulged mightily. Then she looked back up at his face and found that he was staring back at her, smiling mysteriously.

Annalise stood up. She towered over Celestine,

and standing beside her proved very much a contrast – the elegant lady beside the saucy little serving-maid. But she too seemed to be enjoying Celestine's lovely display. She was eyeing the girl's breasts with a great deal of interest. She reached out a silver-taloned hand and lightly stroked the breast that Dominic was not caressing.

'So soft!' she marvelled in her husky voice. She was French, and when she spoke English – as she did most of the time – her accent, like Armand's, was absolutely entrancing. Jemma, so sensitive to beautiful surroundings, good tastes and lovely smells, found much to her surprise that elegant Annalise appealed to her physically in a way few women had before.

Seeing Annalise's thin, smooth hand on Celestine's bountiful breast caused surprising sensations in Jemma. Her dewy opening became even more wet, her clitoris hardening as if sharing its owner's fascination for this little scene and anything that would follow.

The fact was, she had never slept with another woman. She had enjoyed only men. Oh, she'd had offers, but had never felt sufficiently intrigued by the person or persons involved to take up the challenge. No, men suited her very well. But now, watching Annalise's coppery head bow and her bronze-lipsticked mouth start to suckle at Celestine's breast, she wondered if she had missed out on a treat.

The girl was moaning with the pleasure of it, and it was very easy for Jemma to imagine Annalise's thin, mobile lips clamped to her own breast, working with tongue and teeth on her nipples, and not on Celestine's plumper mounds.

Annalise's head raised at last, and she kissed Celestine's throat where the pulse beat frenziedly beneath the soft skin, then she nibbled the girl's ear, licking its shell-like shape briefly, and then kissed her full on the mouth.

Dominic sat back now, watching while Annalise worked her sensual sorcery on the girl. With a murmured plea, Celestine took Annalise's hand and guided it beneath her little skirt. Annalise happily obliged, then exclaimed in pleased surprise:

'Dominic! What a reprobate you are. The girl is naked under this skirt.'

'And what does that make you, Annalise, for finding out?' returned Dominic, taking a sip of his wine.

'As big a reprobate as you,' Annalise admitted cheerfully, her hand lost beneath Celestine's skirt but clearly busy, judging by the gratified moans coming from Celestine's mouth.

'Isn't that very expensive gown of yours getting in the way somewhat, my angel?' Max asked Annalise with a purr in his voice. He was sitting back in a leisurely fashion, Jemma noticed, very obviously enjoying what he saw and getting ready to see more.

Armand came from the sideboard and deftly removed the rest of their main course dishes. Jemma, with a mounting feeling of excitement, knew what was going to be for afters – Celestine.

The girl was trembling with arousal as Annalise's hands and tongue continued to work on her, and when

Annalise paused at Max's remark, the disappointment on Celestine's young face was almost comical to behold.

'Perhaps it is, a little,' she agreed and, wiping her fingers fastidiously on a napkin from the table, she called Armand to her side, indicating the zip on the back of the lovely gown she wore.

Armand obligingly unfastened the zip, and Annalise, aware that she had the attention of fellow diners, teasingly lowered the gown first from one shoulder, then the other. Coquettishly she caught the soft material over her breasts, and then after a moment's hesitation she let it drop to the floor.

Jemma caught her breath. Annalise did indeed have a lovely body, a dancer's body. Her skin was quite pale and fine, her muscles clearly defined beneath it. Annalise's breasts were more boyish than Jemma's own, and certainly far more so than the buxom Celestine's. It was interesting, she found, to compare the two: Celestine's big, hearty mounds and Annalise's dainty, cinnamon-tipped delights.

It always astonished her, the diversity of the shapes, sizes and colours of the female breast; and she saw, with some amusement and quite a lot of excitement, that it was a matter of some fascination for her two male companions.

Annalise's pale, tender body looked untouched by the sun's damaging rays, as if she had lived her life under sunshades and beneath several layers of sunscreen, while Celestine's was burnished to gold, her blonde hair bleached almost white in places. Jemma thought that the fact Celestine was so tanned made her naked breasts – which had obviously been covered by a bikini top while she sunbathed – look even more naked, and much plumper too in their stark whiteness.

All that Annalise wore beneath her discarded gown was a pair of dove-grey silk lace-trimmed French knickers. Jemma found her eyes drawn irresistibly to Annalise's long, strong and supple body. She was sorry she was wearing the knickers; she found herself wanting to see everything, to strip the scrap of silk out of the way and then to stretch the imperious Annalise out on a bed – supposing Annalise would allow it, of course – and examine every desirable inch of her.

'Glorious, darling,' Max said, taking another sip of wine and enjoying the sight before him with a connoisseur's pleasure. Glancing down at his lap, Jemma saw that the napkin there was standing up because Max's penis was obviously erect.

Surprising herself, Jemma discovered that she was wondering what it would be like to be in bed with both Max and his wife, Annalise. She blushed a little, suspecting that her thoughts might be betrayed by the rapt expression on her face, when Max turned to her.

'And what about you, new muse, eh?' he asked.

'What about me?' Jemma asked cautiously, trying to hold down her rapidly escalating excitement.

Max's eyes dropped to her gown. 'Why not take it off?' he suggested.

Jemma looked from Max to Dominic. He was watching her carefully, almost assessingly. Wondering if she'd have the nerve, Jemma thought acidly. From there she looked at Celestine and Annalise. Celestine looked almost drugged with desire and seemed uncaring of what Jemma did or did not do; but Annalise was watching her, and on that cat-like face she seemed to see a challenge.

Jemma found herself rising to the challenge with a survivor's natural instincts.

'Why not?' she agreed sweetly.

She beckoned to Armand, who came swiftly and pulled back her chair as she stood up. Very aware that she had the attention of the entire company, Jemma unfastened the hooks at the shoulder of the gown and, with a studiedly nonchalant shrug, she let it hiss down over her body to lie in a silky scarlet puddle on the floor.

There were several indrawn breaths from around the table. Not from Dominic, of course – he had seen her body before. Not from the watching Armand, either, who, standing behind her as he was, enjoyed a full view of her sweetly curving back and beautiful firm buttocks Buttocks many men would have envied.

Max gasped, and so did Annalise. Perhaps this was because Jemma was totally naked beneath the dress, and they had doubted she would display such confidence as to strip so completely before strangers.

Jemma stood there proudly, her hands held loosely at her sides, one foot placed gracefully before the other. She could feel the heat from the crackling fire like a sensuous touch upon her naked skin, and could feel her nipples standing shamelessly erect. Between her legs, she could feel her little bud stirring hungrily, and knew that she was getting wet. Her eyes met Dominic's, and the heat between her thighs became an inferno.

God, how she wanted him!

But she must play these subtle games of his, instead of enjoying his magnificent body as she longed to do.

Well, so be it. She could wait. And for the moment, let them look! Let them burn their eyes upon her beauty.

'You were absolutely right, Dom,' said Max a bit thickly. He reached out a warm hand and placed it upon Jemma's flank, smoothing the skin there as if it were priceless fabric. Beneath his touch, the skin quivered. His hand slid on to her belly, rubbing gently, as one might run one's hands appreciatively over a particularly beautiful thoroughbred filly. 'She's exquisite,' he breathed, his eyes fastened to her silky bush.

Jemma had to smile at this. They were all looking so serious while she felt liberated by the act of stripping away her clothes, and quite jolly, in fact. Subtly, the balance of power in the room had moved; it had passed from Dominic to Annalise, and now the power was hers. Her body, this body that was so accustomed to a state of undress in the course of her modelling work, had claimed the power for herself. They were all riveted by it, as if she were Venus, the very embodiment of earthly love, or a lesser goddess come down to earth in a shower of gold to mate with a mortal man.

And, like a goddess, she felt powerful. She touched Max's questing hand with her own and then grasped it firmly, lowering it until it covered her darkly furred pubic mound. He gasped again as she pressed his hand against her hot, hungry flesh. Her eyes, half-closed with the intensity of the feelings this wonderful pressure caused, met his. 'Max, if you will oblige me?' she said huskily.

Max took only a moment to recover himself, while the others around the table took a little longer, amazed at her audacity. Even Dominic seemed taken aback. And, glancing at Annalise's narrow face, Jemma saw that she was seriously put out at having the attention so rudely drawn away from what she was doing with Celestine.

As good as his word, Max rose with a courtly bow to her. Jemma was aware of Dominic settling back to watch this with interest; of Annalise and Celestine craning forward to see; and of Armand waiting in the background to enjoy the view. But the power was hers, and she had never lacked nerve.

'In any way you choose, sweet Jemma,' said Max smoothly.

Smiling, Jemma turned and wriggled her bottom up on to the table. She lay back and, in doing so, just as she had planned, she was lying right in front of Dominic, close enough for him to touch her if he wished. The wood beneath her back was a sudden shock of cold, but the curious look in Dominic's eyes, and the way his gaze kept skimming irresistibly up and down her body, warmed her considerably.

'I choose this way, Max,' she said, but her eyes were on Dominic's. 'And you without your camera,' she murmured teasingly to him.

'There'll be other times,' said Dominic.

'Times like this?' She stretched her arms languorously above her head. 'For Max, probably. For Armand, too. But for you?' She shook her head a little. 'I don't think so.'

Chapter Nine

'And what does that mean?' Dominic leant forward and looked down at the naked woman stretched across the table in front of him.

'That you can't have me,' said Jemma, and she drew in a shuddering breath as Max gently pushed her legs apart and feasted his eyes upon the treasures revealed to him.

'Max, can you wait a minute?' asked Dominic, sounding a trifle irritable.

'My dear Dom, I can't even wait a second,' said Max. When he unzipped his fly Jemma saw that this was no exaggeration. His penis was brown-skinned and stocky, just like the rest of him, and sprang from a nest of curly golden-brown hair. If Annalise avoided the sun to keep her looks, Max clearly did not share her worries. His rampant cock reared against his healthily tanned skin, with no tell-tale white line where bathing trunks would be.

Jemma pulled back her legs so that the soles of her

feet rested upon the table. She adjusted her position a little, and her hips came to the very edge of it. Carefully Max clasped his penis, looking down at it and almost seeming to admire it for a moment, before he lowered the reddish-brown helmet toward the entrance it so eagerly sought.

'If you can't have me, Max can,' Jemma sighed wantonly and, for an instant, she saw again beyond the mask of composure that Dominic so often assumed. Again she saw a type of torment; she also saw his eyes flicker up and lock with Annalise's for a second.

Jemma's view of Annalise's face was distorted, and upside-down. Did she really see the slight shake of the head, a look almost of censure, of a stern mother telling her son what was possible and what was not?

Jemma hated mysteries, and this one was seriously beginning to bug her. However, there were other experiences to be enjoyed, and Max was one of them. She felt the head of his prick nudging at her warm, wet opening, and she spread her legs a little wider for his convenience. She felt amazed at herself for her daring, but then she was among the sort of company that seemed to expect free and easy sexual behaviour as the norm. She felt no shame, only a growing, glorious fireball of arousal filling her belly as Max pushed quite roughly into her with a grunt of satisfaction.

She was so close to Dominic that she could smell his cologne and hear that his breathing was growing heavy. She was taunting him with her body, and she knew it. But the sensations that Max was producing with his stocky and serviceable cock overrode all other considerations. With his eyes on her rhythmically bouncing breasts, Max was thrusting his hips to a steady, powerful beat that set up a delicious friction within her.

Panting with pleasure, she rolled her head to the right and stared straight into Dominic's eyes. His were blank now, as green and as inscrutable as jade, but she could still hear the uneven breaths that issued from him. His eyes drifted from hers and then travelled slowly down, lingering over her engorged nipples, over her narrow waist and softly indented belly, until they found the thick black curls on her pubis, and the wide-open slit beneath it. He sat transfixed by the stimulating sight of Jemma's wildly aroused body as Max pounded in and out of her cunt.

'Harder, Max,' encouraged Annalise from across the table.

Max obliged, increasing the depth and frequency of his thrusts, much to the interest of all the assembled company.

'Ah, delicious,' he groaned, pumping with manic speed.

Jemma heard Armand give a stifled moan of desire and glanced past Max's bulky presence to where their waiter stood, his hand thrust down the front of his trousers and working busily.

Dominic seemed to have more self-control than that.

Too much self-control, thought Jemma. Then her orgasm hit her, and Dominic's composure was the last thing on her mind as she lost her own. She clawed at the cool wood of the table, and her hips bucked lustily at Max's, drawing his cock ever deeper inside with each pull. Suddenly Max found this too much to bear, and shouted triumphantly with the force of his own pinnacle of pleasure.

Max's wild spasms inside her soon made Jemma come again and, at last, gratifyingly, she saw through hazy, ecstatic eyes that Dominic was on the verge of giving in to the pent-up passion he was feeling.

Her ecstasy died instantly when Dominic pulled the willing and already wet Celestine across his lap. She heard the sharp purr of his zip as he undid himself, and then she watched as he rummaged under the cover of her frilly little skirts to position himself ready to slip his big cock into the lucky girl.

He had wanted *me*, not Celestine, Jemma brooded angrily. And in a moment or two, he could have had her. So why delay matters by grabbing for Celestine instead?

As Max withdrew from her, and Jemma sat up, dabbing at her thighs daintily with one of the saucy napkins, she saw that Annalise had come around the table and was looking down at her speculatively. Annalise's nipples were fascinating to Jemma, like little cinnamon-coloured buttons, standing out so proudly from the soft fabric of her white, perfectly formed though rather small breasts. Max was tucking his cock back into his trousers, then pausing to caress Jemma's breasts briefly.

'Isn't she beautiful, this new muse of Dom's?' he asked his wife huskily.

Annalise nodded slowly. Her attention was fixed solely on Jemma, not Max. Even the busily copulating couple at the head of the table did not deflect her glance for an instant.

'She is very beautiful, and very bold,' Annalise agreed over Celestine's sighs and gasps of pleasure. 'And now, since you have had your fun with her, Jemma and I will withdraw. Enjoy your brandy, and have a good chat with Dom. Jemma and I have things to discuss.'

Do we? wondered Jemma, but she found Annalise so enticingly bossy – positively dominating, which to her surprise was something of a thrill – that she followed willingly when Annalise plucked up one of the gold, *putti*-encrusted candelabra and led the way from the room.

Annalise did not stop to retrieve her fallen gown, and neither did Jemma; she didn't wish to appear coy. Jemma gave one last regretful look back at the fully engaged Dominic and at the ecstatic girl bouncing up and down on his lap, before following Annalise out into the dark hallway.

The candles flickered in the sudden draught of the door closing behind them, and suddenly Jemma felt uncomfortably like the drowsing sleeping beauty, entranced and following the wicked witch to the room where she would be pricked with the spindle and sleep for a hundred years.

But Annalise wasn't wicked – was she?

She followed the older woman into her own bedroom without a murmur of protest. If Annalise really had something to say, then she wanted to hear it. Annalise might be able to throw some light on the mystery of Dominic's reticence, after all.

And what if she has something entirely more physical in mind? Jemma wondered briefly.

Jemma had to admit to herself that she was quite curious about that, too. Either way, she felt she had nothing to lose, and everything to gain.

When they were inside her room, Annalise flicked on the table lamp beside Jemma's bed, and placed the still-lighted candelabra upon the other table. The glow these two sources cast was soft and seductive, all a pleasingly erotic part of a carefully set scene that included the cool swish of the ceiling fan above them, and the deep bass throb of the ocean that issued through the slightly open sliding doors. Even the flowers on the balcony added their lush perfume to the warm ambience of the moment, and Jemma inhaled deeply, enjoying their fragrance.

She could smell Annalise's fragrance, too, a musky, almond perfume that she found curiously alluring, concealing as it did the heavier musk of the woman's body beneath teasing layers.

Annalise sat down on the bed, her back to the light spilling from the candelabra, and gently patted the coverlet beside her, indicating that Jemma should sit, too. Very aware of her own nakedness and of the perfume of desire that exuded from between her thighs, Jemma hesitantly sat. She felt confused by her own desire to touch Annalise's breasts, to continue the pleasures that

Max had so satisfyingly begun. But how, she wondered, did one go about seducing a woman?

And really, should she even be thinking of seduction when it was answers she really craved – answers to the continuing puzzle of Dominic's behaviour?

Although she tried to keep her eyes upon the severely planed face of Annalise, to her embarrassment she felt her eyes continually straying to the finely toned body beneath, to the gracefully sloping throat, the small but enticing breasts, the amazingly small waist where her gaze was interrupted, annoyingly, by the grey silk French knickers. Annalise's legs, draped casually sideways upon the bed, were incredibly long and thin, but shapely. Her ankles were slender and she still wore her silver high-heeled sandals.

Maybe she was self-conscious about her feet. Dancers often were. She had once heard a ballerina remark that she had the body of a twenty-year-old, and the feet of a woman of ninety. The dance might be ecstasy, but it was also pain, a delicious torture that dancers must endure because they loved it so.

'You like my body. It intrigues you,' remarked Annalise, resting her hands comfortably upon her thighs, where the muscles bulged from the pressure of the bed beneath them.

Blushing slightly, Jemma nodded. 'But I want to know about Dominic,' she said determinedly. She almost added: 'First.'

First before what? If seduction was in order, she had no idea how it might proceed. With a man, she knew exactly what to do. But women were entirely new territory to her. Best not to even consider it; she would only make a fool of herself.

'Ah, Dominic.' To Jemma's consternation, Annalise sighed and suddenly lay back upon her elbows. The flattening out of her stomach over the delicate arch of the ribs, the lengthening of the taut little breasts, the tightening of the muscles in the long, pale-skinned throat, all drew her eye maddeningly. 'And what is it you want to know, *ma chère*?' she asked, in a manner that suggested they must quickly clear this other business out of the way before attending to the real agenda for the evening.

'Why won't he make love to me?' Jemma asked flatly, determined that she would not be deflected from her purpose by the strong allure of Annalise's body.

She leant toward Annalise, and was distantly gratified to see the cool grey eyes flicker down to the heavy sway of her breasts as she did so. 'He's had the opportunity. I've even asked him to. And I sense that he wants to, very much. But he just won't,' Jemma told the older woman.

Annalise's eyes narrowed. It was as if, Jemma thought, this was a familiar refrain to the woman, as if she were slightly bored with it. New muse, old muse, she thought, her mind racing. Had the old muse, whoever she might have been, confided in Annalise exactly as Jemma did now?

With her eyes slitted like that, Annalise did look slightly wicked. Well, perhaps more than slightly.

Very wicked. Likely to eat a comparative innocent like Jemma alive, in fact, and spit out the bits, supposing any were left.

The woman's eyes were still on Jemma's breasts, and she felt an answering shiver go through her, stiffening her nipples in response to that cool grey gaze. Annalise's mouth curved into a vulpine smile as she saw this gratifying evidence of her seductive power.

'You are his muse,' she shrugged, pouting. 'Why ask for more?'

'Because I can't help it. I want him.'

Annalise nodded slowly. 'And it torments you, this desire you have for him?'

'Yes.'

'But, *chérie*, do you not think that, if Dominic had you as you wish him to, the desire that is between you would soon diminish, spoiling your artistic rapport?'

Jemma's eyes sharpened and locked with the grey ones. 'Is that what he thinks? Because I certainly don't. I think we could be very good together, so what on earth is the point of denying it, and fighting it down the way he does?'

Again that irritatingly Gallic shrug. 'Jemma, sweet Jemma. You are after all only an employee, just like that rather delicious little maid Celestine, but in another capacity, do you follow? So Dominic calls the shots. And if he wishes to keep his distance, to observe you and to be inspired by you in that way alone, then how can you argue with that?'

Jemma's back stiffened. When Annalise had said

'observe', her eyes had drifted away from their obvious enjoyment of Jemma's body to the wall behind them. She stood up restlessly, aware of Annalise still watching her nude body with avid interest, and walked over to that wall. Her own reflection peered back at her from the big gilded mirror there. Beyond her own flushed face, turgid nipples and lightly tanned skin, she saw only Annalise, reclining on the bed with the flickering lights of the candelabra flatteringly rim-lighting her severely coiffed red mane so that it glowed like fire.

Dominic himself could not have lit the woman better.

In fact, from where she stood, the bed was exquisitely lit, whether by candelabra or by the table lamps themselves.

Jemma knew that Annalise and Max were staying the night in the guest suite at the back of villa, so why had Annalise led her straight to this, her own room? Out of consideration for Max's sensibilities? She didn't think so. Max was a rake, and would not only applaud if Annalise seduced Jemma; he would almost certainly want to watch.

Idly she tapped the mirror's highly polished surface. Perhaps Max was watching her right now. Perhaps Dominic was too.

Or perhaps, she thought wryly, perhaps I am getting paranoid. Perhaps lust is making me crazy. The thought that this might be a two-way mirror, and that Dominic and Max might be settling down in Dominic's room to watch the entertainment, must surely be purest fantasy.

Quite a stimulating fantasy, though.

She stared at her reflection. Her make-up needed refreshing and, reaching down to the table beneath the mirror, she unzipped her little black satin cosmetics bag and took out a pencil-thin lipstick in that deep, sexy tulip-red shade she loved. Idly, she applied the colour to her lips, and then dotted a little on to her finger and rubbed it into her cheeks. As an afterthought, she dotted a little lipstick on to the dark tip of each breast and, with leisurely, caressing strokes, rubbed it in.

She stood back, assessing the effect, wondering if others assessed it with her. Yes, the colour made her nipples seem even more pronounced, and made the pale skin around them appear even more silky and lush than before. Thoughtfully she put down the lipstick and slid her hands over her ribcage so that they each cupped a soft, full mound.

Was she driving Dominic mad with desire right now? Or was he still with Celestine?

'Tell me more about Dominic,' she said, turning back to Annalise and walking with slow seductiveness over to the bed where she so elegantly reclined. If Dominic or even both the men were watching – which was unlikely, crazy even, but nevertheless, if they were – then let them enjoy the view; let them relish the languid sway of her buttocks, the strong and supple grace of her back, the erotic swing of her hips and legs.

As she moved she reached up and undid the top-knot that fastened her hair. Tossing the clip carelessly aside, she shook out her hair like a dark waterfall, running her fingers through it with sensuous enjoyment. Annalise watched, clearly entranced. And perhaps others watched too. Well, let them. Jemma rather liked the idea, anyway. In fact, it made her feel horny as hell.

'Like what?' asked Annalise lazily, but Jemma could hear the slight quaver in her voice as she fought the power of her own arousal.

'Like who discovered him? Like when did he start taking photographs, and when did they begin selling well? When did the art world admit that they had a genius on their hands?'

'So many questions,' breathed Annalise, but her voice was perfectly steady now, and a suggestion of concealment had come over that fine-boned face. She moved her leg, crossing it slightly over its twin, as she gave Jemma's words consideration.

'It was I who discovered him,' she admitted finally. 'He was working in a run-down studio in the East End of London and my car broke down right outside, can you believe that? No, I see that you cannot, *chérie*, but nevertheless it is true. My chauffeur was quite rude to him when he came out and offered to have a look under the bonnet, but I overrode him. He was a horrible man, so brusque. And he'd got hopelessly lost. And, of course, his pride was hurt when Dominic came out of the studio, looking so wonderful, and tried to help. You know how silly, how territorial, men can be.'

Jemma sat down on the bed again, intrigued.

'So what did you do?' she prompted.

'I dismissed the driver and left him to make his own arrangements for the removal of the car, then I went with Dominic into the studio and telephoned from there for alternative transport. And while I waited . . .'

'Yes?' nudged Jemma eagerly.

'I looked at his portfolio. His work had a raw power, a depth of vision. I can't tell you how exciting it was. Max is very wealthy, you know, and when I married him I gave up my dancing career. Sometimes I got a little bored. The children we'd expected never came along. So I dabbled in the arts, promoting people whose work I liked. And I liked Dominic's. Very much. While I was in the studio I telephoned Max, and within three months Dominic was exhibiting in one of the better West End galleries.'

'A rags-to-riches fairytale,' said Jemma, a touch cynically.

'No, it took some time until he began to be truly appreciated.' A smile quirked the corner of Annalise's thin mouth. 'But Max saw the talent Dominic had, and he drove him very hard to achieve his best work. So, for a while he was a little ragged, yes. But soon the riches came.'

'So you discovered him,' breathed Jemma.

'That is correct.'

Jemma saw the pride in the woman's eyes as she agreed.

'And of course he was very grateful.'

Annalise's eyes met Jemma's in a moment of complete female understanding. 'Magnificently grateful,' admitted Annalise, with a sigh of remembrance. 'Right there in the studio while we waited for my car. Up against a wall, of all things. As I told you, he was young and quite untutored.'

Jemma found herself wanting to ask questions like a guiltily aroused girl in the dorm after lights out. Was he good? He's so big. Did it hurt? Was it exquisitely painful? All she could think of was Annalise spreadeagled against the wall with Dominic's glorious cock buried in her. Was his hair so long then? Was he boyish to look at, or has he always looked so lean, so dangerous, so alluringly hard?

With an effort, she restrained herself. She was no sophisticate, but she was not gauche either, and certainly not gauche enough to afford Annalise a private laugh later in bed when she confided the new muse's schoolgirlish questions to Max.

Jemma restrained her curiosity. Instead she said: 'There was another muse, before me.'

Annalise's eyes narrowed again, keeping secrets. 'Ah yes.' She glanced away dismissively. 'Briefly, yes.'

'Who was she?' asked Jemma urgently. 'And why did she stop being his muse?'

Annalise's head swung round and now her eyes were distinctly unfriendly as they stared into Jemma's. The woman sat up and leant close to Jemma. Feeling threatened, Jemma nevertheless sat still, refusing to be cowed.

Annalise's silver-nailed hand lifted and the back of it rubbed lightly against one of Jemma's rouged nipples; then her hand turned and she had the tender little bud between her thumb and forefinger. Her grip tightened a little, until Jemma crossed the narrow bridge between pleasure and pain. She flinched.

'Those things are not for you to know, my beautiful Jemma,' Annalise's lips purred softly against the skin of Jemma's shoulder. She dropped a kiss on to the pearly skin there, and Jemma gave a shudder of hopeless arousal as Annalise's tongue briefly touched her flesh.

Annalise's eyes were downcast, the coppery eyelashes sweeping against her sharp-boned cheeks as she watched her own hand kneading Jemma's delicate flesh. Again there was pain, and this time Jemma gasped aloud.

'Were you his muse?' Jemma panted, wincing slightly. 'Is that it?'

'Jemma . . .' sighed Annalise, giving her head a little shake of irritation.

'Or did you just want to be?'

'All right!' Annalise leapt to her feet and rounded on Jemma angrily, her little breasts quivering enticingly in her irritation. 'Now that's enough of these questions. Is that understood? Yes, all right. I wanted to be, but I was not. It hardly matters any more. One cannot choose where inspiration comes from, it just does. You inspire him. You are a lucky, lucky girl. It could have been any other woman in the entire world, but it is you. You will be immortalised in the photographs he takes of you. Future generations will see you and marvel at your power and your beauty. Isn't that enough?'

Jemma stood up, too. Annalise was a fair bit taller than her, but she faced her down boldly.

'No,' she said. 'Actually, it isn't.'

And when Annalise seemed about to protest again, Jemma reached out and, fired by anger and by curiosity about the feel of another woman's flesh, she took a cinnamon-coloured nipple between her thumb and forefinger.

Annalise froze in shock. Oh, thought Jemma, so she thought she was the one who was going to dominate! Just to even the score a bit, she tweaked the pert little nipple quite sharply. Annalise gave a gasp and raised her own hands protectively to her breast.

However, instead of pinching as Annalise had pinched her, Jemma softened her touch so that she rubbed the nipple. As she watched appreciatively it stood up under her touch. She felt Annalise's hands trembling a little as they rested lightly over her own. Brimming with power at this enjoyable turning of the tables, Jemma drew closer to the woman and firmly pushed her hands aside.

To her surprise, Jemma realised that Annalise was cooperating with her unexpected ascendancy. Annalise's hands fell to her sides as, swiftly, Jemma came closer still. For a moment Jemma felt like a beautiful vampire about to suck blood from Annalise's throat, so savagely eager was her approach. Annalise, suddenly made aware of Jemma's healthy strength and knowing that it could easily match and even surpass her own, cringed fearfully.

Seizing the woman around the waist, Jemma dipped her dark head and fastened her lips upon the breast she still grasped in her hand. She cupped it now, holding the engorged nipple proud so that her lips could taste it more easily.

Oh yes, thought Jemma. It tasted good. She tickled the very tip of it with her tongue and was gratified to hear Annalise's moan of pleasure. Becoming more sure of her ground, Jemma lapped the nipple hungrily, feeling Annalise's back arch into her, feeling those bony hips and the woman's hard pubic mound grinding against her belly.

'Oh, that's good,' groaned Annalise, and Jemma had to agree.

Or she would have, if she didn't have her mouth full of Annalise's delectable little tit. Now she drew the whole nipple into the hot, wet cavern of her mouth and sucked greedily upon it, pulling firmly until Annalise started to look concerned that this was more punishment than pleasure.

Breathlessly Annalise grasped Jemma's head and, with an effort, pushed her back. 'Gently, *chérie*,' she begged, looking into the passion-glazed eyes of the younger woman.

Jemma's lips were parted and she was panting lightly. Her mouth was very red from the lipstick she had put on, and Annalise shuddered at the thought that yes, this girl could be sucking her blood, sucking her life and soul from her. And furthermore she would let her, and would actually enjoy letting her. Suddenly Annalise understood Dominic's fascination with Jemma. The girl had a will of iron. What she wanted, she took.

At this thought, Annalise trembled anew. She couldn't understand how this reversal of their roles had occurred so quickly. *She* was always the dominant one, the one who played the man's role – that of aggressor and seducer. But Jemma had snatched the initiative from her. Just this once, Annalise was prepared to enjoy the experience.

Jemma's hand was sliding inside the waistband of Annalise's silk drawers, and she noted the lovely texture of the fabric. Only natural fibres could feel that warm and hang so wonderfully well. Jemma loved the feel of silk, and cotton, and even finely polished wood, and the cool brilliance of gold. She was, unashamedly, a sensualist.

She moved her hand around to clasp the taut little buttocks and to knead their soft flesh, then pulled Annalise in tight against the front of her hot young body. Jemma's fingers then lingered at the peachy split in Annalise's bottom, before running inquisitively up and down the alluring crack, much to the squirming Annalise's delight.

Then Jemma was pushing the soft fabric down Annalise's hips, baring her gorgeous little navel. Jemma stared intensely at the tiny indentation, then quickly bent and licked at it. As Annalise moaned she straightened, her eyes still glued to what she was revealing. This would be her first woman, and she was determined that she was going to enjoy Annalise to the full.

Annalise's waist was pleasingly narrow, Jemma noted with interest. Her hips flared quite sexily outward where they met her seemingly endless legs. Impatiently, Jemma pushed the grey silk down a little more, gasping in delight as she uncovered Annalise's bush, which was hot, red and as thick as a fleece.

'I love your bush,' she said admiringly, her fingers busily stroking it as if it were an exotic animal.

'And I love yours, *chérie*,' panted Annalise. She reached out and grasped a hank of the thick black triangle of hair that hung between Jemma's legs. The sensation was intensely enjoyable, sending shafts of arousal into Jemma's belly and up into her breasts. Her nipples rose and rose.

Oh yes, this was good, she thought. So good. And there was a bonus, too, wasn't there? If Max and Dominic were watching from his bedroom, they would get a shock to see Jemma taking the lead, and Annalise meekly playing the submissive role.

Eagerly she pushed Annalise's knickers down, divesting the redhead of what little covering she possessed. The silk garment drifted to her slim ankles and lay there in a silvery pool. Gracefully, she stepped out of them. Jemma stared at her nakedness hungrily, making her quiver with anticipation.

'Spread out on the bed now,' instructed Jemma. 'I want to see you.'

Annalise complied, gracefully reclining upon the big bed while Jemma stood over her, watching imperiously with hands on hips.

'No, I want your legs open,' she instructed impatiently when Annalise made no move to reveal herself more fully. 'I want to see everything.'

With a little moan Annalise parted her legs slightly.

The woman was obviously unused to being sexually dominated and Jemma was entertained by how blatantly Annalise seemed to be enjoying it all. Coyly she covered her mound with her hands, and as she spread her legs wider Jemma was frustrated to find that Annalise's hands crept further down, covering the portal she so wished to see.

'I shall have to punish you for this, Annalise,' she warned her lover sternly. Snatching up a creamy coloured candle from the gold candelabra with its decoration of huge-phallused *putti*, Jemma held the flickering flame high above Annalise's quivering belly. She had tried this before, with Steven, but Annalise was not to know that. Annalise looked fearful that she was about to be burned by the droplets of hot wax.

Jemma knew better.

Annalise screamed as the wax dripped on to her flesh, and then was still. Jemma smiled into her eyes. She too had been amazed when Steven had played this particular game of 'punishment' with her.

'But it feels like kisses,' panted Annalise in relief. 'Like hot little kisses.'

'So it does.'

Jemma put the candelabra aside and knelt upon the bed. She forcibly removed Annalise's hands from between her legs, pushing them back on to the coverlet and holding them firmly. Then she sat back on her heels as she crouched between the long legs of the older woman, and looked.

The turgid little clitoris was the first thing she

saw, poking out lustily from its rose-petalled frills of gleaming wet flesh. Further down was the dark-slitted opening she sought, and, beyond that, the little portal to the anus that could be, she knew from her own experience, so sensitive, so very responsive.

The dark red hair fringing Annalise's delicious opening was dew-dotted like grass on a cold English morning. Jemma bent her head and slowly, delicately, lapped at the salty moisture. Annalise's hips lifted from the bed, whether in protest or in aquiescence Jemma neither knew nor cared.

She licked enthusiastically, then turned her attention to the needy little clitoris and sucked it lightly. Then she nibbled at the petals surrounding it, all the while aware of Annalise writhing and crying out beneath her, and then, deliberately – and even a little brutally – she stabbed her tongue into the salty slit of Annalise's vagina. She pushed it in as far as it would go, lapping the silken walls with small circular movements.

Jemma's hair fell forward to tease and tickle at Annalise's belly. The sides of her breasts hung firm and full against the woman's trembling inner thighs. Releasing Annalise's hands, Jemma pulled the woman's legs up over her shoulders. Annalise, gasping and shivering with the intensity of her pleasure, grabbed the brass rails of the headboard and gave herself up to the needs of the extraordinary young creature who loomed over her, hair a wild tangle of darkness, breasts swinging wildly. Moving her body forward slightly, Jemma pressed herself hard against the woman's sex.

With a firm grip on her ankles it was just possible for her to grind herself against Annalise's hot cunt. It felt gloriously naughty and very different from any sex she'd had before.

Then Jemma, not easing up the pressure on either of them, slipped her right hand between their two straining bodies, smoothly inserting two fingers into Annalise's wide-open cunt, while her thumb played over the woman's clit.

Such extremes of ecstasy could not long be borne. Annalise bucked crazily as her orgasm took her. While her partner was still crying out with pleasure, Jemma brought her hand to her own sex, the fingers still moist with Annalise's juices, and began frantically rubbing herself off until she too was satisfied, crying out loudly and pumping at the supine Annalise until finally she grew still. Sated, she sprawled out beside her conquered lover.

'That was good,' she sighed blissfully.

'Mmm, it was,' Annalise murmured in reply.

But her voice was speculative and edged with the faintest of challenges. It seemed to say, yes that was good, but next time I shall be ready for you and I will be in control, my pretty aggressor.

Jemma smiled as sleep started to fog the edges of her perceptions. It would be quite a tussle, she was sure of that.

And great fun.

Chapter Ten

Jemma was roughly dragged from sleep next morning by the ringing of her mobile phone. Pushing the hair out of her eyes, she sat up groggily, reached for her bag which was on the floor beside the bed, and dragged the phone out.

'Yes?' she murmured, stifling a yawn. She looked around her, coming slowly to her senses. The lamp had been switched off, although the ceiling fan still turned slowly. The candles on the candelabra had all guttered and finally gone out, their melting wax pooling on to the cherubs and, she noticed with a smile, hiding their lewdly rampant members.

Annalise was gone.

Jemma stretched out a hand. The pillow that bore the indentation of the woman's head was cold.

'Jemma?'

'Steven? How's Munich?'

'Full of boisterous blonde Valkyries,' said Steven, and there was giggling in the background.

Jemma smiled, pleased that he was enjoying himself. Then her eyes wandered to the sliding door, which was a little open so that the salty morning breeze lazily caressed and stirred the muslin drapes. Last night, the door had been closed. And since there was only one other room that led off that balcony, there were two possibilities to consider. One: that Annalise had left not by the interior door but by the balcony door, and gone into Dominic's room to continue the evening's fun. Or two: Dominic had been in here while she had been asleep.

Whichever, she hardly cared. She had been sprawled out totally naked on the bed when she fell asleep, and the thought of Dominic standing over her, perhaps becoming excited by the sight of her, was definitely stimulating.

'Tell me some more about Dominic Vane,' she said, not caring if Dominic was watching her through a two-way mirror; not even caring if her room was bugged, which was a possibility, given that she was an object of such fascination for the photographer. She was interested; she wanted to know more. There was something going on here with this crazy abstinence of Dominic's, and any information would surely help her to crack the code and unlock his secret.

'Angel, I've told you nearly everything I know,' said Steven.

'That he hasn't exhibited for over a year,' said Jemma, remembering Steven's words and that very enjoyable evening in the flat with him.

'That's right. And I read in one of the art reviews that the critics were saying he'd lost it. Something to do with his muse having deserted him.'

The muse again!

'Well apparently I am his new muse,' Jemma said lightly. 'But I am trying to find out who the old one was, and why she deserted him, whatever that might mean.'

Steven drew in a sharp breath, and Jemma smiled at the phone.

'I hope you're paying attention to what I'm saying, Steven,' she teased.

'It's difficult,' admitted Steven, gasping a little as he said: 'There is this beautiful blonde lady, absolutely ravishing, and right at this moment . . .'

'Yes?' Jemma prompted, intrigued.

'She has my cock halfway down her throat.'

'How does it feel?' asked Jemma, wanting to share in the experience.

'Glorious. Hot. Wet. Very tight.'

'And here I am, all alone,' sighed Jemma.

'What, no Dominic?'

'Dominic refuses to touch me,' pouted Jemma, pulling her knees up to her breasts and linking an arm around her legs as if to comfort herself at this thought.

'He's mad,' gasped Steven.

'Apparently he's as sane as you or I,' Jemma replied tartly. 'So the question I have to ask myself is, why won't he touch me?'

'Have you asked him?'

'Yes, and no go.'

'Other people there?'

'Yes again. And again, just a cut-off.'

'They haven't, for instance – God, Greta! – they haven't told you he's gay or bi or anything like that?'

'He's hetero. I've seen him in action.' Jemma paused, listening to the interesting sounds coming down the line to her. 'What's Greta up to now?'

'Squatting on top of me, and just lifting herself up and down on my cock.' Steven's breath was becoming harsher, his words more disjointed. 'God, that's so good.'

'Does she have big breasts?'

'Enormous,' gasped Steven in satisfaction.

'And they're right in front of you now?' prompted Jemma when he broke off, panting hard.

'Mmm. She's got these huge nipples, very pale pink like opening rosebuds. Jemma, I really have to go.'

Disappointingly, the line went dead. Jemma tossed the phone back into her bag, got off the bed, stuck her tongue out at the mirror, and went to shower.

As she sat on the shaded deck of Max and Annalise's motor cruiser two hours hater, Jemma had to admit that she could easily get used to a life like this.

A life of indolence. A life of being an icon, a source of near-worship. Woman as goddess, she thought, and had to suppress a smile.

She sipped the wine that the crew had provided and lounged back to have a good look around. The yacht was about sixty feet long, which was not big by Cap

Ferrat standards. There were many moored nearby that were a fair bit bigger; a couple of them even sported helicopters, perched like toys upon their landing pads at the stern of the yachts. But Max and Annalise's yacht was nevertheless luxuriously appointed and very well stabilised. Moored at anchor in the bay, the *Annalise* moved only slightly in the soft swell of the water. The dazzling sun glinted off the aquamarine sea and a soft breeze tickled her skin where it was not encumbered by the skimpy white bikini she wore.

Max, Dominic and Annalise were also dressed in bathing clothes, since it was too hot up on the deck – despite the huge canopy rigged above the lunch table to protect them from the full glare of the Mediterranean sun – to wear more.

Jemma looked at Annalise, who was sitting opposite her. Annalise always chose metallics, Jemma noted with interest. Her bikini, as minute as Jemma's own, was of a shimmering bronze lycra mix, and her lips and nails had been meticulously painted to match. Her russet hair was hanging loose today in a neat, shining, shoulder-length bob that seemed to catch and hold the hot fire of the sun. She wore sunglasses, to shield her eyes and, perhaps, Jemma thought, also to hide her expression.

From behind her own sunglasses Jemma found herself admiring Annalise's long, strong body and thinking about what she had done to it last night, caressing it, overpowering it, making it writhe and scream. But from the cool welcome she had been given by the woman today, she suspected that Annalise's recollections were not so fond. She was aware that she had pleasured Annalise beyond the woman's expectations, but was aware too that the woman's pride had been dented by their steamy interlude.

Annalise liked to be in control; it was as simple as that.

And Jemma had snatched control from her.

Wondering if Annalise might be planning to make her pay for her transgressions, Jemma shivered deliciously. If there was a price to be paid for such exquisite delights, then so be it. She would look forward to her punishment. Meanwhile, she watched the toss of Annalise's hair and the glint of light on the sunglasses that hid all expression, before lazily turning her attention to the two men who stood by the rail.

Both men wore the requisite Continental black briefs, revealing in Max's case a compact and well-toned body and, in Dominic's case, a body that many men would gladly sell their souls to the devil for.

He was taller than Max, his shoulders broad, his hips enticingly narrow. His chest was gloriously muscular, and his stomach looked hard as steel. Jemma could barely take her eyes from the oil-smeared brown skin of his thighs, where the dark hair grew in abundance. The wind was catching his long, dark gleaming hair and tossing it this way and that. He looked like a pirate, she thought with relish, stripped and ready to dive into the ocean, a cutlass between his teeth. She could imagine him boarding another vessel and making off with the most beautiful woman on board.

God, I wish he'd make off with me, thought Jemma, heaving an irritated sigh.

Perhaps that was what Dominic had done. Like Faust, he may have sold his soul. Made a bargain with God or the devil – who knew which? Perhaps he had said to some all-seeing, all-knowing deity: 'Please, give me a new muse and I promise I will not consort with her.' So the muse became both a pleasure and a pain, delightful to behold and also a torment, because to touch her would be to break the bargain and perhaps wreak havoc.

Sheer fancy, thought Jemma, laughing at herself. And thinking about the pleasure and the pain of their peculiar relationship, she had to privately admit that there were advantages to it. The continuing itch of Dominic's denial was a hot, heavy presence between them. If they had had sex, perhaps they could have put that to one side to some extent – although, with Dominic, Jemma did wonder if that would be possible. She couldn't easily imagine remaining aloof in his presence. Because of their continued forced abstinence from the fleshly delights they could so easily have shared, Jemma was finding that she had never felt so outrageously sexual.

She knew that Dominic felt the same.

Watching him moving about the deck, sipping a long cool drink as he chatted to Max before lunch was served, she felt his eyes on her. When she glanced at him, she found that she could read nothing in his face. Annoyingly, he too wore sunglasses to protect his eyes from the dazzle of sea and the light, and they hid his thoughts from her.

But nothing could hide the sudden lustful surge at the front of his bathing trunks.

Yes, he felt the same.

But he also felt restrained; obliged in some way to resist.

Annalise, watching her as she gazed entranced at Dominic's arousal, said: 'You can't have him, you know.'

Jemma clinked the ice around her glass and smiled sweetly at Annalise. 'Why, because you want him first?'

'No, you know why. You're his muse.'

'I may be that, but I am also a woman with needs and feelings.'

Annalise chuckled dryly. Dominic was leaning against the rail talking to Max, and his erection was still evident. 'As you can see, stubborn one, he is fully aware of that.'

Jemma took a long draught of her drink and put her glass down on the table between them. Calculatingly, she raised an arm so that the back of her hand rested across her brow. Tiny beads of sweat were forming there, and she casually wiped them away, aware that as she moved so did her breasts. Licking her lips invitingly, she lifted her hair free of the back of her neck for a moment to let the breeze play over her moist skin.

All the while, her eyes were on Dominic. And it was clear that Dominic's eyes were on her, judging by the rearing outline beneath that tiny triangle of black material he wore.

'I think I'll slip this off, it's so hot,' she said casually. 'You don't mind, do you?' she asked Annalise.

'Not at all,' shrugged Annalise, her mouth curving in a knowing smile. 'Upping the stakes, are we, *chérie*?'

'I really don't know what you mean,' replied Jemma with studied innocence, and reached behind her to unclasp the white bra top. It unclipped easily, and just as easily her dark-tipped, lushly full and naked breasts fell free.

'Well, what is sauce for the goose . . .' said Annalise smiling, her eyes avidly taking in this unexpected treat. With slow, deliberate movements she unbuttoned the halter top of her own bikini, then unfastened the back. She placed the discarded scrap of material in her rattan bag on the deck beside the table and sat back casually, her charmingly perky little breasts with their puckered cinnamon-coloured nipples seeming almost to salute those larger, more womanly orbs across the table.

Annalise glanced at Dominic and let out a throaty, excited laugh. 'Look!' she whispered to Jemma.

Jemma looked over at Dominic. The tiny briefs were under a great deal of pressure. Clearly both women could see the full outline of his cock beneath the spandex fabric. Peering more closely, Jemma thought she could even see his cock's delectable pink helmet questing above the top of the material. Wetness seeped hungrily between her thighs, and she almost groaned aloud with wanting.

'God, I wish he'd take them off,' she moaned.

'Do you see the head?' hissed Annalise, watching raptly.

'Yes.' Jemma's mouth was so dry with lust that she had to take another drink. 'Yes, I do.'

Max turned around at that moment, saw that their two female companions had divested themselves of their bikini tops, and grinned broadly in appreciation. His penis too jerked in delighted response. He said something, laughing, to Dominic, and tapped the front of Dominic's bathing trunks. Dominic glanced down, laughed too, and laboriously tucked his unruly organ back beneath its covering.

The two men approached the lunch table and sat down, Dominic beside Jemma, Max beside Annalise.

'This is very pleasant,' said Max, smiling around at his three companions, paying particular attention to the two women who were naked to the hips. 'Very pleasant indeed. Like Manet's *Déjeuner sûr l'herbe*, only more sexy.'

'More?' Annalise looked at her husband curiously.

'Yes, my darling. Because those ladies were totally naked, while you two are not yet ready to reveal all your secrets. And a little mystery is very stimulating.'

'Hardly much mystery in my case, Max. After all, I am your wife.'

'And you know how much I love your lovely little red bush.'

They exchanged teasing glances. Even Dominic smiled. Jemma felt at once that she was almost surplus to requirements here; that these two men and this woman were a unit, working and loving together, and that she was no more than an intrusive accessory.

The thought annoyed her.

No, she was important here. She was not going to let their little games affect her own usually solid self-esteem – no way.

'But I shall forego the pleasure of feasting my eyes upon it, for the moment,' said Max gallantly. 'If you insist on keeping it covered.'

'Oh, Max, what a libertine you are,' laughed Annalise, standing up and holding her arms aloft in a pose of abject surrender.

She looked like one of those exquisite Art Deco bronze and ivory figures, thought Jemma, feeling her own juices beginning to flow faster at the sight of Annalise's delicate beauty.

'Come then, if you must,' she sighed prettily, and Max pulled her unprotesting form between his hairy, muscular thighs and eagerly unfastened the ties, one at each hip, of the bikini bottom.

Jemma looked to her right and saw that, up on the little flybridge of the motor yacht, the three young suntanned males that constituted three quarters of the crew were ogling both her and Annalise shamelessly. She was amused by their fascination. One of them, a particularly handsome sun-bleached blond wearing cut off jeans and nothing else, waved shyly. She raised her glass to him discreetly but, when she turned back to the lunch table, she found that Dominic had noticed the exchange and was smiling wryly at her.

Max meanwhile had achieved his objective. With the ties undone on the little bikini, Jemma was afforded an excellent view of Annalise's taut white buttocks as the material fell away from them and the garment hung loose, trapped only by the snug pressure between her thighs. She caught it at the front with her hand, teasingly, so that her hand covered the mound Max so wanted to see.

'Now darling, don't be coy,' Max chastised her lightly, his voice husky with desire.

Annalise smiled and dextrously slipped the scrap of fabric out from under her concealing hand.

'Anna,' complained Max.

'Oh, all right,' she said, and revealed herself with a great show of reluctance.

'Look, isn't she lovely, my little red fox?'

Max affectionately ran a hand over her neatly clipped fiery bush while Annalise squirmed with delight.

Dominic clapped this performance enthusiastically, and Annalise gave a dainty little bow, then sat down. 'She is lovely,' he agreed. Annalise nodded slightly in thanks for this compliment.

Jemma wondered what the hell was expected of her now. Did they expect her to pull off her knickers, too, like a schoolgirl enraged at unfair competition and desperate to impress? Well she wasn't going to.

Not unless Dominic asked her to.

'It's so hot, Jemma. Why don't you . . .?' he then said, shocking her so much she almost choked on her drink.

For God's sake! What was he doing this for, putting

them both through hell again and again? Later, he was going to take pictures of her on board; he had brought all his gear with him. So was this a necessary part of his creative process, this incredibly frustrating sexual buildup? Or was he just a masochist?

Irritable, blushing, aware of the watching boys on the flybridge and of the intense attention she was attracting around the table, Jemma stood up. Dominic had taken off his shades and his lime-green eyes now watched her with challenging directness. She started to slip her fingers inside the bikini bottom to pull it down, when Dominic halted her with a hand on her wrist.

Puzzled, Jemma felt him pulling her between his knees. Then she understood. He was going to do to her what Max had done to Annalise. He was going to strip her.

Suddenly she could hardly breathe. His thighs on either side of hers felt hairy, hot, very strong. They held her like a statuette clamped into a vice.

Dominic's eyes were almost on a level with her breasts. Putting her own sunglasses on to the table as a gesture of defiance, Jemma stared boldly into his eyes and almost dared him to continue.

But of course, he would. Self-torture seemed necessary to him.

Which was okay by her, if that's what turned him on. But unfortunately his games also tortured her, damn him. And she found the silent watching by Max and Annalise unnerving.

Dominic's hands went not to her bikini bottom

but rested lightly upon her hips, where they lightly smoothed over the silky skin there. It was the first time he had touched her. Jemma found herself unprepared for the sheer power of her own passion when he did. His hands were big, long-fingered, and they were pleasingly dry. She hated clammy fingers on her. But Dominic's were lovely.

His hands were sliding over her belly, making the skin there flutter wildly, then up to her waist, lingering there as if caressing an instrument of great worth. They then travelled slowly up over the deep curve of her ribcage until they rested just under the full thrust of her breasts. Her nipples tingled with hungry need. Jemma's head went back in anticipation of pleasure, and her eyes closed. A tiny groan escaped her.

When he hesitated, she opened her eyes and looked down into his. Go on, she thought, and there was an encouraging twinkle in her eye. Don't stop! But his eyes had changed. They wore that blank, closed-off expression again. His hands retraced their route instead of rising to cup and caress her breasts. They slid back down over her ribs, under which her heart beat a furious tattoo. They paused again at her waist. Then they travelled on, and there was something almost deliberately brutal and uncaring in he way his fingers hooked into the fabric of her bikini bottom and swiftly dragged it down.

Jemma stood utterly still, almost panting with the strength of her desire. She looked down at Dominic and saw that, despite the sudden blankness in his eyes, he was extremely aroused. The bold pink head of his penis was again showing a little above the line of his black bathing trunks.

She could feel her sex swelling, too, wet and straining and desperate to be touched. Slowly, very slowly, his hand was rising, stretching towards it. He was going to touch her bush, perhaps slip a finger into the dewy little slit that so ached for his attention.

Oh yes, she thought eagerly. Do it!

'This has gone far enough!'

Jemma turned her head, startled.

It was Annalise who had spoken, leaping to her feet on the other side of the table, her breasts quivering with agitation.

'Anna . . .' warned Max lightly.

'No, it has,' she snapped at him, and then she leant on the table and looked across at Jemma with unconcealed spite in her taut little smile. 'I think the time has come for you to pay for your transgressions, my beautiful Jemma.'

Jemma looked at her, then back at Dominic. He shrugged, seemingly unwilling to come to her aid. 'I wasn't aware that I had committed any dreadful sins,' she said.

'Where is that boy with the lunch?' Max asked, trying to defuse the tension around the table.

'To hell with lunch!' said Annalise, who had the bit well between her teeth.

'Annalise, calm down,' suggested Dominic.

'When she taunts you with her body, and endangers

all that you are, all that you could be? No, it's time she realised what her position is here.'

'And what is that?' enquired Jemma coolly.

'Subservient,' Annalise hissed back.

'I was hardly that last night when I had you on the bed, was I?' Jemma returned goadingly.

'You see?' Annalise said angrily to Dominic. Then, regaining her self-control a little, she looked back at Jemma. 'It's time she learned her lesson.'

She turned to the dark-haired boy who was nervously approaching the table with a tray of starters, and waved him impatiently back to his galley. 'Later, boy. Can't you see we're busy? For now you can make yourself useful in other ways. Bring me some rope.'

The bewildered boy sent a fearful, blushing glance around at the naked and near-naked diners, and managed to say: 'Rope, Mrs Klein?'

'Rope. R-O-P-E. Bring it.'

'What are you going to do, Annalise? Tie me up and force-feed me?' Jemma could almost have laughed at this farce. 'I'm quite hungry, actually.' She addressed her next words to Max. 'Your wife has taken offence because I took the sexual initiative last night, Max.'

But Max was not his usual jocular self today – that was clear. Not smiling, he replied: 'No, I think the offence goes a little deeper than that, Jemma.'

The boy had returned at a run with the rope. He hesitated beside Annalise, intimidated and also obviously aroused by the tall naked woman.

'Good,' she purred at him, giving the tempting bulge

at the crotch of his white denim trousers an encouraging tweak. 'Tie her hands behind her back.'

Jemma almost laughed aloud in disbelief. But the boy meekly came around the table, almost apologetically pulled her hands back, and proceeded to tie them firmly together at the wrists with the tough chandler's rope he'd brought.

Her eyes went to Dominic, and then to Max, in outrage, but they both looked away. Angrily she strained her wrists against the bonds, but the boy had been thorough. She could not get her hands free.

'That's good. Now bring her,' instructed Annalise, snatching up the fruit knife from its dish on the table.

Jemma felt a distinct twinge of misgiving. What the hell was the knife for? She didn't mind indulging them in their bondage games, she suspected she was in for some fun, but why the knife? The boy was grasping her arm and tugging her along in Annalise's wake. The tall, copper-haired woman was hurrying towards the stern of the boat, and the boy quickly followed with his captive.

Jemma glanced back. She saw that Dominic and Max were following more slowly. And the boys up on the flybridge were hooting and cheering as if this were all part of some lewd entertainment.

The boy yanked her forward again, and she almost fell, but he caught her, then dragged her up. Panting, she collided with the front of his hot young body, and felt the furious thundering of his heart and the hard poke of his erection. He was frightened of Annalise, but not without sympathy for Jemma, she could see that.

Annalise had gone down a short stainless-steel ladder to the small bathing platform at the stern. Earlier, they had dived and swum from this point, and the diving-board was still there, hanging out over the sea.

The boy, realising that she could not manage the ladder because of her bonds, lowered Jemma carefully down on to the platform with surprising strength.

'Go now,' ordered Annalise, and he quickly disap-peared in the direction of the galley, grateful to get away from these employers of his with their sophisticated games.

Annalise approached Jemma, her eyes assessing rapaciously the full, healthy beauty of Jemma's lush young body. Jemma too was enjoying giving Annalise the once-over. She loved that silky red bush, just as Max did. And those cinnamon-coloured nipples – how sweet they had tasted last night! Had her hands been free, she would have reached out to caress the other woman. Such close contact with Dominic had made her feel extremely eager for sex.

'On to the board,' ordered Annalise, licking her lips greedily at the feast before her. 'You're going to walk the plank, my beauty!'

'Annalise, this is ridiculous,' sighed Jemma. 'Untie my wrists and let's go to your cabin. You know how much pleasure I can give you.'

'On the plank!' repeated Annalise, and to Jemma's amazement she dashed round behind her and pricked her buttock lightly with the fruit knife. A little arrow of pain shot through her, and she flinched. 'Ah, did I prick you?' crooned Annalise by her shoulder.

'Only that's not the sort of prick you want, is it, *ma chère?* You want Dominic's, and not here.' Her hand skimmed over Jemma's trembling, delightful buttock, which showed only a faint indentation from the knife's pressure. 'You want him here.'

Annalise's slender hand slid into the deep peach-like cleft of Jemma's arse and found the tight little bud of her anus. It moved on slowly to the wet, eager opening, and her fingers teased and pinched lightly at the jaunty little bud of Jemma's clitoris, Jemma moaned with pleasure and opened her legs a little so that Annalise could proceed more easily.

'Ah, no,' Annalise murmured as Jemma's back arched willingly. Her buttocks pushed at Annalise's hand, presenting her aching, empty cunt to the taller woman. 'No, beautiful one. First you learn discipline.'

Again the point of the knife pricked at her, this time on the other buttock. Jemma gasped with the slight pain of it, and glanced back as she heard movement. Dominic and Max had come down the ladder and were standing a little apart from the scene Annalise was playing out. Both were watching avidly, and both were clearly very aroused by her performance.

As Jemma watched, Max said: 'You know, these things are far too restricting,' and pushed his bathing trunks down around his ankles, stepping out of them neatly. 'That's better,' he said in relief, looking down at his towering, chunky brown penis and giving it a light, admiring stroke with his hand. His eyes met Jemma's, and he winked at her encouragingly.

'You're right,' said Dominic, and even Annalise paused from administering punishment to Jemma so that she could watch him strip.

As he pushed down the trunks, his cock loomed up tight to his waist. It was of almost identical thickness to Max's, but longer. Dominic stepped out of his trunks, making his balls stir heavily beneath their thick furry covering. Unlike Max, he did not touch himself; he folded his arms and leant back against the ladder, preparing to enjoy the spectacle these two very different but exceedingly alluring naked women presented. The head of his fine pink cock was open slightly, and a pearly glint of seed sparkled there in the sunlight.

Jemma wanted to lick it off. Then she wanted to lick his cock, every proud inch of it, and then his balls, and then take that lovely thing into her mouth and bring him to screaming ecstasy as she knew she could.

Glancing at Annalise, she could see that she too was enthralled by Dominic's mighty organ. But suddenly Annalise was all business again, goading her with the little knife along the plank. Jemma, her balance affected by her bound arms, obligingly made her way in wobbly fashion along the thing until she reached the end.

Here was where this very stimulating game had to finish. With her wrists tied, she would be unable to swim if she went off the end of the plank. She half-turned to speak to Annalise and, at that moment, a particularly

sharp lunge from the little fruit knife made her jump
and let out a shriek. She lost her balance instantly, and
fell into the deep blue water.

Chapter Eleven

'Sometimes,' Max said to Jemma as they sat in a luxurious restaurant in Monte Carlo two hours after her ordeal, 'Annalise goes a little too far with her jealousies.'

Jemma nodded in agreement and forked disinterestedly at the excellent dish of salad and chargrilled goat's cheese that had been reverentially set before her by an immaculately dressed waiter.

She was still a little dazed at Annalise's actions. Of course, the woman had not meant her to fall from the plank. It had up until then been an erotic game without a hint of real danger, and certainly Dominic and Max had enjoyed it too, until Jemma had actually lost her balance and fallen in.

Then – and this grated a little on Jemma, even now – it was Max who dived in; Max who untied her hands so that she could swim back to the platform. And it had been Max, not Dominic, who had – while they were still in the water – slipped his hotly aroused penis into the waiting depths of her cunt, and brought them both to a very satisfactory orgasm.

When they finally separated and climbed back aboard the *Annalise*, the woman the boat had been named for had disappeared into her stateroom with Dominic, although the crew were still up on the flybridge, and they applauded warmly as the naked pair crossed the deck and went below to shower and change.

Max nipped into his dressing-room, which adjoined the master stateroom, and could not avoid hearing the noises of lovemaking coming from in there. He could not resist a peak through the slightly open door, either, and relished the stimulating sight of Dominic's taut buttocks pumping up and down energetically between the wide-open legs of Annalise.

Smiling, he selected some suitable clothes for a little trip up the coast, and then joined Jemma in her shower. They were going to take lunch, just the two of them, in a little place he was very fond of in Monte Carlo. Best leave Anna and Dom to it, for now, he thought. Let tempers cool.

Jemma, letting Max soap her breasts as he wished to do, happily agreed to this plan. For her part, there was no question of temper. She had simply slipped and ruined Annalise's very sexy game, which would probably otherwise have ended with the four of them in bed together.

She kept telling herself that Annalise had not intended her to fall.

Certainly not.

And, anyway, if Annalise had Dominic – for the moment – she had Max, and he was a very good substitute. As he soaped between her legs, pushing his wrist delightfully against her clitoris while his fingers explored deeper, she reflected that lunch with Max alone might be a much more pleasurable bet today.

She stroked his towering cock admiringly as the hot water cascaded soothingly on to their tangled bodies. When he had used the hand attachment to rinse the soap from her bush and from the dark valley between her thighs, she tenderly rubbed a thick lather of apricot-scented soap into his lustily twitching organ while he groaned with the exquisite pleasure of it.

Not willing to rush so enjoyable a task, she then gently soaped his balls, matting the dark hair there with the lather. Her deft fingers ventured further, smoothing over his deliciously firm thighs and up to swirl around the tight little bud of his anus. Then she rinsed Max thoroughly while he kissed her neck and avidly caressed her gleaming wet breasts.

Finally he lifted her against the tiles, pulling her thighs open and wrapping her legs around his waist. The intrusion of his hot, wet penis into her eager sex was a physical shock of huge contrasts as her back was pressed against the cold tiles. It was a delightful contrast, like being steamed in a hot sauna then plunging into a crystal-blue and well-chilled plunge pool. Sexy. She loved it.

Max's hips rocked busily back and forth, and they kissed beneath the teeming water, mouths open, tongues meeting and caressing. Their mutual climax was sudden, and extremely good.

Later, as they dressed, Max caught Jemma's hand as she went to put on a pair of white silk panties.

'No pants,' he said huskily, kissing her with warmth. 'I want to know, as we travel around today, that there is nothing covering your lovely little cunt; nothing to keep you from me.'

'All right,' said Jemma, both amused and aroused by this. She returned his kiss, and left the pants off. She put on a lemon-coloured linen shift dress, and nothing else except her gold sandals and a casual straw carryall slung over her shoulder, containing her purse, her mobile, her travellers' cheques, her identification, her hairbrush, perfume, and a small bag of make-up.

Max left a note for Annalise, and then he and Jemma were taken ashore in the tender by one of the crew. There Max picked up his sporty red Mercedes convertible and, with the top down and the sun beaming like a hot caress upon them, they drove along the spectacular cliffside corniche to Monte Carlo.

And now here they were, in the restaurant, and the very last thing on Jemma's mind as she looked across the table at Max Klein was food.

She thought how handsome he was, how suave. So different from Dominic. Dominic was a bit of a wild man; his walk was a naturally seductive swagger, his hair usually hung long and loose, and he favoured jeans and open-necked shirts with the sleeves rolled up rather than worn in a formal style.

It was as if clothes were an irritating restriction to Dominic.

But Max! Max wore clothes with panache, and he only wore the best, the most exquisitely tailored and most refined of fabrics: silk for his shirts, fine linen for his trousers, cashmere for his socks. He relished the rich, the fine, the expensive. Just like this restaurant, Jemma thought. Sighing impatiently as he finished his meal, Jemma realised it was Max she was hungry for, not food.

She wriggled deliciously on the soft velvet banquette. Not wearing any pants in public was a far more erotic experience than she had bargained for. It gave her a feeling of vulnerability, and also the urge to shock. In fact, it was driving her half-crazy with desire.

The velvet of the banquette was soft but so firm on her thighs. What would it feel like, she wondered, if she hitched her thin linen dress up – just a little, for it was extremely short, daringly short, with no pants on – and let her nude behind come into close contact with the dark, ivy-green velvet?

Max placed his knife and fork together and pushed his plate aside. Watching her intently, he dabbed at his mouth with the fine damask napkin and then tossed it carelessly on to the plate.

'What are you thinking about?' he asked her huskily.

'Oh, nothing,' said Jemma with a shrug.

'Come on, tell me. You're looking a little flushed, you know. And your nipples are standing up. I can see them right through that thin linen shift you're wearing, and it is making me feel rather excited.'

'Max!' hissed Jemma, both scandalised and delighted because he had spoken in his normal tone of voice and several heads had turned.

'All right, I'll speak lower. Is that better? Now tell me what is on your mind.'

Jemma let out a trembling breath. 'I was thinking about the velvet on the banquette and what it would feel like . . .' Her voice trailed away. She felt herself beginning to blush.

'If you pulled up your dress?' encouraged Max. He sat back, obviously enjoying this conversation enormously. 'Go on then. Do it. Only you and I know that you are naked underneath.'

Glancing nervously around, Jemma made sure that she was unobserved. Then, discreetly, she lifted her buttocks a fraction and pulled up the thin lemon fabric. The sensation of the thick velvet pile upon her exposed cleft was so exquisite that she let out a gasp of shock.

'How does it feel?' prompted Max.

'Wonderful.' Jemma moved a little, pressing down harder on to the banquette. Ah, exquisite! she thought, and could not help but press her thighs together as that hard, hungry pulse began to beat between her legs.

Max was watching her avidly. 'No wonder Dominic chose you,' he said.

'He chose me because I enjoy sex, apparently,'

returned Jemma, trying not to pant as the sensations became more intense. 'But I'm not his first muse. There was another. Annalise told me.'

'And should I tell you more? Should I tell you about Vena?'

Jemma was stilled for a moment, distracted from her very pleasurable encounter with the nubby velvet seat. 'Vena? So that's her name.'

Max smiled. 'Obviously you know very little about the art world, Jemma. Her image was everywhere in the eighties. Did you not see Dominic's interpretation of Vena as Venus, rising naked from the waves? It was incredible.'

'No.' Jemma was feeling increasingly aroused and desperate for an orgasm, so stimulating was the sensation of the material beneath her swollen sex. She pressed down harder, gripping the edge of the table to increase the friction.

'Or the one of Vena playing squash wearing nothing but a headband? Or the one of her washing between her legs with a sponge? Those sold in limited editions to collectors all around the world.'

It was no use; she was not concentrating on what Max was saying. She began to rock slightly back and forth, biting her lip and feeling flushed.

'Oh, Max,' she cried suddenly and came, clenching her buttocks hard, pushing her clitoris down on to the velvet pile. She suppressed a cry of pleasure.

Max's smile broadened. 'Good?' he enquired softly.

'Marvellous,' sobbed Jemma, slowly returning to

her senses. What was she doing, masturbating in a restaurant, in full view of the other diners? Dominic's words came back to her. 'People seem to drip sex here. It's the climate.'

Suddenly she was embarrassed. 'Max, can we go?'

'Of course, my darling,' crooned Max, and Jemma was amazed to find that she wanted him again soon – very soon.

Max settled the bill and they left to wander along the gilded shops that lined the prosperous streets of Monte Carlo. All the designers had their wares on display here, and there was one particularly alluring little emporium, sporting very daring lingerie and evening wear, that Jemma lingered in front of, her arm tucked through Max's.

'That would suit you,' said Max, pointing out a very revealing white lace teddy. Suddenly he was pushing open the door, making a bell chime inside the thickly carpeted and seemingly empty shop, pulling her along with him. 'Come on. Try it on. Let's see what it looks like on you.'

Jemma hesitated. 'You were going to tell me more about Vena.'

'And I will, my darling. Later.'

The shop assistant was a neatly groomed and well-proportioned woman in her thirties whom Max seemed to know already. She wore her thick dark hair in a French pleat, and Jemma thought that she had lovely blue eyes and a very sensual mouth. It was a mouth made for fellatio and cunnilingus, very wide for her face, with bee-stung lips glossily painted with fuschia-pink lipstick.

'Yvette, my little companion wishes to try on that beautiful thing you have in the window. The white one,' Max said to the woman with easy familiarity. 'And maybe that one, too? That little leopard-skin-look number. And the black one, also.'

'But of course,' said Yvette with a deferential nod of the head. She asked him to please be seated, and Max sat on the spindle-legged gold chair she indicated. She then smiled at Jemma, and escorted her to the back of the shop. There she drew back a thick brocade curtain set on a pole with brass rings, and ushered Jemma into a brightly lit cubicle, which was mirrored on three sides.

As Yvette went to fetch the flimsy garments for her, Jemma put down her bag on the tall stool to one side of the cubicle and eagerly stripped off the lemon linen shift. She beheld three naked Jemmas in the mirrors, each one heavy-breasted, slender and dark-bushed – and each one had a very naughty smile on her face, the smile of a beautiful young woman who was being pampered and spoilt by a host of admirers. For the first time since her arrival in France, she felt free of Dominic's hold over her.

Behind her, suddenly, the curtain drew aside and Yvette appeared holding the lace teddy. The woman's eyes roamed over Jemma's nude body with extreme interest, and Jemma found herself wondering if Yvette was busy speculating on what her relationship with Max could be. Well, she wanted no more of a relationship with Max than she already had – that of a free-loving and pleasant companion. Any further involvement would surely mean crossing Annalise, and she was surprisingly reluctant to do that. Besides, the enigma of Dominic would be enough to occupy her thoughts on her return to the villa.

Losing your nerve, Jemma? she taunted herself lightly as she realised that she did not want to cross Annalise again. For once, no ready answer came.

Maybe she was. Maybe, in certain situations, retreat was the best solution.

Thoughtfully she watched as the woman coloured a little and averted her eyes from Jemma's glorious nakedness. She placed the three garments upon the chair, giving a courteous nod to Jemma as she withdrew, closing the curtain behind her.

Jemma picked up the first garment with interest. Not the white one Max had taken such a fancy to, but the animal print she preferred. She removed the ensemble from its hanger, then slipped on the panties. They fit her snugly, and she turned her back on the mirrors to admire the thong. Her pearly buttocks were completely revealed, but the thong concealed the mysteries of her cleft and rubbed her in a most enjoyable fashion.

Breasts swinging free, she reached out for the matching stretchy brassiere top then wriggled into it. With some amusement she found that the garment had a feature she had not noticed when it was draped across the gold satin backdrop in the window – nipple holes! She teased her breasts into the right position so that each rapidly hardening nipple poked jauntily out from its little hole, then surveyed herself in the mirrors.

Perhaps a touch obvious?

Grinning at her reflection, she tossed back the curtain and walked into the shop, where Max and Yvette were waiting. 'What do you think, Max?' she asked him, walking over to where he sat. She slowly turned this way and that before him.

Jemma paused, facing him, and held her hair back with one hand, placing the other on her hip, which she tilted slightly forward, as her model training had taught her. The pose was deliberately provocative, and Jemma was pleased to see that Max seemed suitably affected. She could see his penis growing lustily in his trousers, and his eyes lingered happily on the naked curves of her hips and buttocks, and upon her perky nipples, which felt so hard they almost seemed to return his stare.

'Luscious,' he breathed admiringly. 'Is there more?'

'Perhaps more than you can handle, Max,' she teased lightly, turning away from him and wiggling her buttocks enticingly as she sashayed back to the cubicle.

There she stripped off the animal print and reached for the black lace garment, which seemed bigger than the other two. Stepping carefully into it so as not no tear it, she found that it was a body stocking, seamless and crotchless, and that it was extremely revealing. The filmy black base with its regular pattern of twin roses skimmed her lithe body smoothly. At the same time it seemed to emphasise her breasts and nipples outrageously, and her bush seemed even blacker beneath its thin covering.

She strolled back into the main body of the shop, posing again in front of Max. 'Well?' she purred.

'Charming,' said Max, crossing his legs to ease his discomfort.

Jemma gave him a secret, seductive smile.

'Mam'selle looks ravishing,' Yvette said honestly, and her high colour clearly revealed the turbulent state of her own emotions as she looked at this beautiful creature before her, lightly clad and yet so cunningly revealed.

'Try the white,' suggested Max.

The white, as Max called it, was a babydoll nightdress and knicker set. Fashioned from the finest lace, its filmy top and little frou-frou skirt would be little more than a tantalising veil over Jemma's healthily glowing skin. She returned to the cubicle and slipped both on. The top fastened with dainty satin bows, and the straps were narrow slivers of pure silk. The knickers, when she pulled them on, she found to have a thong-strap, like the animal-print ensemble, which bared her behind; but these were slightly different in that they tied at the sides with bows.

This, she thought, assessing her reflections, was what a bride might choose to wear on honeymoon to stimulate the libido of a nervous young husband.

'Now that is very appealing,' said Max, surprising her by pulling back the curtain of the cubicle. She heard the shop bell ring and, over his shoulder, saw Yvette welcome a new female customer. Giving him a seductive smile, she turned back to her reflections.

'Do you think so?' she asked critically.

Max came into the cubicle and pulled the curtain closed behind him. The cubicle was very small, and Max seemed to fill it almost entirely, bringing with him a whiff of Trumper's Lemon and aroused male that Jemma found extremely pleasing.

Max leant back against one of the mirrored walls, arms folded, his eyes caressing her. He nodded. 'But perhaps with the bows undone?' he suggested.

'Like this?' Jemma reached down and slowly released the four tiny bows that secured the front of the garment, starting from the top.

Max seemed to hold his breath until the last one was undone. Finally the white lace hung open, falling from the precipice of Jemma's breasts in a snowy white swathe that was as insubstantial as spun sugar. Her nipples were just visible as darker circles beneath the white, and the crease beneath each full breast was suggested rather than seen. What had been revealed was a central strip of soft, sheeny flesh: the valley between her sumptuous breasts, the dip of her stomach, the soft indentation of her waist, her smoothly inverted navel, her belly.

Then the knickers interrupted his view. Her bush was a dark fuzz beneath the white. Her thighs gleamed invitingly. Max caught his breath, feeling every pulse in his body hammering like crazy.

'You like this one best,' Jemma said archly. 'I can tell.'

'Can you?' Max's dark eyes were exchanging teasing glances with hers. 'How?'

Jemma's eyes travelled down the front of his body.

'Your cock,' she said.

'And what about my cock?'

'It's standing up,' Jemma pointed out, her eyes lingering on the front of his trousers.

'It would stand up even better if you pushed the sides apart a bit more,' said Max.

'I will, on one condition,' replied Jemma.

'Name it.'

'That you will tell me everything I need to know about Vena before we get back to the yacht.'

Max lifted a brow at her. 'Yes, all right. Of course I will.'

'Then that's a deal,' said Jemma, placing a hand on each edge and pushing the sides of the white babydoll nightie open with taunting slowness.

First the slope of her breasts was revealed, then the fuller, deeper curve where the skin gleamed like rich, pale satin stretched over a padding of swansdown. She paused for a moment, for effect, then eased the flimsy fabric back over the turgid nubs of her nipples and back, back further, until the fabric lay beside her arms, just brushing the sides of her naked breasts.

'Enchanting,' Max said in appreciation, his eyes drinking in this stimulating sight with enjoyment. He reached forward, grasping her upper arms, and turned her around so that she could see herself in all three mirrors – and there she was, her breasts jutting proudly back at her.

Behind her, so close behind her, she could feel Max's cock pushing restlessly against her buttocks. It felt very arousing, to stand there half-naked while Max, fully clad, pressed his erection against her.

'Look,' he murmured huskily in her ear, 'look how beautiful you are, Jemma. What a splendid muse for any artist.'

Worshipfully he dropped a kiss on to the base of her throat. His lips progressed from there to the soft, sensitive skin beneath her ear, kissing, his tongue flicking out to touch her, to feel the mad beat of her pulse. As Jemma's head went back on to his shoulder and she gasped in lazy appreciation of his attentions, Max slid his arms beneath hers and cupped her breasts in his strong brown hands, lifting them, stroking them.

Each stroke made Jemma's flesh quiver wildly. As they both watched, her nipples grew harder as the blood raced eagerly through her body. They darkened, too, through rose and violet and almost to purple with the depth of her arousal. She arched her back a little, straining her twin globes into Max's manipulating hands, and straining her buttocks against his hard, moving thighs. She could feel her sex unfolding like the petals of an exotic flower, her juices flowing to dampen the soft fabric between her legs. She groaned in pleasure, her breath catching as Max pushed harder against her in an irresistible rhythm.

Oh, but she wanted him now. This instant!

And Max knew it. He freed one breast and reached behind her. She heard the jingle of his belt being unbuckled, and then the soft hiss of his zip. Almost immediately, she felt the hot rod of his penis pressing against her bottom.

'Do it to me,' she urged him. 'Hurry, Max.'

But Max only released her. He moved past Jemma, positioning the high stool in the centre of the cubicle. As he turned back to her, she was riveted by the sight of his naked penis bobbing about, springing from the opening at the front of his trousers like a weapon. She caught it, and caressed it briefly, but Max was intent on getting behind her. As he did so, he said: 'Put your elbows on the stool, Jemma.'

He was panting.

Well, so was she! Jemma was enjoying this enormously. She complied happily, placing her elbows on the stool amid the tangle of discarded garments. She waggled her bottom invitingly at Max, who laughed a little breathlessly.

'Won't Madame Yvette be scandalised if she catches us fucking in her changing room?' gasped Jemma, feeling Max's fingers fumbling at the sides of her knickers.

'Madame Yvette is a broad-minded woman,' Max reassured her, busily unfastening the little bows that were holding the garment together. 'She's French.'

Jemma felt cool air on her bottom as Max succeeded in undoing the bows. The little wisp of fabric was whisked away, then tossed into a corner. She felt suddenly very exposed. She looked up into the mirror, seeing her breasts hanging bell-like between her arms; seeing her own feverish eyes. Behind her she saw Max pushing his fine brown cock down between the cleft of her naked buttocks.

Instantly she felt his penis nudging her cleft open with its warm, damp head, then its whole hot length pushing in past her anus, nudging, probing, then finding the opening of her already well-lubricated cunt. She moaned in utter bliss and moved her legs apart, granting him access in one single, deep, powerful surge.

He was in.

God, it felt so good. Distantly she heard the bell ring as one customer departed or another entered – who knew or cared? Her whole focus was on Max's magnificent cock as it pushed with rapid, deep thrusts in and out of her. Her dewy lips and wet sex sucked eagerly at his penis, as if wishing to drain every last drop of seed, every last ounce of enjoyment, from him.

Jemma relished the feel of the cool material of his shirt brushing her back as he bent over her. Beneath that fabric, she could feel the heat of his chest where his heart was pounding furiously, keeping time with every thrust. Muttering endearments, his breath on the back of her neck hot and arousing, Max put his arms around her and clasped her breasts once again, more roughly this time, more desperately, squeezing and kneading them until Jemma let out a half-stifled cry of ecstasy.

Max's hand slid urgently down over her naked belly and buried itself in her cunt, his fingers grasping the needy bud of her clitoris and rubbing gently, his palm pressing hard upon her furry mound, giving her sensations that were outrageously stimulating. Jemma felt her orgasm building unstoppably; it was out of her control; and at that instant she was aware of the light jingle of the brass rings on their pole as the curtain was drawn back.

Madame Yvette put her head into the cubicle – Jemma could see her, reflected in the mirrors – and said: 'Is everything satisfact— oh!'

Panting hopelessly, Jemma could see the poor woman blushing beet-red with embarrassment at having interrupted them like this. But her own physical needs were overriding all propriety. She could focus only upon Max's cock and Max's hand, and what he was doing to her.

She saw Madame Yvette's eyes widen in shock as she took in the scene: Jemma almost nude, bending over the stool, flushed with passion and with her breasts swinging wildly with each thrust; and Max, his trousers down around his well-muscled thighs with his cock buried deep in the moist cleft between Jemma's dainty buttocks.

Max halted mid-thrust, showing rather more control than Jemma herself, who hungrily pushed back to reclaim him.

'Monsieur, I do apologise,' stammered Madame Yvette, her eyes glued to the activity between Jemma's thighs. 'I had no idea that you were . . . busy.'

Jemma could only admire Max's sangfroid.

'Not at all, madame,' he said with what looked to her in the mirror more like a grimace than a smile. 'We are just finishing our business. Please stay. We won't keep you a moment.'

Madame Yvette nodded her agreement to this plan, and soon Max was thrusting away again quite satisfactorily, unworried by the watching woman. In the mirror Jemma saw the woman flushing, her eyes fastened to Max rather than to Jemma.

That mouth, thought Jemma in distant amusement. She was in no doubt that Madame Yvette wished that Max's cock was in her mouth and not in Jemma's cunt.

But it *was* in Jemma's cunt, and Jemma took full advantage of this now, pushing back mightily to meet every thrust of Max's. Her climax, which had been quivering on the very brink of completion when Madame Yvette had made her unexpected entrance, now reasserted itself.

Her arms on the stool began to quiver, the muscles straining to support her and to bear the weight of Max's hearty assault. Her thighs too shook, and the taut muscles over the smooth flatness of her belly trembled. Each thrust, each groan of Max's, was a delicious incitement now, pushing her ever nearer her own ultimate goal.

When Max again clasped her breasts, squeezing her nipples quite violently, a shriek of ecstasy escaped her and her fists clenched. Max's breath grew faster and faster, and she felt, unmistakably, the sudden hardening, the outpouring, the rapid and almost desperate strokes that meant he had come.

Panicking, not wishing him to leave her in this state of extreme need, Jemma clamped her vagina harder on to his still-full penis. It was her undoing; the sudden intensity of all those marvellous sensations seemed to explode in her brain, signalling a message that shot from there to her breasts, to her clitoris – and she came, too, lunging back with helpless passion on to Max, letting out a series of wild cries until there was nothing but calm, stillness and the heavy throbbing of two mutually delighted hearts.

Slowly, Max withdrew his sated organ. In the mirror, Jemma watched him dazedly. He drew out his handkerchief and carefully mopped his red and distended cock while Madame Yvette looked on with appreciation. Thoughtfully, he then tucked the handkerchief gently between Jemma's legs as she straightened. She grasped it, thanking him with a nod and a kiss.

'So, madame, I think our business is concluded for today,' said Max as he tucked his penis back into his trousers. Madame Yvette looked regretful to see it go. His eyes twinkled at her. 'We'll take all three garments, please. And, if you are open next week . . .'

Yvette nodded eagerly.

'Then I shall return. Alone, I think? And perhaps we can conduct a little more business, of a mutually satisfactory nature?'

'Oh yes, monsieur,' gasped Yvette, and gathered up the garments and hurried off to make up the hill.

Jemma carefully deposited the handkerchief in her straw carryall, then slipped her lemon linen shift back on. Languorously she brushed out her hair and then applied lip gloss. Max watched her with amusement in the mirror.

'You are an extraordinary woman, Jemma,' he considered. 'Nothing throws you.'

'I'm certainly single-minded,' Jemma agreed, shrugging her shoulders as they went back into the main body of the shop.

Back at the car, Max slung the pretty red and gold bag of purchases in the back seat and they drove in relaxed silence for some while back the way they had come; then Jemma said: 'Stop the car now, Max.'

Max complied, pulling into a rare safe spot on the towering, precipitous corniche. They sat for some time, saying nothing, looking down at the plunging cliffside and the sea stretching out beneath that. The curve of the bay was clearly visible and, from where they were positioned, their destination – Cap Ferrat – was in view. Boats were moored out there, but there was a blue haze on the water now as dusk crept in, so it was impossible to distinguish which one of them was the *Annalise*. Seabirds cried overhead, soaring effortlessly on the thermals.

'Now tell me,' said Jemma at last, 'all about Vena.'

Chapter Twelve

'Is she still alive?' This was Jemma's first and most urgent question. Having been on the sharp end of Annalise's jealous rage, this seemed to her to be a pertinent query.

Max turned sideways in the driving seat and looked at her in blank surprise before letting loose a bark of surprised laughter.

'*Alive?*' he repeated in amazement. 'Of course she's alive. And well, so far as I know. What could make you think otherwise?'

'Annalise,' Jemma replied flatly. 'Did she make Vena walk the plank, too?'

Max tutted impatiently and smoothed a thoughtful hand over her cheek. 'Dear Jemma, that was a game. Nothing more, nothing less. She knows very well that both Dominic and I are strong swimmers. She knew you were in no danger.'

'Pity she didn't let me in on that,' Jemma said dryly. 'But did she? Make her walk the plank?'

'No. But there were other things, of course. Annalise

has been possessive about Dominic ever since the moment she first discovered him. And when he took Vena to be his muse, she was outraged.'

'Because *she* wanted to be his muse. I know that. She told me so. Max?'

Jemma gazed at him intently.

'Yes, my sweet?'

'Did they sleep together? Vena and Dominic?'

'Ah.' Max looked away, his expression troubled. 'Yes.'

Jemma leant back upon the soft buttery leather of the car's luxurious upholstery and sighed, her head thrown back to the sun's glare. She closed her eyes a moment, pondering. 'It's hot,' she complained mildly.

'Then slip off your dress. Up here, no one will see.'

Jemma willingly pulled the shift up over her head and placed it at her feet. The kiss of the sun upon her naked skin was glorious, and she tilted the seat back, enjoying the sensation of heat and the fragrance of sex that her warm body exuded when subjected to the sun's balmy rays.

'Are you sure these won't burn?' asked Max, leaning across to lazily caress the nearest full breast, his hand deliciously cool against her hot skin as it passed lightly over her quiescent nipple.

Jemma shrugged, making her breasts jiggle enticingly. Her smooth belly entranced Max's connoisseur's eye, and the dark triangle of fur between her long legs drew him like a magnet.

'I don't have any suncream with me,' she sighed.

Max leant further over, unsnapping the glove

compartment and taking out a little tube of cream. 'I always carry some. It gets very hot here.'

'I know. And everyone drips sex,' said Jemma, as he unscrewed the top and applied a little to his fingertips.

'Are you trying to distract me from the subject, Max?' asked Jemma a little breathlessly as he began to rub the cool cream into her breasts. 'Oh, that feels good,' she groaned.

'Of course I am not trying to distract you,' grinned Max as she looked up at him questioningly. 'Vena is alive and well, but she parted from Dominic on bad terms.'

'What bad terms?' queried Jemma, relishing the leisurely touch of his fingers on the soft, mobile flesh of her breast. His palm grazed her nipple and it stood up, hard and questing, inviting the next caress. 'Don't stop,' she begged.

Max applied himself diligently to the task in hand while he spoke. 'Dominic felt that he lost his artistic power when he slept with Vena.'

Jemma gazed at Max steadily as he started on her other breast, sliding the cream over it with long, caressing movements. Cars passed them on the mountainous road, but it was sheltered where they were parked, and the real world seemed far away.

'Do you think that is what happened?' asked Jemma with interest.

'Me?' Max shook his head. 'No, I don't. She was – is – very beautiful, Vena. As you are. But hers was a very different beauty to yours. She had long silky blonde hair, and she was tiny – really petite. She looked almost like a child when she stood beside Dominic, and Annalise and I did speculate as to whether she could actually accommodate him at all, in a sexual way. You know that Dominic's penis is very big.'

'Yes,' breathed Jemma, thinking about Dominic's penis. If Vena had had trouble taking him inside her, she certainly would not. She would relish it.

And suddenly she saw that she would not get the chance to do so. Dominic was afraid.

Looking at Jemma, taking pictures of her, had rebuilt his confidence, returned to him the talent he was so proud of. And, if sleeping with his last muse had disempowered him, the same could happen again. It was a mental thing, a conviction in Dominic's own mind. But the mental could affect the physical. If she continued to pursue him, continued to hound him into bed with her, she could do him damage.

Troubled, Jemma sat up straighter. The sun slipped briefly behind a cloud and suddenly she felt chilled. She clasped her hands around her knees, an action which pressed her breasts together most appealingly and caused Max to adjust his clothing in some discomfort. He put the cream back in the glove compartment and laid a hand upon the pretty curve of her back.

'What is it, Jemma?'

Jemma turned her head and looked into Max's eyes. 'I want him, Max. I want his big cock inside me. I want all of him. But I don't want to ruin his talent.'

'Well, then –' Max took a long, thoughtful breath '– perhaps the one need not affect the other.'

'Max, if Dominic believes it does, then it will.'

'When he slept with Vena . . .' pondered Max.

'Yes?' prompted Jemma, turning to him eagerly, her breasts swinging engagingly. He was gratified to see that her nipples were dark and jutting now, and when he glanced down, he saw that her sex was glistening against the black thatch, obviously aroused and ready for attention. Did I do that? he wondered. Or was it the thought of that oversized cock of Dominic's that excited her so much?

'When he had sex with Vena,' Max went on patiently, reaching out a hand to tease a tempting nipple, 'it happened suddenly. They worked together for months, with no intimation that the relationship would become a sexual one. Then they both got rather drunk at a beach party at the end of a shoot, and Vena straddled him right there on the beach after a swim. I saw them. I was there, although they were unaware that I was. They were unaware of anything at that time. I saw them come out of the water, laughing and jostling each other, and then Vena said something to Dominic and pulled down the front of his shorts. He was erect, and she took him into her mouth. She wore only the bottom half of a bikini, and her breasts were splendid, very small but exquisitely formed. They fell to the sand together – they were some distance from the fire and the dancing that was going on at the party. I saw her take off her bikini, then she was holding his cock in her hands, then squatting over him and easing herself down on to it, just a little bit at a time. I can still remember the way she cried out when she took him fully inside her. She was so tiny, you see. But she took him. She was determined and, as I say, very drunk.'

'And then, suddenly, it was over,' murmured Jemma thoughtfully. 'Max, do you suppose this loss of power of Dominic's was something that came from him? Or . . .' Jemma hesitated.

'Or was it something Annalise put in his mind?' finished Max for her. 'It's all right, Jemma. I am not offended on my wife's behalf. I know that she loves to manipulate him, and retain her hold over him. It's possible she did suggest to him that sex with Vena would rob him of his inspiration. It sounds like her, don't you think?'

Jemma nodded dumbly.

'And it seems to me that if we – you and I – could create a little space between Annalise and Dominic, we would all be better for it. Dominic would be free of her, you would have the object of your desires, Annalise could pursue a more well-rounded life, and I could have my wife's attentions rather more often than I do.'

'And how do we create this space?' asked Jemma.

'You create it, sweetheart,' said Max, tweaking a nipple gently. 'Prove that it isn't true. Seduce Dominic. But do it gradually; do it in such a way that he realises this loss of power is all rubbish.'

Jemma gazed at him thoughtfully. 'That sounds so easy.'

'I don't think it will be. I'll help, but Annalise will fight it to the last, be sure of that. And Dominic, when he realises your intention, will panic. I've seen some of the work he has done with you. It's very good work. Of course he will panic. He doesn't want to lose it all again.'

'Well,' Jemma said lightly, straightening purposefully, 'I will just have to make sure that he doesn't.'

Max smiled at her. He reached down and gave her clitoris a friendly rub, then looked at his watch with a sigh of regret. 'Put your dress on, muse. Time to get back.'

Dominic was setting up reflectors and fill-in flashes on deck when they reboarded the *Annalise* in the late afternoon. He was working busily, totally absorbed in setting a scene that was already in his mind and, because of this, Jemma was able to watch him unobserved for a little while. Max had gone below, Annalise was nowhere in sight, and the crew were on the flybridge and up in the prow. From the galley came wafts of spices and herbs – the rich fragrant sauces that would make their dinner taste exotic.

Jemma leant against the table under the awning and watched the warm light of sunset play upon the loose, healthily bouncing hair of Dominic. He wore only jeans, and his well-muscled chest and arms were tanned, making him seem leaner, harder. His face was shadowed and intense as he bent and peered into the camera on the tripod.

She felt again that distinct physical tug as she stood there watching him; it was a signal that passed through every sexual channel in her body. When he looked up, lancing her with those vivid green eyes, she shivered in reaction.

'What took you and Max so long?' he asked her angrily, coming over to the table with that long, restless stride of his, pushing his hair back with one hand. 'The light's almost gone.'

He walks like a jungle cat, she thought. 'Oh, we went shopping,' she said aloud, finding that the fresh impact of Dominic's physicality was like a punch to the stomach. She felt breathless. When he stood close, she could feel the heat radiating from his naked torso. She wanted to touch it, to feel its texture beneath her fingertips.

And why not?

Jemma reached out and placed a hand on the centre of his chest. Instantly she felt his heartbeat, strong and regular. The hair was scrunchy beneath her hand, the texture of his skin smooth, a fine contrast to it; and yes, he was hot. Very hot. A light sheen of sweat was mingling with a thin coating of oil. She could smell the oil, like coconuts and summer holidays, and the light grassy scent of his cologne, and the muskiness of his sex. His nipples were the colour of dark chocolate. She stared at them in wonder.

'Shopping for what?' He still sounded angry, but his tone had altered subtly to include a measure of fond male exasperation for the vagaries of the female psyche.

He's as affected by my closeness just as much as I am by his, thought Jemma. Her eyes ran down his body,

following the dark arrow of hair to his navel and beyond.
The stonewashed jeans he wore were snug-fitting and
rested on his hip. They outlined the bulge of his penis
rather than concealed it. And yes, it was standing up a
little, as she knew it would be.

'Clothes,' Jemma said huskily, allowing her hand to
trail down that intriguing arrow of hair where oil had
gathered.

She could imagine him smoothing it on while he lay
naked in the sun, the oil running down in rivulets over
his hot flesh, pooling in his navel, dripping down into
the fork of his thighs where the hair grew very thick and
coarse. Were cocks, like nipples, prone to burning?

If so, he would surely smooth oil into it.

'Jemma?' Dominic said impatiently.

Jemma snapped back to the present with a start. She
stood up straighter, aware that her body was running
riot again; aware of the steamy heat that was being
generated between her legs by the mere thought of
Dominic lying naked in the sun.

'Sorry,' she mumbled, then glanced at the table where
a cellophane-wrapped bouquet of flowers lay, tied with
an ivory satin bow. 'What are these for?'

'Oh, Annalise bought them for you. As an apology,
she said. She didn't mean to frighten you.'

Jemma gave him a taut smile. 'You may tell her
that she didn't,' she replied, and examined the blooms
cautiously, looking for the catch, the poisoned apple.
There were ten velvety white arum lilies packed amid
ferny foliage. Jemma had never before noticed how

erotic these lilies looked, their smooth sides like the petals of the female opening, the long single stamen in each one dark and firm and upright, like a man's sex.

'You were right about the climate,' she said on an unsteady breath.

'What about it?' He had obviously forgotten what he had said, but he was standing very close to her now, caught in the spell of a chemical attraction he would always do his best to deny.

'You said it made everyone feel very sexual,' said Jemma, and she brushed past him to where he had set up ready to shoot. 'You want me over here, yes?'

Dominic turned slowly and walked after her. 'Yes,' he said, and his voice sounded thoughtful.

Jemma turned at the rail. The hot, salty breeze caught her hair and turned it into a streaming black banner, flecked with red from the dying sun. The skin of her arms and legs gleamed like polished bronze.

'So, what should I do? Just stand here?' asked Jemma, effecting her best wide-eyed and innocent act. It was time to start dismantling Dominic's defences, one by one.

Her words seemed to galvanise him. He nodded, and bent over the camera. The flashes squealed as he switched them on, then they began to beep intermittently. He adjusted the focus on the camera, intent on the subject before him.

Dominic glanced up at her. 'Come on, then, take the damned dress off,' he growled.

'Yes, sir,' she said sweetly, and slipped the shift off

over her head in one easy movement. She was about to toss it on to a nearby sunbed when Dominic said: 'Wait.'

Dominic gazed at her full breasts which in this subdued light seemed tipped with purple. Her hair blew this way and that, at one moment concealing a nipple, at the next revealing it. Jemma had paused, the lemon-coloured shift held loosely in her hands at the juncture of her thighs. There was something achingly vulnerable about the soft curves of her hips, and the smooth indentations on either side of her belly, but her bush, her mound of Venus, was hidden from view by the fabric.

'Stay like that,' he ordered, and Jemma did.

The camera fired, again and again, the motor drive winding on furiously.

'Now sit on the sunbed. Straddle it.'

Jemma did so. Again, she would have put the dress aside, but Dominic said no. She sat up on the sunbed, the little ball of fabric modestly covering what would otherwise have been clearly revealed between her wide-open legs.

'You obviously feel more comfortable when this is covered,' she commented, glancing down past her naked and rather cold breasts at her thinly concealed sex as the flashes fired and the camera shutter clicked.

'Do I?' Dominic was adjusting the focus, darting forward to flick her hair back, moving a flash umbrella, very intent on what he was doing.

Oh, very cool, she thought. But he couldn't conceal

the fact that he had an erection. Not in those jeans, anyway. His cock was rearing up like a stallion's, and the hipster fit of those jeans was making watching him work an endless tease. Would it poke over the top of them in a moment, as it had over his bathing trunks?

'Jemma, concentrate. Don't move.'

She had wriggled a little to try to alleviate her sudden state of acute arousal. 'Sorry,' she muttered, shivering a bit. 'Dominic, my tits are freezing,' she complained lightly.

'Cover them for a moment, then,' he said, as he was busy changing films.

When Dominic turned back to her, she had the linen shift dress clutched in a thin line like a bandeau bikini to her breasts, but her black bush, clearly on show to him, was naked. Her thighs were splayed by the sunbed and, at that moment, he wanted nothing more than to push her back on to the bed, unzip himself and plunge his cock into her up to the hilt.

Instead, gritting his teeth with the effort of restraint, he kept shooting, moving around the sunbed, telling her to turn this way and that, lean forward, move back. Finally the light faded to the point where it was not good enough any more, and Jemma was shivering. Dominic straightened.

'That's a wrap for today,' he said, holding out a hand to her to help her get up.

Jemma took it gratefully, her thighs aching from being stretched over the damned sunbed. She stood up, and his grasp brought her rather closer to the front of his body than seemed wise, just at that moment. Still, wasn't she going to set about dismantling his defences, starting right now?

She let the dress she had been hugging to herself fall, and snuggled in close to the front of his big hot body to warm herself up. Dominic slipped his arms around her obligingly. She pressed her face into his chest, relishing the heat that radiated off him as the chilly night drew down about them.

The stern and aft lights to warn other shipping of their presence flickered on at either end of the *Annalise*, lightening the gloom of night a little.

'Are we eating here?' she murmured, her lips on his chest.

'Mmm,' said Dominic in reply, and with a thrill of satisfaction Jemma felt his hand softly stroke her head.

She looked up at him, her teeth gleaming white in the dying light as she smiled.

'That's nice,' she said encouragingly.

A shiver shook her, not from the cold this time, but from an animal arousal so intense she could hardly bear it. Dominic rubbed her back soothingly, pulling her even closer. Jemma cuddled closer still, wriggling her soft breasts with their hard points of pleasure into his skin.

And suddenly she could feel every inch of his cock standing proud and upright beneath the thin covering of denim. Glancing down, she saw the pink head of his aroused penis peeking out over the waistband.

'Oh look,' she cooed in admiration. Her fingertips

lightly touched the silky head, and it was Dominic's turn to shiver.

But he made no objection.

This was progress, surely? she thought. They stood that way for long moments, her fingers lightly rubbing the exposed head. In the dim light, she could see the little eye at the tip of his cock open, and then it grew moist. She felt her own moisture flowing in reply, her heartbeat speeding up to fever pitch.

Still Dominic said nothing. His heart was pounding fast in his chest – she could feel it. Boldly her fingers moved to unfasten the buttons at his fly. She held out little hope of achieving this. As each button was released, she was certain he would stop her. But he didn't. Finally she held the exposed length of his penis tenderly against her belly. And it was at that precise moment that a female voice said from feet away: 'Goodness! I am not interrupting anything, am I?'

Chapter Thirteen

'Of course not,' said Jemma with false brightness. 'We were just finishing up for the day.'

'So I see,' Annalise said sarcastically.

Dominic was tucking his cock back into his jeans. The moment was ruined, and so Jemma stepped away from him and smiled confidently at Annalise, showing none of the animosity she felt. And Jemma was gratified to see the woman's eyes flicker over her body, assessing her from head to toe.

Annalise herself was dressed lavishly for dinner, in gold this time, a shimmering satin drop-waisted shift dress in a colour that matched her cymbal earrings and a necklace that looked so heavy, so pagan, that Jemma was surprised she could lift her head.

Annalise looked wonderful. Confronted with cat-like sleekness, Jemma felt very aware of her own windblown hair, of her nakedness.

Instinctively she snatched up her crumpled dress and held it against the front of her body like a shield.

'Why hide perfection?' purred Annalise, walking slowly around her so that she could peruse the long curve of Jemma's back and the two round, perfect buttocks.

Decent again, Dominic turned back to the two women.

'Jemma, why don't you go and change?' he suggested.

Jemma saw that Annalise's eyes were resting with suspicion upon the front of Dominic's jeans. His erection, though hidden, was still obvious to anyone who cared to look.

'And what's this?' enquired Annalise, walking slowly up to him and patting the bulge at his crotch.

'What does it look like?' snapped Jemma, unable to restrain herself.

The woman was talking to them as if they were a pair of guilty teenagers. Oh yes, she was trying to protect Dominic's artistic power; but she was also trying to keep him for herself.

Annalise turned her head, unperturbed, and gave Jemma a cool smile.

'It looks like an erect penis,' she answered with sweet malice, 'and when I came up on deck it looked like you were handling it, Jemma. And you know that's not on.'

'I know no such thing,' Jemma said icily.

'Then you should.' Annalise let the subject go with an apparently careless shrug. Turning away from Dominic, she held out a hand to Jemma and smiled. 'Come. Let us not be enemies, *cherie*. Did you like your flowers?'

Jemma watched Annalise warily. What sort of game was the woman playing now?

'Yes,' she said with caution, although she had not particularly liked the blooms. She had found them, in fact, almost threateningly sexual. 'Thank you for them.'

Annalise's smile widened.

'It was a pleasure. And I am forgiven for that silly business earlier?'

'Well . . .' Jemma hedged. When Annalise turned on this hundred-megawatt charm of hers, it was difficult to be surly.

'Jemma?' Dominic prompted anxiously after a moment.

'Yes. All right,' she conceded, more for Dominic's sake than anything else. 'Of course you are forgiven, Annalise.'

'Good.' Annalise clapped her hands together, as happy as a child with this news. She extended the hand of friendship again, and this time, feeling coerced, Jemma took it.

'That's it,' Annalise cooed gently, as if tempting a wild horse with sugarlumps. Her silver-grey eyes wandered appreciatively up and down Jemma's shivering body. 'Let's go below and get you dressed for dinner, yes?'

'Yes,' said Jemma, but it sounded more like a sigh.

Jemma had been briefly shown the main stateroom on the *Annalise* when she had first come aboard. Max had given them the grand tour, very much the proud owner. But Jemma hadn't really absorbed the grandeur of the cabin where Max and Annalise shared a bed. All she had noticed was that it was red, with highlights of gold.

Now she was able to take a closer look. The large bed was covered in scarlet satin and scattered with jewel-coloured cushions. The ceiling was tented in huge quantities of red fabric, giving the cabin the look of a sheikh's tent. There were two big brocade-covered chairs edged with decorative wood carvings painted bright gold. Looking closer, Jemma saw without surprise that those carvings, like those at the head of the bed, depicted a multitude of satyrs and nymphs joined in the act of copulation.

'The wardrobes are concealed behind these walnut panels,' said Annalise, guiding her through the stateroom. She opened a door, and there was a bathroom to match: corner bath, double sink, bidet, toilet, shower cubicle – all were in red with heavy gold fittings.

'Max loves red,' Annalise said in her ear as they stood in the doorway looking around. 'It's the colour of passion.' She reached out and lightly caressed Jemma's naked nipple where she had incautiously let the shift drop a fraction. 'Like these. They are red now, but sometimes they are much paler. They grow red, of course, when you are stimulated. Is that what Dominic was doing to you up on deck? Touching you like this?'

Annalise's cool fingers stroked and gently pinched the hungry nub, and Jemma leant back against the doorway with a little moan of pleasure.

She was dimly aware that Annalise had asked a question, and she ought to answer, but her state of sexual readiness was so acute after that unsatisfactory encounter with Dominic that she could hardly form a sensible word in reply.

She let the shift dress drop further, slowly baring her breasts, her belly, her hips, until it was covering only her pubis.

'Oh, goodness, aren't they glorious, these breasts of yours?' breathed Annalise shakily.

'You like them?' breathed Jemma. Her back was arching of its own accord as Annalise's fingers grew more demanding. Annalise's hand cupped one full orb and lifted it as if testing its weight, then her head dipped.

With only the crown of Annalise's sleek red head in view, Jemma felt the woman's hot breath sear her breast, then Annalise's tongue flickered out – like a serpent's, thought Jemma, in fascination – to lick at the heated tip of it.

'Suck it,' she begged hoarsely.

'Should I?' asked Annalise teasingly between licks. 'Or should I just drive you crazy by doing this?'

Jemma felt a tiny nip from Annalise's teeth, and again she was licking the needy nipple, now touching its outermost tip lightly with the point of her tongue; now lapping it as a cat would lap water; now avoiding the very tip and anointing only the areola.

'Do it,' Jemma instructed her breathlessly.

'What is it, *ma cherie*?' asked Annalise, her voice distorted by contact with Jemma's soft, mobile flesh. 'Did that naughty Dominic drive you to the point of distraction, only to leave you unsatisfied?'

That much was true, thought Jemma, but it was
Annalise's interruption that had broken the mood
up on deck. Without it, who knew what might have
happened? Certainly he had seemed more receptive to
her this time.

'Look how hard they grow when you think of him,'
Annalise noted silkily.

As Jemma looked down at what was being done to her,
Annalise took a nipple fully into her mouth and sucked
hard upon it. The almost painful tugging of that soft,
passionately moving mouth upon her breast seemed to
shoot a message of hot need to every cell of her body.

And it was almost amusing, wasn't it, that the husband
had pleasured her and now the wife was doing the same.
She gave a deep, animal moan and clasped Annalise's
head with one hand.

'That's it, beautiful one, enjoy it,' murmured
Annalise, but Jemma needed no such encouragement.

Letting the crumpled dress fall to the floor, she slid
her other hand warmly up and down Annalise's flank,
pushing up the hem of the gold skirt until her hand
was underneath it. Happily she found that Annalise was
wearing no underwear to get in the way. Eagerly her
fingers sought out the fiery bush she so admired but,
when they reached their goal, she found only smooth
skin beneath her hand. She let out a gasp of surprise.

Annalise's head raised and the grey eyes with their
widely dilated pupils smiled into Jemma's.

'Shocked, *ma cherie?*' she teased. 'I did it on a whim.
Let me show you.'

Annalise lifted her skirt obligingly, and Jemma looked down in fascination.

Her pubis was completely nude, like a child's. Clearly now Jemma could see the two pouting lips of Annalise's sex beneath the smooth roundness of her mound of Venus, and the enticing slit between them where Annalise's clitoris and the soft petals of her innermost sex were concealed.

'This little thing does not stand up so boldly as yours does,' said Annalise, flicking her clitoris affectionately with a finger. The tiny thing stirred a little – clearly stimulated – but Jemma had only to focus her attention on her own body to realise that Annalise was right. Her own clitoris was swelling, eager as always to proceed.

Jemma thought that Annalise's naked, shaved crotch was one of the sexiest things she had seen in a long time. Enthralled, she ran her hand gently over it, then slid her index finger into the warm naked slit, and it was Annalise's turn to moan.

'Ah, *cherie*,' she sighed as Jemma probed more deeply.

Annalise's juices were flowing freely as Jemma continued this delightful investigation. Unable to help herself, Jemma found the opening she sought and slid her finger inside. Instantly Annalise shivered and opened her legs wider. They were such long, alluring legs, and the flat boyishness of her belly was so tempting, and the vee indentation on either side of it was like the head of an arrow, saying, yes, go on, do it, do it now, that Jemma could not resist her.

Bringing the front of her own body closer to

Annalise's, Jemma let the warm fur at her crotch brush the naked, vulnerable flesh at her partner's, while her fingers continued to caress the woman avidly.

But then, suddenly, Annalise pulled away. Jemma's fingers came free of her cunt with a tiny sucking sound.

'You are so hard to resist,' complained Annalise, gasping to catch her breath, one hand to her chest as she stared at Jemma.

'Then why resist?' reasoned Jemma. She could feel the desperate heat building between her own legs, and was sorry that Annalise had moved away from her. Annalise's dress was in place again, concealing her glorious pussy.

Annalise gave a taunting smile. 'You want me to continue, then?' she asked. 'You want me to show you what other delights I have, beneath this gown?'

'There can't be more, surely,' Jemma said shakily. All she knew was that she wanted Annalise to take it off, to be across that big bed, to open herself to whatever she chose to do to her.

'Well, there is,' purred Annalise, regaining control of herself.

'Then show me,' said Jemma. She held her arms out from her sides, indicating her own sumptuously naked body. 'As you can see, I am hiding nothing.'

Annalise grasped the hem of the dress and, with one tug lifted it over her head, revealing that she was naked apart from one thing – a bra. But it was like no bra Jemma had seen before.

It was fashioned of black leather, thick with metal

studs and loops and staples, and fastened at the middle of the front with three heavy straps pulled in to the last notch. The effect was to hoist Annalise's excellent little breasts higher so that a full, tempting cleavage sat above the bra's cleverly fashioned cups.

At the centre of each cup, there was a hole, and through each hole peeped a naked cinnamon-coloured nipple.

'What do you think?' asked Annalise, standing with hands on hips, her naked and shaven cunt thrust out challengingly.

'I like it.' Jemma strolled over and lay back on to the bed. It undulated under her, much to her surprise. A waterbed on a boat! she thought. How typical of Max's over-the-top style. She propped herself on one elbow and gazed at Annalise.

'But?' Annalise asked.

'But I like you better without it,' admitted Jemma.

'Then undo it for me,' said Annalise, coming over to the bed and sitting down close to Jemma. 'And then we shall see what you look like in it.'

Amused by the idea, Jemma cheerfully complied, unbuckling each strap with tortuous slowness until the leather bra fell open. Annalise's breasts dropped a tiny bit as the last buckle came free; the thing had been pulled in very tight, slightly chafing the tender flesh under her breasts. Jemma soothingly rubbed the sore red line before slipping the bra off Annalise's shoulders.

'There they are, your lovely little tits,' she exclaimed, and dropped a kiss on each nipple.

'Come on, try it on,' said Annalise, her voice sounding excited.

Humouring her, Jemma slipped the straps into place upon her own shoulders and pulled the thing closed over her breasts.

'The thing to do,' instructed Annalise, taking charge, 'is to do up the bottom buckle first, then position the nipple-holes correctly, then fasten the other two.'

'Does Max like this sort of bondage gear?' Jemma asked with interest as she followed Annalise's instructions carefully. It was surprisingly difficult to centre her nipples on the holes in the middle of each cup, and trying made her laugh a bit at her own ineptitude.

'Max loves it,' said Annalise, stretching out her long naked form beside Jemma as Jemma struggled with the thing. She watched as Jemma fastened the last buckle and sat back on her heels to show off the effect.

'There! What do you think?' she asked.

'I think, *ma cherie*, that you are exceedingly beautiful.' Annalise eagerly drank in the sight before her, lingering on Jemma's naked hips and belly. The black leather bra, hoisting her full breasts to new heights of voluptuousness, matched her bush to perfection.

'It looks better on you than on me,' sighed Annalise, reaching out to tweak an erect nipple.

Jemma leant back against the headboard. 'It feels very erotic,' she admitted. 'Very tight. Restrictive. And yet at the same time it shows these.' She touched her own nipples.

Annalise sat up beside her, fiddling with the headboard. For a moment Jemma wondered what on earth she could be doing, then she saw a small hidden panel pop open at a push, and a chain emerged in Annalise's quickly moving fingers. A chain which she hastily fastened to the right-hand strap on Jemma's bra.

'What –' began Jemma, but Annalise was straddling her quite suddenly, popping open another little compartment. Another length of sturdy chain was released, and she clipped that into the metal loop on the other shoulder.

Belatedly, Jemma tried to move but found herself securely fastened to the headboard.

A moment's panic washed over her, and then she thought: what am I worrying about? This is ridiculous. Let Annalise have her fun. All I have to do is slip the bra off if the going gets too rough.

Annalise remained straddling Jemma, crouching over her with a triumphant grin on her face.

'I have you now, my beauty,' she crowed.

'So you do.' Languidly, Jemma leant back against the headboard. 'Now what are you going to do with me?'

'Punish you,' said Annalise, her eyes gleaming. She ran her tongue over her lips in anticipation of pleasures to come.

'Oh? For what?'

'You know. For touching Dominic's cock the way you did.'

'He wanted me to,' returned Jemma, untroubled. So much for bunches of lilies, so much for 'let's be friends'! Annalise was still grinding away at the same old thing.

'Why? Because you wanted to touch it?'

'I can touch it anytime I like,' Annalise said proudly.

Jemma shrugged easily. 'He wanted me to touch it. He did not object. If you hadn't interrupted us, things would have gone on from there.'

'What would you have done?' Annalise demanded.

Jemma thought it over. 'I would probably have got him to sit on the rail, and then I would have caressed him until he was very excited, and then I would have taken him into my mouth.'

'I keep telling you, just like I told Vena, this mustn't happen,' Annalise said angrily.

'Why? Because you had already warned Dominic that to sleep with his muse would cause him to lose his artistic powers?'

Two bright spots of colour sprang up in Annalise's cheeks, and Jemma knew that she was right. Annalise had poisoned Dominic's mind before any seduction had occurred and, after the seduction by Vena, his worry over his artistic prowess had turned his loss of them into a self-fulfilling prophecy.

'And what if I did? It was only the truth,' spat Annalise.

'It was a lie that became the truth because Dominic believed it,' Jemma pointed out.

Annalise glared down at her, anger making her breasts heave magnificently. With her legs wide open, Annalise's nude sex was clearly visible and very tempting to the chained Jemma. She reached out a hand, sliding it up one long quivering thigh until she reached the juncture

she sought. She briefly touched heat and wetness before
Annalise sprang back, away from her caressing hand.

'No, this time it is I who will set the pace, lovely
Jemma,' said Annalise firmly. 'Now open your legs for
me.'

Enjoying this game, Jemma complied. She sucked in
a breath when Annalise suddenly ducked her head and
gently licked at her clitoris. She strained upward towards
her deftly moving tongue, but she could not move too
much as she was chained to the headboard, tightly
chained. All the movements would have to be Annalise's.

Jemma was enjoying this game, although just occa-
sionally the deadly serious look on Annalise's face
perturbed her. There was no doubt that the woman
meant every word she said: that she wanted Jemma to
stay away from Dominic, and that, if Jemma did not,
some dire consequence would follow.

Thinking of the plank, Jemma wondered about
that, but only for an instant, because now Annalise had
reached down beside the bed and was holding a curious
object in her hand.

It was a succession of three tomato-red egg-shaped
objects, linked together with a durable-looking red and
white cord. At one end there was a loop, and Jemma
watched in fascination as Annalise placed this over her
wrist. Jemma looked up, and Annalise smiled archly
when she saw the look of frank curiosity on Jemma's
face. What were these? Jemma wondered. Instruments
of torture to use on someone who would not obey
Annalise's wishes?

'Haven't you seen Japanese love-balls before, then?' Annalise looked surprised.

'I've heard of them.' Jemma's voice was a trembling whisper. Her cunt seemed to vibrate with longing where Annalise's tongue had touched it, and she wanted that tongue back again.

But Annalise was playing with her – punishing her.

She caressed the Japanese love-balls, running them between her hands to warm them. 'You see how considerate I am, *ma cherie*? I warm them first. Now keep quite still, and do exactly as I say.'

The coppery head bent low between Jemma's thighs. Jemma felt but did not see the first ball slip inside her. She gave a little gasp and pushed down on to the slick little thing. Annalise chuckled in amusement at her keenness, and then pushed in the second.

A sense of fullness began to permeate Jemma's sex, and with the insertion of the third she felt gratifyingly full; so full that a fourth would have been out of the question.

Glancing up at her, Annalise gave the cord a tug; with a soft sucking sound like the ocean pulling back from the shore, Jemma felt her eager sex pull the contraption back up almost to the neck of her womb.

She let out a cry of surprise at the sweetness of the sensation. The balls inside her felt so mobile, unlike the hard, questing cock of a man. Again Annalise pulled, and the sensation was one of the sweetest Jemma had ever experienced.

Panting, she clasped the headboard tight with both

hands. With passion-glazed eyes she watched the naked woman manipulate her to the point of frenzy. Annalise's silvery eyes were fixed to Jemma's breasts, which bounced with every steady jolt she inflicted. Deep eddies of pleasure were rippling around Jemma's thighs as the love-balls were pulled ever faster in and out of her.

Jemma watched in complete acquiescence as Annalise straddled Jemma's thigh and, without breaking the rhythm with the balls, proceeded to rub her nude muff with its dainty, eager little clitoris, up and down the strong, shapely length of Jemma's leg.

The woman began to groan as the sensations of impending orgasm caught her up. Jemma's arms were shaking and, without the least intention of doing so, she found herself pushing her hips down on to the balls in a wild progression that could end only one way.

Annalise's nipples were standing right up, and the flesh of her flat little belly quivered as she rode Jemma's thigh. Watching the hypnotic jerk and bounce of Annalise's breasts, feeling the woman's heat and wetness against her own flesh, was finally enough to overcome any resistance that Jemma might have had to Annalise's overtures.

In sublime ecstasy Jemma cried out as her climax took her, her cunt gripping and kneading the balls, her hands clutching frantically at the headboard. Her hips leapt wildly up towards the hand of the woman who was pleasuring her so well.

Annalise's fingers were buried in the crinkly hair of

Jemma's cunt, and her own sex was soaking wet. Within an instant, she too was screaming out and surrendering to the heat of orgasm. Then, at last, she was still, and she crumpled to the bed, her limbs entwined with Jemma's, her breathing harsh.

Releasing her tight grip on the headboard, Jemma sighed as she came back to herself. She was staring at Annalise's very smooth features – surely the work of some excellent plastic surgeon, she thought – as the woman lay, eyes closed, right beside her. Annalise's fingers idly plucked at Jemma's now-smooth nipple where it protruded from the leather bra.

As if sensing Jemma's attention, Annalise gave a tug, and Jemma felt each of the very stimulating egg-shaped love-balls plop out from her in succession. Jemma felt her heartbeat gradually slowing down. Gently she stroked Annalise's narrow flank as they revelled in the soft afterglow of satisfactory sex.

'So, you will not attempt to seduce him again?' Annalise said softly in her ear.

Jemma's head turned in surprise. Annalise's eyes were open, and staring piercingly into her own.

'I can't promise that,' she said honestly.

Annalise's expression hardened briefly, then she turned away from Jemma with a shrug.

'Well,' she said casually, 'you can't say you weren't warned.'

Chapter Fourteen

The long, hot days passed in a pleasurable haze after I that, and while they were on the boat Jemma took the feelings of her hostess into account and did not attempt to seduce Dominic.

At least, not directly.

However, she knew there were a thousand and one things a woman could do to seduce a man, without actual coupling taking place: the kiss, the flirtatious glance, the brushing of her body against his as they danced on deck to a smoochy number played on Max's state-of-the-art sound system. Jemma had learnt a whole battery of tricks to use in this subtle battle. And though Annalise was almost certainly aware of what was going on, there was nothing concrete she could point the finger at, nothing overt.

After all, Jemma thought, she had been warned. Best, for the moment, to take some notice of that warning.

Dominic and Jemma returned to the villa a few days later, alone, borrowing one of the crew's powerful motorbikes for the journey from quay to villa. His camera gear had, for the moment, been left on board. Dominic wore only his tight-fitting jeans; his bare chest and splendid torso and excitingly muscular arms were naked and darkly tanned now.

'It's all right for you,' said Jemma as she prepared to ride pillion.

She was wearing jeans, too, and a decorative white shirt. It was far too hot for a bra. Her long, lustrous hair – like his – was hanging loose.

'In what way?' Dominic kick-started the bike and the lion's roar of the engine filled the quiet summer air, driving seabirds away squawking in alarm.

'You can go bare-chested. It's cooler.'

Dominic glanced around the quay. The place was quiet, almost deserted. The millionaires' yachts and power cruisers bobbed peacefully at rest on their hyper-expensive moorings.

'So can you.' He sent a challenging glance back at her over his shoulder. 'If you've got the nerve, that is.'

Jemma returned his stare with a teasing glint in her eye. 'You'd like that, wouldn't you?' she accused huskily.

'What man wouldn't?' Dominic admitted.

He half-turned on the seat to watch as Jemma slowly unbuttoned her shirt. With a cautious look around, she opened the front of the shirt to reveal her naked breasts, their nipples puckering slightly in the cooler air of morning. Then she slipped it from her shoulders and quickly turned to tuck the garment into the pannier behind her.

Turning back, with an impish grin across her face, she hugged herself and gave a little shiver, making her breasts tremble deliciously. A pulse started to beat heavily between her legs as she saw that Dominic's attention was still focused hungrily upon her breasts.

'What is it?' she asked, swallowing nervously.

'Good job I've got a spare camera back at the villa and a few rolls of film,' he said, his voice hoarse with desire. 'I'm going to shoot you like that, on the front of the bike.'

'All right,' said Jemma. After all, that was the work she was being paid for. 'Can we get moving now? Someone might see.'

'Chicken,' he said mildly, and looked forward again, gunning the engine. 'If you hold on tight to me, it'll look like a boy and a man on a motorbike,' he shouted over the noise of the engine. 'That's it. Cuddle up close. God, your nipples are hard.'

'It's because I'm cold,' said Jemma, realising her excuse was hardly believable. She snuggled against Dominic's broad back, which gave off heat like a furnace. Cold was obviously not the reason her nipples were hard.

'Cold, or aroused?' he asked.

'All right, I'm aroused,' Jemma admitted, rubbing her breasts against him in a teasing rhythm. 'Aren't you?'

Dominic gave no answer, so Jemma slipped her hands downwards over the soft, worn denim that covered his crotch. It was bulging impressively.

'Now, if you carry on doing that, we really will

attract attention,' Dominic said with a laugh, replacing her hands firmly around his hard-muscled middle.

He revved the engine, and they set off at a fast pace. Jemma, tucked in against his hot body, saw only the blur of the countryside shooting past, a mixture of greens and sands and terracottas that dazzled and whirred like a kaleidoscope.

She was glad when they reached the villa. Dominic went inside while she positioned herself as he wished – at the controls of the bike. Fortunately, the front of the villa was well-concealed by the thick shrubs and trees which grew so lushly in the grounds. If anyone did pass by, they wouldn't be able to see a thing.

Presently Dominic re-emerged from the villa, wearing a 35mm Nikon on a strap around his neck. No tripod this time. He set up in front of where Jemma patiently sat, naked to the waist, and quickly started to work.

Jemma watched him as he moved around her, shooting busily, working through film after film.

'Slip the jeans off,' he said after a while, and, professional model that she was, she stepped down from the bike without complaint, kicked off her flat sandals, unzipped her faded jeans and stepped out of them. She wore a plain white thong underneath.

'What about this?' she asked him.

'Off, I think,' said Dominic, and Jemma pushed the tiny covering down around her ankles, and stepped free.

Naked, she remounted the bike, feeling the sexual buzz of having him there while she was in the nude;

feeling the leather, heated by the pressure of his body and the engine, touching her cunt.

The sensations this contact invoked were warm and sexy. Despite her best efforts to concentrate on holding the pose for him, Jemma felt stimulated. Her sex was swelling and becoming moist. Her legs were open, straddling the bike. There was a slight flush on her chest and her nipples were as hard as acorns. Her state was obvious to Dominic.

'This hardly seems fair,' she complained lightly as Dominic worked frenziedly around her.

'What?' He clicked the shutter again, then refocused, and clicked again.

'Me naked and you clothed.' She pouted at him seductively. 'I'd feel so much more comfortable if you took your jeans off, Dominic.'

'You'd only get hornier than you already are,' Dominic said wryly.

'That,' Jemma informed him, 'is a risk I'm prepared to take. Now who's lacking nerve, hmm?'

'You think I won't take them off?' enquired Dominic, lowering the camera for a moment.

'That's right,' Jemma said firmly. 'I suppose Celestine and Armand are indoors, and would be shocked? Or perhaps that would be a sort of treachery against Annalise, since we sneaked away before she was awake, like a couple of schoolkids playing truant?'

'That's wrong,' Dominic returned calmly, his green eyes very intense as they held hers. 'Celestine and Armand have gone into Nice, as they often do on their day off, which this is. And Annalise has no say in what I do.'

'Perhaps you should tell her that.'

Dominic shrugged. 'Perhaps I should.'

They locked eyes for a moment, but Jemma thought, no, this is getting too deep, too fast. I don't want to bully him or frighten him. Gently, gently – the stallion must be coaxed to the mare.

She deliberately smiled and, propping her hands on the bike's highly polished casing, waggled her breasts enticingly at him.

'We're getting off the subject,' she said, enjoying watching the outline of his cock beneath the jeans rise and rise.

'What *was* the subject?' he asked as if hypnotised.

'Your jeans,' Jemma sweetly reminded him. 'Drop them, Dominic, or I'll think you're a sissy.'

'Well, I can't have that,' said Dominic. He bent and untied the laces of his deck shoes, and then kicked them off. He straightened.

Jemma gazed at him expectantly. Everything seemed suddenly quiet, waiting. Even the birdsong that usually filled the little glade where the villa was situated seemed distant, and muted.

Dominic returned her stare while his hands went to the heavy buckle on his plaited tan leather belt, undoing it slowly.

'This is better than the Chippendales,' Jemma said wryly, sitting back to enjoy the show, her arms folded over her waist.

'I don't have their sense of rhythm,' said Dominic, undoing the button fly with deliberately teasing stops and starts.

'Oh, I bet you do,' sighed Jemma, stirring restlessly.

She understood now why men looked so intent when they were on stage in strip clubs; but all that howling and shouting the women seemed to do *en masse* was not her, somehow. This was serious business – a truly ravishing man stripping off for her own personal entertainment.

When the last button popped undone, Dominic bent from the waist, obscuring her view momentarily, and pushed the jeans down in one smooth movement. She watched the strong naked curve of his back, and the poetry in the motion of his rippling shoulder muscles, as he stepped out of the jeans. He straightened.

Had she forgotten how beautiful his thighs were, so hairy, so powerful, with long, dense muscles? She couldn't help but stare at them.

His belly was equally enthralling, perfectly toned, and very flat and hard.

But his penis was the most gorgeous part of all, standing up like a cathedral spire, so rigidly aroused at this moment that it lay flat against his belly, pointing to his navel. It pulsed with life, the big vein on its underside glowing almost purple in the shadows cast by the trees, its softly rounded head shining pink.

'Does that feel more comfortable?' Dominic asked her, one eyebrow raised in amused enquiry.

Hastily Jemma raised her eyes to his face. She felt herself blush lightly with the libidinous feelings that were rushing through her. 'Yes,' she lied, having to lick her lips and swallow to moisten her suddenly dry mouth.

'Well, good. Now can we get on?'

It was a rhetorical question. Dominic started working again, slowly circling the bike, telling Jemma to move her arm this way and that, sit forward, or turn in the saddle – all of which she did automatically. She was a true professional, and even when her mind was not fully occupied with the job – even if the job was tedious or downright dull – still she did her best.

Well, this was hardly dull. Or tedious. But it certainly was distracting.

His balls, for a start. She seemed unable to take her eyes from his balls as they bobbed so beguilingly beneath their mat of dark hair. And when he circled her, turning restlessly to get a better angle, the hard muscles that bunched in his buttocks made her long to reach out and touch them.

How different a man's buttocks were from a woman's, she thought. Annalise's were so delicate; but Dominic's looked Herculean, and she could not take her eyes from the dense feathering of dark hair that ran down the slit between them.

'Jemma, could you look up please?' asked Dominic.

Her eyes quickly raised to his face. He smiled.

'Your eyes are too low. Look up about tree level, could you? As if there was something important on your mind.'

'There is,' sighed Jemma, but she complied cheerfully.

Dominic worked on, altering her position, moving the bike, changing films, for about an hour. Finally Jemma had to ask for a rest, and Dominic agreed readily. When she stretched her arms above her head to release tension, she felt her spine crack.

Remembering some old horse-riding exercises she'd learnt in her teens, she lay back along the saddle and pillion, stretching, then straightened and leant forward over the handles.

'Sorry, did we go on too long?' Dominic grinned ruefully, watching her delightful contortions with interest. His cock, which had grown quiescent over the last fifteen minutes, now started to stir again as he had time to look at her as a woman, and not as an inanimate subject for photographing.

Jemma jumped down from the bike and stretched again, standing up on her toes and reaching for the sky and the thick canopy of trees that surrounded them.

'Oh, that's bliss,' she purred as her spine started to unknot. 'Could you do my shoulders for me?'

Placing the camera carefully on the bike's saddle, Dominic complied, standing behind Jemma and gently kneading the muscles in her shoulders.

'Good?' he murmured against her shoulder.

'Mmm,' she moaned. 'Very good. Harder.'

Jemma moved a little, just the merest fraction, and she could feel the heat coming off his body. Another furtive half-step back and she felt the head of Dominic's hard, hot penis digging into the small of her back. She stayed there, knowing that having his most sensitive flesh in direct contact with hers must be unbearably arousing for him.

Dominic paused in the massage for the merest moment as Jemma moved against him, then he continued; with each move of his strong fingers on her shoulders, she felt his cock lift and fall. It was lovely, but it was also very stimulating. She longed to reach back and push that big, hard member of his down between her thighs.

'That's fine. Thanks,' she said at last, and turned around.

They stood very close together now. Jemma's desperately aroused nipples were brushing against his skin. Dominic's breathing was frankly ragged. His cock, trapped between their bodies, loomed moist-tipped against her belly. He was discovering what a barrier, what a protection, clothes could be. Jemma knew that the sight of her nude before him when he was fully clothed was relatively easy for him to cope with. But when, as now, they were both naked, nature began to assert herself.

Jemma knew he wanted to be inside her now.

Gently she reached down. She wanted to touch his penis, but she resisted, despite how wet, how eager, she was for it. Instead, she took his hand and brought it slowly to her breast. Dominic resisted for a split second, then allowed her to lead his hand. Smiling into his eyes, she placed his hand over the firm globe of her breast, letting him feel its softness, its sponginess and the thrilling hardness of the needy little nub at its centre.

When his hand started to move on her breast of its own accord, she took hers away, then rested it lightly, tracing deft little circles on the hot skin of his hip.

The feeling of his hand caressing, touching, kneading her breast was almost more than she could stand. With a little moan of pleasure she brought his other hand to claim the other breast. Then she had to endure the pressure of both his hands as they weighed and played with them, his fingers gently pinching her nipples.

'These glorious tits of yours have been driving me mad,' he muttered, and in triumph Jemma felt his hips move forward; felt his full naked cock straining against the front of her body. His balls had lifted, ready for mating; she felt those, too, in their hairy covering, pressing against her – it was a wildly erotic sensation.

'Why, because you wanted to touch them like this?' gasped Jemma, her hands moving encouragingly on his restlessly surging hips.

'You know what I've wanted to do to you,' he murmured against her throat. He was nibbling the skin there with his teeth, sending feelings of shocking intensity from her scalp to the tips of her toes.

'What?' she coaxed shakily. 'Say it; please say it.'

'Why, when you can see?' He drew back just a little, one hand dropping to clutch at his cock. 'Look at it, Jemma. It stands up and begs every time I look at you.'

'It's gorgeous,' breathed Jemma. While his hand held the thick stem of it, Jemma encircled the fat, aroused tip with her fingers. Daringly, hoping he would not stop her, she placed the pad of her thumb over the wet, open eye of his penis and rubbed gently.

'But it doesn't need to beg,' she said softly, as Dominic's mouth opened on a gasp of pleasure. 'It can have me. Right now, right here. In any way it wants. In any way you want, Dominic. You were telling me what you wanted to do to me. Don't stop.'

Dominic swallowed heavily. He let go of his penis, leaving it in Jemma's hand. Relishing this, she pushed the foreskin back a little, letting it strain towards her. She bent from the waist and blew softly on the wet tip. Dominic groaned.

Jemma let her tongue lap across the little pearl of love-juice quivering there, like a cat lapping the last luscious mouthful of cream. His penis twitched in acute arousal. His hands clutched at her heavy breasts, squeezing them.

'Fucking doesn't cover it,' said Dominic between gritted teeth as Jemma straightened against him.

Deliberately, she let her bush tickle his cock, rubbing it against the great naked stem of his flesh until he cried out in torment.

'It's a start, though,' said Jemma, whose own pulse was racing tumultuously; whose cunt was so open, so needful, that she thought: yes, now. Right now, I want him now.

Throwing caution to the four winds, she placed her hands over his, guiding them away from her breasts. There was a bonus in this. He could look down at her tits again and enjoy the sight of their full delicious nakedness, then feel them pressing against the hot skin of his chest.

Everything in the glade seemed quiet and cool. Like Adam and Eve in the garden of Eden they stood there, so close together, ready and eager to devour the apple. He was erect; she was open. It was time.

Jemma fastened his hands beneath her buttocks. He caressed them instantly, acquainting himself with their soft texture, and the way the flesh moved under his questing hands.

His fingers soon found the damp slit between them and paused there to explore. Jemma endured this for several seconds, feeling herself trembling on the very precipice of her climax as he touched the little opening of her anus, then dug deeper to find the jewel of her vagina, so wet; so open to him.

She was about to tell him to do it, to lift her, to open her to him, to split her with the hard rod of his flesh, but Dominic was, if anything, slightly ahead of her.

He was caught up in the moment now, fears forgotten, nothing mattering to him except these feelings and their natural conclusion. His hands clasped together under the flesh of her buttocks, and he lifted Jemma up against the front of his body.

Obligingly, her breath coming in short hungry gasps, Jemma opened her legs and fastened them around his waist, placing one arm tight around his neck. His cock nudged at her cleft, seeking the opening; Jemma reached down and took the hot shaft in her hand, placing the tip where she wanted it, against the waiting mouth of her cunt.

Dominic half-turned, and Jemma felt her back connect with the nearest tree. Pressed hard against it by his weight, she felt his glans slip easily inside the wet and welcoming depths of her. He had her pinioned now; he was all aggressive male and not to be denied. Not that she had the slightest intention of doing so.

Even the tip was big. She gasped in delight at its intrusion, her hips lunging forward strongly to take more.

Then there was a sudden, awful crash as if of shattering glassware.

They both froze, eyes locked. Jemma licked her lips so that she could speak. 'I thought that Celestine and Armand were out?' she managed to whisper. The sound had undoubtedly come from one of the rooms on this side of the villa.

Dominic dropped his head on to Jemma's shoulder. As he moved his legs, the better to support her weight, his balls swung heavily against her pubis. His cock, lodged in her portal, nudged deeper despite his best intentions.

'There was a note on the hall table, in Celestine's writing. We'll both be back at four, it said. Oh, you're wet, you're so wet.'

'They didn't set the alarm?' muttered Jemma, torn between the delicious feeling of just wanting to plunge ahead – let him ride her as he was ready to do – and the worry of who could be in the villa not twenty yards from where they stood coupled.

Dominic shook his head, his dark hair feeling silky as fur against her throat. Jemma shuddered with desire. He lifted her a little higher. The bark of the tree scratched her back lightly. His hugely aroused cock sank slightly deeper into the hot open shaft of her pussy. Oh, he felt so good! Bigger than Max.

But what if there were burglars in the villa? nagged her worried mind.

Who cares! flung back her libido.

But her brain was asserting itself. Such people could be dangerous – and she and Dominic were at their most vulnerable right now. Suppose they were watching, enjoying the sight of Dominic's naked buttocks surging heavily between her widely parted legs?

'Dominic. Stop,' she murmured hopelessly, but he was committed now, completely and utterly.

With a gasp that might have contained the word 'no' he pushed in. Unable to help herself, Jemma let loose a shout of ecstasy as Dominic's big penis at last filled her wide-open sex to its fullest extent. His balls, that had so fascinated her throughout the shoot, slapped hard against the mouth of her cunt as he drove recklessly in. His shaft was so hard, so hotly aroused, that Jemma was dimly surprised she could take it so effortlessly.

But then, she was very open. In this position, she supposed any man might feel exceptionally good.

Dominic was thrusting. His hips pumped mightily. Jemma let her head fall back against the tree, her mouth open in complete pleasure, eyes closed. What if there was danger? She couldn't bring herself to care right now.

Her whole being was centred upon his endlessly moving crotch as it pushed savagely against her, driving that magnificent penis ever further into her. The fur that covered his balls and the front of his crotch tickled her open petals and teased her own tiny penis – her clitoris – in a furious counterpoint.

First his fur tickled it, then his pubic bone ground against it.

It was hypnotic, this rhythm, as old as time and quite irresistible.

'That's it, that's it,' she found herself murmuring in his ear. 'Do it to me, Dominic.'

Another crash. A vase or something, it sounded like. Dominic's head turned this time, and suddenly he broke away from her, pulling his reddened penis free from her with a heavy sucking sound. 'Jesus,' he cursed in frustration, knowing that he must stop, but unable to do so.

Outside of Jemma's body, still his own needs drove him. As Jemma leant weak-kneed and desperate for satiation against the tree, Dominic applied his own hand to his needy member, massaging it roughly with deliberate and expert strokes. He gasped, stifling a cry, as his come began to spurt from his cock within seconds, jetting like a foaming fountain from the open eye.

Finally he was still. He turned his head and looked at Jemma. 'Sorry,' he said inadequately. 'Put your jeans on. Stay out here, and I'll go and look.'

But there was no need. At that moment Celestine appeared at the front door wearing a black mini-skirt and a white chiffon blouse with – if Jemma's dazzled eyes were not mistaken – no bra beneath it. Her hair cascaded, messy and streaked with blonde, on to her shoulders. She carried the shards of a blue glass ornament in her fingers.

'So sorry, monsieur,' she tutted in annoyance, taking in Dominic's bare-arsed nakedness with an interested look, then staring at Jemma, who was also still naked.

Jemma absolutely refused to cover her breasts or her bush like a guilty teenager. She walked forward and stood beside Dominic in front of Celestine.

'Did I disturb you, monsieur?' Celestine enquired anxiously. She glanced down at the shattered article in her hands. 'I am so sorry. I dropped one vase, can you believe it? And then, a few moments later, I dropped another. You know that's not like me.'

'I do know it, Celestine,' said Dominic, his eyes suspicious as they gazed at the innocent-faced girl. 'I thought you and Armand were in Nice for the day?'

'I felt a little unwell, and returned early and alone. I came through the back gate,' Celestine explained. 'I thought I would just potter around a little, do some dusting. I didn't even know you were here until I glanced out of the window.' Celestine coloured becomingly. 'And then I could see that you were busy, and I admit I was so busy watching that I . . . I dropped the vase.'

'And then you stopped to watch again, and you dropped the second one,' filled in Dominic.

'I was envious,' Celestine admitted lightly. She glanced at Jemma, and her glance was a trifle hostile. 'I saw that you were having this lady, and I remembered how big and good you feel, and I got a little . . . well, a little excited.'

Jemma glanced down with some amusement at Dominic's penis. Although recently spent, it was beginning to rear lustily once more. Perhaps this was because Celestine's extraordinarily large pink nipples were showing clearly through her chiffon blouse, their aroused tips poking at the sheer material in invitation.

'Shall I tell you what I think, Dominic?' Jemma offered into the sudden silence. 'I think Annalise saw us leaving the boat this morning, and called Celestine on her mobile phone to tell her to interrupt us at all costs. So, Celestine, you hurried back from Nice, leaving Armand there, and broke first one vase, hoping that would stop us. When it didn't, you broke another, and that did.'

Celestine blushed guiltily, but addressed her reply to Dominic.

'No, monsieur!' she cried. 'That is not true.'

Dominic looked dubious.

'Oh yes it is,' Jemma said calmly. 'But don't fret, Celestine. You just carry on with your work, and don't overdo it. You can even watch us again – from Dominic's room – if you like.'

Smiling at them both, Jemma reached out and trailed her fingers along the now considerable length of Dominic's naked cock, from stem to tip. Then she clasped it, and moved past Celestine, leading Dominic by his penis towards her bedroom.

'And I suppose you'd better phone Annalise back and tell her it didn't work,' she flung over her shoulder.

Chapter Fifteen

'Perhaps this isn't such a good idea after all,' said Dominic, as the door to Jemma's bedroom closed and locked behind him.

'What, you think Annalise is going to come steaming back from the boat to rescue you from my clutches or something?' Jemma laughed gently and led him inexorably to the bed.

'I think she might try it,' sighed Dominic, allowing Jemma to push him back down on to the pillowy softness of the bed.

Above them, the ceiling fan turned, cooling the air and casting shadows. All was quiet and peaceful – unless Celestine got desperate and dropped another vase! And even that wouldn't stop this from happening, not now they knew that it was only Celestine and not burglars rampaging through the villa.

Jemma left Dominic on the bed for a moment. The sliding doors to the terrace were open. She closed and locked them. There was no entrance now, and no exit either. No entrance for Annalise; no exit for Dominic.

She went back to the bed, admiring the play of light and shade over his wonderful body. And yes, despite all his fears, his cock was up again, ready for her. He was watching her as she walked; watching the swing of her breasts, the way the shadows moved over her silky skin, and lingering on the dark, inviting triangle between her long legs. His penis was twitching with eagerness; his eyes, however, were doubtful.

'If you are so unwilling,' she joked lightly, sitting down beside him and running an admiring hand along his naked flank, 'perhaps I will have to tie you down. Annalise tied me down, you know.'

'Jemma.' He was leaning up on his elbows now, one leg bent at the knee. His green eyes were troubled. 'When I slept with Vena . . .' he began.

'When you slept with Vena,' Jemma finished for him, 'nothing untoward happened. Except for Annalise going mad with jealousy and succeeding in convincing you that your artistic powers depended upon you not seducing your muse. Dominic, don't tell me you still believe that. Don't tell me that silly woman still has such power over you.'

'All artists are superstitious.' He shrugged.

'They don't all have cocks as beautiful as this,' said Jemma, her hand clasping his big erection.

She leant forward, enticing him with her breasts; his eyes left hers and went to them. He lay back and his hands came up to clasp them. Jemma sighed blissfully as her nipples tingled and rose irresistibly against his palms. Their eyes met. Jemma smiled.

'Still worried?' she cooed.

'Of course. But I want you too much. Ever since I first saw you in that darkroom in London, being so thoroughly fucked by Neil, I've wanted you. You know I get a hard on every time I look at you. I had one then, and I've got one now. It's driving me crazy.'

'Then just lie back. Let me take full responsibility, Dominic,' purred Jemma, surreptitiously reaching for her stash of silk scarves in the small open-fronted cupboard by the bed. She closed her fingers around two.

While Dominic still kneaded and caressed her full breasts, she lightly straddled his middle. Leaning forward, she attached first one scarf to the bedhead, and then the other. Dominic took this opportunity to replace his hands with his tongue and teeth, distracting her considerably.

Gasping a little with the sensations he was starting up in her, she gently grasped first one of his hands and then other, tying each by the wrist to the bedhead.

'That's not fair,' Dominic complained mildly when he realised what she'd done. 'I can't touch you.'

'No, but I can touch you,' grinned Jemma, deliberately lowering herself so that her thick bush tickled his hard-muscled stomach.

She felt his cock rear hotly between her legs and moved back a fraction, enough to be able to tickle that too, and to rub its whole silken length with her damp and needy cleft. The feeling was exquisite. Her clitoris was being constantly caressed by the pink helmet of his cock as she moved gently back and forth upon him.

'Jemma,' he growled in complaint, looking down at what she was doing to him.

'Hmm?' Jemma was distracted, centred upon her own desires for the moment. 'Oriental lovers use this as a form of birth control, did you know that?' she said dreamily. 'It's very pleasurable, isn't it? But there's no penetration. Only close contact.'

'It's *too* close, Jemma,' Dominic said wryly. He groaned and strained up against her, arching his back from the bed. 'I'll come like a train in a minute,' he panted.

'Well, we wouldn't want that,' agreed Jemma, feeling quite ready for him in any case.

God, he was big! She knelt up above his crotch and grasped his cock, taking time to admire it thoroughly and to administer a little slow-down magic, encircling the top of his scrotum with her thumb and fingers. She squeezed gently and pulled down, holding it for a while. Dominic groaned again and strained up against her once more, but didn't complain. After all, this was for his benefit, too. He wouldn't want to rush this any more than she would.

Jemma then shifted her hand to clasp his penis's hot, pulsing shaft. Gently, almost tenderly, she guided its engorged tip to her wide-open cunt, lowering her hips a couple of inches so that he was able to push up inside her.

Dominic pushed, just a little.

Jemma felt herself open further to accommodate

him, and it was her turn to groan. She looked down at where they were joined; the head of his cock was inside her, the shaft still revealed to her sparkling eyes.

'Good?' panted Dominic, as their eyes met in mutual but restrained hunger.

'Oh yes, good,' she moaned in agreement.

'Better than the vibrator?' Dominic tried to smile but it was almost a grimace. Every cell in his body was telling him to thrust upwards, now. This took a lot of self-control.

Jemma's mouth opened in a shocked exclamation that ended in a smile. 'You watched me through the mirror,' she said.

'How did you know?' Dominic pushed, unable to help himself. His cock intruded a little further. Teasingly, Jemma lifted her hips higher, denying him full measure.

'I guessed,' she said, swirling her hips in a circular movement that all at once caressed, stimulated, but denied.

'Oh,' said Dominic, but it became a groan of pure need.

Jemma was rotating her hips like a belly-dancer, her naked and aroused breasts bouncing lewdly as she did so. The tip of his cock was being treated to a hot, wet and extremely erotic massage inside her. He strained against his bonds, cursing her lightly, but he was securely tied. If he hadn't been, he would have pushed her straight over on to her back and rammed himself into her as hard as he could.

Dominic watched in helpless thrall. Her breasts were moving, bouncing, shivering, and her nipples showed every sign of total arousal, their skin puckered and dark, their tips hard – an invitation to suck and bite.

And he would have done, but she was keeping them out of his way for now, driving him mad instead with all this hip-play.

'Did you enjoy it, watching me?' she panted, dipping her hips tormentingly so that for one brief, glorious moment she enclosed him almost to the hilt.

'Yes,' he moaned. A light mist of sweat was forming over his body and rubbing on to hers where it joined with his. 'Of course I did.'

'Did you fantasise that you were doing it to me, and not just watching me using the vibrator?' she teased, dipping her hips again.

Dominic pushed up wildly, enjoying the hot wet clasp of her vagina around his cock.

'Yes,' he groaned.

'And now you are doing it to me,' she said.

'You're doing it to me, you mean,' Dominic corrected hoarsely.

'Oh, and you want to change that, do you?' she teased, pushing down again, full measure, feeling his incredible size opening her sheath to its fullest extent. She let out a little scream of delight.

Imagine him riding her unrestrainedly, she thought; that big cock pushing into her just like that, again and again, sending her berserk with pleasure.

Suddenly, she wanted just that. She reached forward,

untying his bonds with trembling fingers. Dominic grumbled because the movement took her hips up again, away from him.

But then his hands were free and, in an instant, he had grasped her hips with them and rolled his whole naked length, hot and hard and heavy, on top of hers. He eased her thighs apart with one knee, insinuating himself swiftly between her legs. Then, moving his hands so that he could rest comfortably above her on his elbows, he grinned triumphantly down at her.

'I am going to fuck you,' he warned, 'until you can hardly stand.'

'Do it then,' Jemma said huskily, because now she wanted him desperately. But something was about to threaten their pleasure. Her sharp ears had picked up a car coming to a stop, and the crunch of stiletto heels on the gravel of the drive.

Quickly, she thought. Do it quickly, Dominic, before the Wicked Witch of the West gets here and breaks the spell.

Dominic, unheeding of everything but the dire need to have Jemma right now, reached one hand down to clasp his rigid cock, then moved it until it vanished into the fur between her wide-open legs. Lying back with her arms above her head, totally ready for him, Jemma felt his hot wet helmet touch her portal first, nudging her open, before slipping deftly inside.

Once he had gained this entry, he pushed on smoothly, victoriously, letting the whole length of his cock slip easily inside her.

'Oh, that's good,' sighed Jemma, reaching down with both hands to clasp his buttocks; to feel the marvellous raw power of him as he started to thrust his huge member into her.

Dazedly her head rolled on the pillow as Dominic's penis pushed powerfully in and out of her. Someone was hammering at the hall door now, but she paid that no heed whatsoever. She was so wet, her sex so hopelessly engorged and eager for him, that the whole focus of her universe was his pumping buttocks beneath her hands, his cock thrusting madly inside her, and his sweat-slicked stomach brushing hers every time he moved.

Dominic too seemed disinclined to accept any interruption, but he did throw a concealing sheet over them with one impatient hand. His head dipped and he caught one hot nipple in his mouth, tugging it gently; then he nipped the other one; then he suckled at them, not once breaking the hard rhythm of his pistoning hips.

Distantly Jemma heard voices raised in argument; the pounding on the door went on.

She didn't care.

This was what she had wanted for too long now, and what she had craved: Dominic inside her, his body twined with hers; his movements driving her to the farthest shores of ecstasy; his groans and grunts of animal need a delicious stimulant.

Jemma felt her orgasm hovering ever nearer, building in steady waves of pleasure that were matched by the mad thrusting of his hips against hers.

'Yes, oh yes,' she urged him on.

She could see faces, figures, through the muslin drapes, standing outside the sliding doors that led on to the terrace. Annalise, of course. Also a worried-looking Celestine – and Max, come to calm things down, with any luck. They seemed dim and distant, like wraiths, their raised voices distorted by the thick shatterproof glass, their impatiently tapping fingers and fists as inconsequential as fairy dust.

Not that she cared right now. She didn't care that they must have come through Dominic's room and seen them clearly through the mirror.

It's too late, Annalise, she thought, surging towards the best, the most final of victories with each answering push of her hips against Dominic's.

At last she came, the muscles of her vagina clamping in violent, needful spasms around his engorged penis. She grabbed the bedhead so that she could thrust more easily, relishing the lovely spasms, the trembling weakness in her arms and legs as the climax came at last and washed over her.

Dominic was no more than a heartbeat behind her; not an instant after her own wonderful orgasm she felt his balls hardening and lifting with the added ferocity of every thrust he subjected her to; and finally, the feeling that he had grown even bigger, impossibly bigger, and then the spasms, the release, the feeling of his big body pressing on to hers, sweat sticking their skins together like glue, his harsh panting for breath in her ear.

They lay like that for long moments beneath the sheet, enclosed in a cocoon of peace while pandemonium went on around them. Suddenly there was a rattle at the hall door. The key in the lock dropped to the thickly carpeted floor, and the door swung open.

Annalise strode in wrathfully, followed closely by Celestine. Max stayed in the doorway, having a little more discretion than his wife.

'I am so sorry, monsieur,' said Celestine hastily, wringing her hands, 'but Mrs Klein insisted I let her in with the master key.'

Dominic looked down ruefully into Jemma's face, kissed her lightly on the lips, then withdrew from her, rolling over on to his back.

The sheet concealed their nakedness, but it could not conceal the outline of the still-towering magnificence of Dominic's member. He leant back on his elbows and looked at his uninvited guests in amazement, while Jemma sat up, decorously pulling the sheet under her chin. Unseen by Annalise, Max sent Jemma a complicitous wink.

'You have gone too far, Dominic,' accused Annalise, advancing like a Fury on the couple in the bed. 'You know the consequences of sexual contact with your muse.'

'He knows what you choose to tell him, certainly,' Jemma said dryly. Her eyes met and clashed with the silvery grey orbs of Annalise, who seemed to be positively shaking with jealous rage. 'And in any case, Annalise –' she decided to bluff it out '– sex didn't take mma opened her mouth to speak again, to press her point, but to her surprise Dominic interrupted her with: 'So what are you going to do, Annalise? Conduct a medical examination of us both? Jemma's right. You interrupted us before we had sex. As you can see.'

He clasped his cock through the sheet. It was still hard enough to convince Annalise, Jemma saw. And even Celestine gave it a look of extreme interest.

'Mrs Klein, I am sure this is the truth,' said Celestine with an anxious glance at Dominic. 'I interrupted Mr Vane and his companion outside, too, as you instructed me to. Sex did not take place. I saw—' She reddened becomingly. 'I saw Mr Vane stimulating himself. With his own hand.'

So Jemma had been right. Annalise had seen them leave the boat, had phoned Celestine and made her come back to the villa despite the fact it was her day off, and had told her to distract them in any way she could if it looked as if intercourse was about to happen.

Annalise stood over the bed, uncertain. What, after all, could she do? thought Jemma. But still she felt a little uneasy in the face of Annalise's wrath.

Annalise seemed almost to be sniffing the air for the salty scent of sex, but the air conditioning was very efficient in the villa, and any faint perfume that escaped from beneath the sheet would soon be dispersed.

And Jemma saw by Annalise's uncertainty that the mirror must have been covered, and that Annalise had been in such a tearing rage that she hadn't stopped to rip the cover off. If she had, she would have clearly seen what was happening in Jemma's room.

'My darling,' said Max, coming forward to clasp Annalise's expensively covered shoulders, 'this is all wild supposition, you know. And Dominic is no fool. If he thought there was any real danger to his artistic ability, he would not make love to Jemma. You must know that.'

Annalise looked dubious.

Jemma tried to keep her face blank, but she felt inclined to shout and scream with delight. Annalise was beaten. She had had sex with Dominic, successful, sublime sex. And not only was Annalise unsure about what had taken place, she also seemed curiously defeated by it, and almost drained of will.

'Well,' Annalise said doubtfully, not sounding like her usual robust self at all, 'if you are sure, Dominic?'

'I am sure, Annalise. And so is Celestine. So is Jemma,' Dominic replied blandly.

'Yes,' said Max and gave Annalise a hug of reassurance. 'My darling, you are too protective of this brilliant boy,' he teased. 'Come now, let's go into Cannes and have a splendid lunch and spend some money in the shops there, all right?'

Gently, soothingly, Max led Annalise away. Celestine stood rooted to the spot, and Dominic and Jemma were very still in the bed as the pair's footsteps retreated down the hall. Then the front door closed and the villa was still. The three remained quiet while Max's car started up, and the engine gave a full-throated roar. Steadily, the car rolled down the drive and away.

Finally, Celestine spoke.

'I apologise again, monsieur,' she said humbly, looking down at the carpet in her embarrassment. 'Mrs Klein was very insistent, but really I have no excuse. I feel ashamed. I will understand if you wish me to leave now, and not return.'

'Celestine,' interjected Jemma urgently, 'is the mirror covered in Dominic's room?'

'Which mirror, mam'selle?' asked Celestine with perfect blue-eyed innocence.

'Come off it, Celestine,' chided Jemma. 'You know which mirror I mean.'

Celestine nodded, chastened. 'It is covered,' she said 'Mrs Klein walked straight past it on her way through to the terrace. She was too angry to think straight.'

Jemma and Dominic exchanged relieved looks.

So that crisis was over. But, Jemma thought, there might soon be another. Dominic had to start work again, immediately, like someone who had just had a car crash or fallen from a horse. He must drive on, remount. Work and work brilliantly. To prove to himself, no one else, that he was the genius of the lens still, that sex with her had not tainted his talent in any way.

'There is no question of your leaving my employ, Celestine,' Dominic said formally. 'But I do have some work I wish you to do right now.'

'Anything, monsieur,' said Celestine with cheerful fervour.

'Good.' Dominic rose from the bed. Celestine's eyes rose appreciatively to his sex-reddened penis, then dipped modestly again to the floor. If she realised the significance of its ruddy appearance, she gave no sign of having done so. 'You can come to my room right now, with Jemma. I'll fetch my camera.'

Jemma got out of the bed, feeling pleased that this most tricky hurdle had been got over without too much pain. But why did she still feel so troubled, so unsure? Annalise was vanquished. She could do nothing to them.

So why didn't she really believe that, in her heart?

Dominic's room was a more or less exact twin of her own: spacious, sparsely furnished and luxurious in an unfussy way. Naked, Jemma stood patiently by the big windows in his room, which led on to the terrace, while Dominic got his camera and loaded some fresh film.

He hadn't bothered to put his jeans back on. His wardrobe was full of pairs of trousers, and yet he continued to stroll quite casually around the room while the two women looked on – one nude, one fully clothed – setting up a small tripod with the camera mounted upon it.

Dominic had the most spectacular male body Jemma had ever seen. He was actually, she thought to herself, quite photogenic himself. He had good bones, which was always the determining factor.

She watched him moving about as he set up ready to work. She enjoyed watching the play of hard-toned muscles under his bronzed skin. His cock was quiescent now, although even at rest it was still of a prodigious size. It bounced heavily between his legs as he moved, and his balls hung loose. Her eyes met Celestine's, and she could see the admiration for his beauty in the servant's eyes, too.

How loyal Celestine had been, siding with Dominic against the rather overwhelming Annalise. Dominic obviously chose his staff well.

'Ready?' said Dominic, and Jemma snapped to attention.

'Where do you want me?' she asked.

'Come and lie with Celestine on the bed,' he replied, and Jemma's eyes fastened on Celestine with a new interest.

The girl gave her a blankly innocent stare, but Jemma was beginning to realise that Celestine was very good at looking innocent, even if she was experienced, despite the fact her body was that of a seductive siren. And hadn't there been a bit of jealousy there once, over

Armand? Still, the girl had helped them today. Perhaps it was all forgotten. Jemma went to the bed and lay down, awaiting further instructions.

'Celestine?' prompted Dominic.

'Yes, m'sieur? What would you have me do?' she asked, trying to take her eyes from Jemma's lush, inviting body on the crisp, white sheets of Dominic's bed.

'Just lie down with Jemma.'

Celestine's blue eyes widened in surprise. But Jemma could see that the girl was not too disconcerted. She wore only a brown leather mini-skirt, a lilac stretchy crop-top that hung out from the shelf created by her large breasts, and sandals. Her streaky mane of blonde hair hung around her shoulders, unkempt just now but giving her a very tempting and bedable look.

Obediently Celestine kicked off her sandals and lay down beside Jemma. As Celestine made herself comfortable, Jemma looked her over. Yes, that little crop-top was very intriguing; the delicious shadow it created where those heavy, delectable breasts pressed against the material needed investigation.

'This is nice,' said Jemma to put the girl at her ease, reaching out to touch the soft lilac material with a thumb and forefinger. 'Have you modelled for Dominic before?'

'No.' Celestine looked a little flustered, but she was sensual enough to look eager to continue with this, too.

'It's quite simple,' Jemma said reassuringly. 'Just move whichever way he wants you to move. He'll tell you clearly what he wants.'

'That's right,' added Dominic, who had set up a small spare flash unit and umbrella beside the bed and was angling it so that the two woman were flatteringly lit. They lay face to face on the bed. 'Now, Jemma, improvise. Just do what you feel.'

Improvise! Jemma hesitated. It was always easier to follow clear instructions than to use one's own initiative.

If she did what she felt like doing, she realised suddenly, she would lift the hem of Celestine's lilac crop-top and look at her breasts. Subliminally she had been watching them earlier, noting the way they swayed so heavily under the top, frankly intrigued by the outline of Celestine's nipples.

She remembered the amazing size of Celestine's pale-pink nipples when she thought back to the dinner party on her first night at the villa. She remembered, most stimulatingly, the way Annalise had caressed the girl's bush, and the way Dominic had had Celestine at the head of the table. And she remembered with a pang of regret how miserably jealous she had been of Celestine's coupling with Dominic, as Annalise had dragged Jemma off to bed.

'Well? Come on, Jemma,' urged Dominic from behind the camera, adjusting shutter speeds.

Do what you feel, he'd said. With an apologetic glance at Celestine's wide-open blue eyes, Jemma reached out and eased up the hem of the top. First, the deep shadow beneath Celestine's big breasts was revealed, then the gorgeous and startlingly white curves came into view.

'Arms back, both of you, don't block the shot,' said

Dominic, and they complied. The camera started to fire, whirring along on the motor wind.

Jemma continued to push up the top. Celestine's breasts were very heavy, crushed together by the fact that she was lying down, which pushed their tips even further forward in a way that was extremely provocative.

As Jemma bared the girl's nipples, all her previous caution and inhibition left her. They were exquisite, just as she remembered, very big and of the most delicate sea-shell pink colour. She pushed the top up further, so that each of the delectable naked breasts were fully on show.

'Goodness, aren't they beautiful?' she said admiringly.

'Too big,' said Celestine, colouring apologetically.

'No.' Jemma shook her head firmly. 'They're magnificent. Lovely and upright. Oh look.'

Jemma drew Celestine's attention to the fact that her nipples were hardening as they spoke. When the girl's nipples puckered in arousal, their tips lengthened as if inviting the appreciative watcher to suck at them.

Jemma, mindful of the camera's angle as she moved forward, chose the breast that was crushed against the mattress for her attention, so that she should not block Dominic's view too much. Do what you feel, he'd said, and yes, she wanted to do this.

Her hand clasped the girl's big soft breast while her mouth fastened upon the nipple. She sucked hard, knowing, as only another woman would know, how good this would feel. Celestine gave a moan of delight and clutched at Jemma's shoulder.

'Arms back, Celestine,' Dominic reminded her gently, and Celestine moved her hand down to rest lightly on Jemma's naked hip, smoothing over the silky skin as Jemma attended to her breast with lush sucking sounds.

'Oh you taste good,' said Jemma at last, lifting her head to smile into Celestine's eyes. 'Powdery and milky.' She dipped her head and took the other nipple into her mouth, circling it busily with her tongue, gently biting with her teeth, and tugging upon the extended bud with every intention of stimulating the girl by her side to the point where she forgot all propriety.

'Slip the top off, Celestine,' said Dominic, crouching naked behind the camera.

As Celestine drew back a little to shrug the top off over her head, Jemma glanced at Dominic and saw with pleasure that his cock was stirring afresh at the sight of all this nude female flesh.

Naked to the waist, Celestine lay back down. 'May I?' she asked shyly, indicating Jemma's breasts.

'Of course,' Jemma said huskily, and lay still while Celestine tongued her own nipples. Lovely sensations rocketed through her at the gentle touch of the girl's hot tongue. Her nipples tingled and stood erect, sending a message of eroticism to the warm cleft between her legs, where her juices began to flow.

Her clitoris began to harden and an exquisite ache was starting up between her legs. Jemma led Celestine's hand there to caress it, which the girl seemed more than willing to do.

Strange, thought Jemma, how soon one became unaware of the watching camera. She turned on to her back, inviting Celestine to continue with her ministrations. Celestine happily obliged, pushing eager fingers into the soft slit so wantonly presented to her.

'Arms above your head, Jemma,' Dominic instructed softly, and Jemma followed his directions closely while almost humming to herself with pleasure at the depth of her desire for this succulent girl.

Celestine continued with her stroking, the whole length of her creamy-skinned body tight against the side of Jemma's, the heavy breasts touching Jemma's smaller and more finely shaped ones. Seeing that Jemma appreciated this, Celestine deliberately rubbed her nipples against Jemma's and insinuated her thin, silky blonde bush between Jemma's thighs to rub up against her darkly covered mound.

Dominic moved around the bed restlessly; distracted by his movement, Jemma glanced at him to see that he was fully erect now. She reached out and touched his penis worshipfully, stroking it from stem to tip. Celestine's eyes followed hers and lingered on the mighty erection.

'It feels very good inside, yes, Jemma?' she giggled, indicating Dominic's cock.

'Wonderful, Celestine,' agreed Jemma, then instantly froze, worrying that she had betrayed their sexual relationship with her thoughtless words. But Celestine shook her head, negating Jemma's fears. Their secrets were safe with her.

Celestine's fingers were inside her now, three fingers or four, and she was full, but not full enough – not after Dominic.

The pressure of those thrusting fingers was, however, very pleasurable, and she spread her legs a little wider so that Celestine could crouch between her thighs and give her more of the same. Jemma moaned and lifted her hips, rocking them back and forth in time to Celestine's thrusting. Her orgasm threatened like an approaching summer storm, soon to burst upon her to drench and refresh her.

She saw Dominic, with a light curse, put the camera and light meter aside and get on to the bed behind Celestine, who still crouched intently between Jemma's spread thighs. Celestine glanced around in pleased surprise as Dominic knelt behind her, nudging her own thighs open.

In an instant he had pushed his cock down, and slipped it into Celestine's hot, wet cleft. Celestine shivered and tensed for a moment, and then Dominic started to thrust with deep, lazy strokes inside her cunt, and she groaned and sighed in delight.

Three-way fucking was something Jemma had never tried before, but she had to admit it did have its good points. She enjoyed the bob and swing of Celestine's breasts above her, and from where she lay she could also see each languorous thrust of Dominic's hips as he took his pleasure in Celestine. Celestine's fingers were now rubbing her clit and pushing into her at the same pace as Dominic's thrusts, and it took only a very little leap of the imagination for Jemma to believe that it was Dominic's cock moving inside her, and not Celestine's fingers.

That thought was her undoing. She came with a scream and a jolt of ecstasy, her thighs clamping around Celestine's waist, her feet resting upon the suddenly rapidly thrusting buttocks of Dominic. Celestine came next, throwing her head back against Dominic's shoulder and howling like a satisfied she-dog.

Dominic's orgasm was last, but it set Celestine going again; ripples of pleasure pervaded her until she slumped forward on to Jemma in utter exhaustion.

After a moment Dominic withdrew from Celestine, caressing her pearly buttocks with pleasure and approval. Jemma watched him, admiring his heaving chest, his hard-packed stomach, his moist pink cock, which still stood as upright as a pole.

'We'll call that a wrap, shall we?' he said huskily, with a rakish grin. Carelessly he dried his cock on the sheet. 'That's the last roll before we do the centrepiece for the Paris exhibition Max has got planned.'

'And what's the centrepiece to be?' Jemma asked lazily, stretching and smiling at Celestine.

'You'll see,' Dominic answered mysteriously.

Then he got up from the bed and took the film out of the camera, before leaving the room to put it safely away with all the others.

Chapter Sixteen

Dominic seemed pleased with the work he had done so far with Jemma; everything had been packeted up and delivered to the professional processing laboratory in Nice that he always used.

Now, apart from this mysterious 'centrepiece' that Dominic had told her about, everything seemed to be coming to an end. Jemma was surprised to find that she was a bit sad about that. Soon she would be back in her London flat, perhaps with Steven, perhaps not. Soon, too, she would be resuming her madcap life of hectic assignments and airport dashes.

Soon, but not yet.

This was her reality for the moment: the hot Mediterranean sun; the breeze sweeping in from the sea; the cool glamour and calm of the villa; and, of course, Dominic.

Unfortunately, most of their days were spent out on the yacht with Max and Annalise while Dominic discussed the fine points of the Paris exhibition with Max.

Jemma found, at times, that the atmosphere on board was stifling. Annalise watched the pair of them with jealous eyes, panicking if they were alone for any length of time, even going so far as to patrol their nightly sleeping arrangements – much to Dominic's amusement and Jemma's wrath.

The fact was, they had found it impossible to get together properly since the day of the motorbike shoot. Jemma had to wonder, because Annalise's paranoia was infectious, whether Dominic was intending to repeat the experience or not.

Perhaps he believed he had transgressed, but got away with it just that once.

Perhaps he had no intention of fucking her again.

Not knowing either way, and being too fearful to ask Dominic flat out, was driving her to a frenzy. It was a frenzy that very often was soothed and sated in the arms of Max Klein, or one of the very able and willing crew members.

There was one particularly ravishing boy, his lithe body toasted to a golden glow, his floppy blond hair bleached almost white by the sun, who only ever wore cut-off jeans as he served lunch up on deck. And, as the four diners were always naked by lunchtime, after a morning spent swimming and sunbathing, it was deemed silly that the boy should have to hide behind the formality of his clothes – scant though they were.

Max suggested it as the main course was served, and happily, the blond boy agreed, although he was a little shy about stripping off then and there.

'Come, Mark,' encouraged Annalise, who was sipping her wine – she had been sipping rather a lot of
wine lately, Jemma thought – while wearing nothing
but her sunglasses. 'As you can see, we are all naked.
Why shouldn't you be?'

'Well, if you insist, madame,' he said, blushing
charmingly.

'I do.' Annalise stood up from the table, swaying
slightly.

The boy's eyes went in small circles from her spice-
coloured nipples to the naked slitted mound between
her legs.

So she's still shaving, Jemma thought with interest.
Glancing at Max and at Dominic, who had both
abandoned their sunglasses in the shade of the awning,
she saw that both men were looking at it. She could not
see their cocks stirring at the bracing sight of Annalise's
nude pubis – they were concealed by the table – but she
knew they were.

Unwilling to let Annalise grab all the control and all
the fun as usual, Jemma stood up too, and went around
the table to where Annalise stood before the boy. She
put a companionable arm around Annalise's shoulder
and smiled provocatively at the boy.

'You look like the Three Graces with the third
one missing,' joked Max, fidgeting slightly to ease his
arousal.

'If Mark will take his shorts off, we will have a full
set,' returned Jemma.

Enticingly, she reached out and ran a finger around

the waistband of the cut-off jeans. 'Or perhaps he wants me to take them off for him?'

'Why not?' suggested Dominic, watching the scene in fascination. The boy was no more than nineteen or twenty, and he was very beautiful in that shining, untouched way that only youth can be. The blush on his cheeks was like the slight pinkening on a ripe pear. He could see why Annalise wanted a peek at what Mark seemed so keen to keep hidden.

'Come on, Mark,' cajoled Annalise, leaning quite heavily against Jemma. 'There'll be a bonus for you.'

The boy's startling blue eyes lit with interest.

'And as an additional incentive,' Jemma added boldly, 'if you do it, you can have us both.'

The boy hesitated, intent on securing a good deal for himself. But Jemma could see he was tempted by the sudden bulge at the front of the jeans.

'Together?' he asked doubtfully.

'Together, if you want,' said Jemma, with an enquiring glance at Annalise. Annalise nodded. Jemma wondered if she would still be awake to fulfil their promises after lunch, or if, instead, she'd be sleeping off all the wine she'd drunk throughout the morning.

'I do,' said Mark a bit hoarsely.

'It's a deal, then?' prompted Jemma with a smile that was sheer provocation. She ran a hand slowly up over her hip, over her waist, up over her ribcage until it cupped and lifted one firm, full, dark-pointed breast. 'You like these, don't you?' she asked.

'Y-yes,' stammered Mark, his eyes glued to her breasts just as Dominic's and Max's were.

'Then do it. Slip those shorts off. You'll be so much more comfortable without them.'

'Here, I'll do it,' Annalise volunteered smoothly.

She went down on her knees in front of Mark, who edged back like a frightened colt. Jemma soothed him with a smile. Annalise's fumbling fingers managed to undo the button at his waist, then she slid the zip down, and pushed the shorts to the deck.

Mark was wearing a pair of white briefs.

'Oh,' said Annalise in disappointment, while Jemma eyed the flat belly with its sexy little indented navel, and the well-muscled thighs lightly covered in gleaming blond hairs, and the prodigious bulge that pushed out the front of the briefs.

'Take them off, Mark,' she instructed and, with Annalise still kneeling before him, the boy bent deftly and pushed the briefs down. He stepped free of the jeans and the briefs in one elegant movement, and straightened.

The four diners were transfixed by the revelation. Mark's chunky penis was standing up like a divining rod, springing from a thick nest of darker blond hair that covered his ample balls. His cock was amazingly pale in contrast to that deep, rich tan on the rest of his body. In fact, all around his hips his skin was white and very fine, and almost vulnerable-looking. Max, who had a side-view of the boy's ivory-white buttocks, found himself handling his own erection rather desperately beneath the tablecloth.

'That's a nice cock, my boy,' he complimented Mark with aplomb. 'Don't you think so, darling?' he asked Annalise, while trying to subdue his own cock a bit.

'Luscious,' agreed Annalise, sinking back on to her heels the better to admire it.

Jemma glanced at Dominic, who was leaning forward with his elbows on the table, assessing the boy's beauty with an artist's eye.

'Quite photogenic,' agreed Dominic. 'What do you think, Jemma?'

'I think it's magnificent,' said Jemma with a sigh of desire.

'And I can have you both? Together?' asked Mark with a nervous swallow, obviously fearing they would now back out of the deal.

'In any way you want,' said Jemma, sashaying back to her seat. 'After lunch.'

The main course of fish and salad was soon disposed of. After that there was coffee, fruit and cheese, if any-one wanted it. Max had the cheese, and so did Dominic, but the two women found themselves increasingly dis-tracted by the beautiful Mark, who was moving around the table serving them with punctilious politeness while sporting an erection of gargantuan proportions.

'Isn't this bothering you, sweetheart?' asked Annalise as he passed. She gave his tumescent prick a loving pat.

'Not at all, madame,' replied the boy in a fluster, quickly gathering up the plates.

'It turns you on, then, serving us in this state? What a shameless boy you are.'

'Don't tease him, Annalise,' said Jemma with a sympathetic smile at Mark. 'You look wonderful, Mark, and why should you be ashamed? Your cock is beautiful,' she told him firmly.

Mark blushed with pleasure at the compliment, but was not sophisticated enough to feel entirely easy with this situation. Shyly, he held an empty tray in front of his burgeoning genitalia.

'Now why is concealment so much more intriguing, even challenging, than an open display?' wondered Annalise aloud as her gaze tried to pierce Mark's defences.

'Perhaps because your tastes are becoming jaded, my love?' jibed Max. 'And this child's innocence is just the kick-start your drink-sodden libido needs?'

Startled by the cruelty of this comment, Jemma looked around sharply at Max. Usually he was so supportive of Annalise, even in her worst moods. Max always smoothed things over, and played the peacemaker.

Well, perhaps he was tired of the role, she thought with an inward shrug. She saw that even Annalise was startled by what Max had said. The woman looked really stung by it, in fact, and Jemma could not help but feel sorry for her.

'Max, are you saying I'm drunk?' she half-laughed, her eyes uneasy as they darted around the table.

'You know you are. You've been drunk ever since you got it into your mind that Dominic and Jemma had sex that day at the villa – which they didn't. And even if they did, so what? The world wouldn't end. The boat wouldn't sink, I assure you. The walls of the villa wouldn't crumble and fall. Dominic's artistic talents wouldn't disintegrate – but your hold over him might.'

Max stood up suddenly. His own usually sturdy cock was now flagging between his legs, Jemma saw in surprise.

'You will have to excuse me,' he said with his more usual politeness. 'I'm in a foul mood today, and I'm not fit company for any of you.'

So saying, he went below, slamming the door into the seating area behind him with a thump.

Jemma looked curiously at Dominic, but he could only shrug in reply. He too rose from his seat. His erection, of course, was still in place, rock-hard against his belly.

'I think I'll catch a little sun,' he said casually. 'Jemma, will you be free by four? The light'll be good then.'

'OK,' she nodded agreeably, wishing he could join Mark, Annalise and her down below but knowing that was out of the question. She hoped that when she and Dominic worked together later they would be able to leave the ship and then make love somewhere.

That thought cheered her up a bit. She went and helped Annalise up from her chair. With Mark supporting her on one side, and Jemma supporting her on the other, they were able to get Annalise down to the main stateroom, where she promptly passed out in one of the big gilded chairs and started to snore loudly.

Jemma looked at Mark apologetically.

'Next door,' she whispered, and led the boy into

the far less ostentatious cabin that was for the moment serving as her own sleeping quarters.

It was furnished in peacock blue and cool white. Jemma found it rather more restful but certainly not as stimulating as the main stateroom. The instant they were inside, Mark was on her like a fury, pulling her body tight against his, kissing her with puppyish eagerness, and kneading her breasts with his hands.

Jemma laughingly pulled away a little, but let her hips and belly remain in contact with the boy's hotly aroused penis, enjoying the sensation quite considerably. Mark was staring openly at her breasts.

'Aren't you disappointed that you are only to have one woman instead of the two you were promised?' she asked with a smile, kissing his deliciously pouting mouth with lingering slowness. His tongue darted into her mouth, flirting with her tongue. His hips pushed against hers inexpertly.

'You're so beautiful,' he exclaimed against her chin, lowering his silky blond head to kiss her throat. 'I think I'm in love with you.'

Jemma pushed him back a little, more serious now. His hands, trembling slightly, continued to play with her nipples and his eyes seemed fixed to the hard, dark buds, as if he could not quite believe what he was touching.

'I don't care that it's just you. I love you,' he muttered ecstatically, dipping his head and briefly taking a nipple between his moist lips. 'It's you I wanted,' he said ardently against her breast. 'You, not her.'

'Hush,' said Jemma, in case Annalise should overhear.

It seemed unlikely, but she didn't want Annalise to suffer more indignity today than she already had. It would be unkind. Mark seemed to be getting a taste for the breast. He was sucking at her nipple quite hard now, and his hands were rubbing feverishly up and down her naked buttocks, pressing her pubis hard against his penis.

Jemma dosed her eyes, feeling desire shoot through her like a comet.

'How old are you, Mark?' she asked on a gasp, her hands settling upon his broad, bony young shoulders.

'Nineteen,' he mumbled against her tit.

'Nineteen?' she repeated dryly.

Mark's head rose. His blue eyes twinkled as he gave a bashful grin. 'All right, seventeen.'

'You mean sixteen, don't you? And I'm the first, yes?' guessed Jemma.

'Of course not,' Mark denied hotly.

'Mark?' Her voice was stern.

'All right, yes.' His face fell almost comically. 'Does that mean you won't let me . . .' His voice trailed away in despair.

'It doesn't mean that at all,' Jemma reassured him.

She led him to the bed and had him lie down upon the silk paisley-printed coverlet. Peacock-blue suited him, she thought. The blond hair on his head and between his muscular young thighs looked white in the subdued light of the cabin. His penis twitched eagerly.

It was obvious that two women would have been beyond him. He did not possess the sexual stamina or the self-control yet to accommodate two female appetities. Just as well Annalise passed out when she did, thought Jemma with amusement. It had saved Mark from embarrassment.

She didn't even dare tongue him, he was so aroused. He would come in an instant. And, as this was his first time, the last thing she wanted to do was humiliate him.

Settling upon a safer option, she deftly straddled him, grasping the stem of his penis to help him slow down. Mark reached up and fondled her breasts cautiously, but seemed even less certain about the prospect of being ridden.

'I want to be on top,' he complained, as if this were of vital importance to his masculinity.

'It doesn't matter who is on top,' Jemma pointed out, 'so long as both of us have a lot of fun.'

'But I want –' For a moment he sounded like the child he no longer was, begging for a treat, pouting and frowning, ready to throw a tantrum if need be.

'Hush, darling,' Jemma soothed him. 'Now don't move or I'll be very cross,' she said in a stern, motherish voice.

As she had thought he would, Mark subsided, yielding to the authoritarian voice of the female, the mother.

'But can't I at least –' he whined, straining restlessly upward towards her bush.

'No,' said Jemma firmly. 'Now don't move. Not a muscle. Or I'll stop and leave the cabin, all right?'

Mark fell back, daunted by her threat.

Perhaps she really would leave, and his fellow crew members would see her leave, and then they would know she had walked out on him. They would know she had left before he could fuck her. He would be a laughing stock!

'That's better,' murmured Jemma as Mark grudgingly complied.

Jemma leant forward against his strongly developing chest, placing her hands on either side of his head. The dark fan of her hair fell forward, tickling his shoulders. Carefully, as if this were a matter requiring great precision, she allowed one nipple to brush against his full, nicely shaped lips.

Mark's mouth opened and his tongue lapped sweetly at the turgid tip. Jemma, enjoying the sensation, allowed the boy to carry on for a while, then, when his lips clamped around it and his arms came up to envelop her, she pulled back.

'Didn't I tell you not to move?' she asked.

Mark squirmed. 'You did. But I couldn't help it.' His eyes were hopelessly locked on to her breasts which swayed so heavily, so seductively, when she moved over him.

'You must help it,' said Jemma 'What I want to teach you, Mark, is self-control. When a man makes love, he needs self-control.'

Dominic, she thought wryly, seemed to have that facility in abundance. After all, he hadn't attempted to fuck her since that time at the villa.

'Jemma?'

Jemma snapped back to the present, pushing thoughts of Dominic to one side.

'No,' said Jemma. 'Whatever you're about to ask, forget it.' She smiled her siren smile at him. 'For now, Mark, I'm in charge. Now tell me, do you like this?'

Jemma had leant back and was positioning herself over his fiercely erect penis. She clasped it lightly, spread her legs to their fullest extent, and gently pulled the good-sized organ back from his belly so that its wet lip caressed her rigid little clitoris.

'I like it,' he gasped, trying not to thrust upward but failing.

'Keep still or I'll go,' Jemma said flatly, and he subsided with a tormented groan.

Jemma waited until he stopped moving, and then continued. She pulled the head of his cock back further, until it rested at the moist, open portal of her vagina.

'Now, is that good?' she asked, dipping down a little so that his cock could part her lips and enter by no more than an inch.

'Oh, it's good,' he groaned, and sweat stood out in tiny beads on his brow and chest, testament to his efforts not to move, not to thrust like fury. The hard six-pack of muscles on his stomach fluttered madly with the force of his restraint.

'And this?'

Jemma pushed her hips down a little more, taking him a fraction further.

'Good.' He nodded, his face a grimace of torment.

'This?' asked Jemma, taking him in more. Her own voice was a little unsteady now. His cock felt so amazingly hot inside her.

'Now this,' said Jemma, and, finally, she had his whole rigid cock lodged inside her. She squeezed it with the hot, tight sheath and held it prisoner. Mark moaned and bit his lip, his eyes darting between her face, her breasts and her bush.

'Good.' He groaned. 'Oh, that's so good.'

Jemma gave him a shaky smile, pleased with his progress.

'Now you can move,' she said.

It was like releasing an avalanche. Mark rose up, grabbed her hips and flipped her over on to her back in the blink of an eye, without once dislodging himself from his snug position between her legs.

With Jemma underneath him, he started pumping his cock in and out of her as if his life depended upon it. Jemma lay back and let him have his fun. His eagerness was extremely stimulating, bringing her to a plateau of readiness for satiation that was soon to find its release.

Mark's balls were slapping against her with each heavy thrust. She felt them harden to rigid little nuts; felt the sudden glorious sensation of extra fullness inside her – and then his orgasm came. He yelled out, riding her furiously for brief seconds and then subsiding in a limp heap atop her.

His cock, however, was not yet limp.

'So now you know how to please yourself,' she murmured in his ear. 'Now do you want to know how to please me? And all the other women you will have in your lifetime?'

Mark, still gasping and grinning, propped himself up on his elbows over her.

'Yes,' he managed.

'Then stay inside me but move forward on your elbows,' instructed Jemma. She had tried this with Steven, and it was a very effective inducer of female climax. 'That's it,' she said encouragingly as Mark repositioned himself.

His cock pulled a little free of her and its stem pressed hard against her clitoris.

'That feels odd,' said Mark. 'Feels like I'm going to slip out.'

'You won't, so long as you don't thrust in and out,' said Jemma, dry-mouthed. The feeling of his penis moving against her clitoris was sheer heaven. 'Now just rock backwards and forwards.'

Mark was very pleased to continue. Being so young, he was ready for more action anyway, and this was a real learning curve for him. His first woman, *and* she was teaching him the mysteries of female arousal.

He started to rock back and forth, hardly moving his cock inside her at all. He closed his eyes in ecstasy, able to take his time a little now that the mad elation of his first fuck had subsided.

His cock had certainly not subsided. It was twitching back to total fullness again, and Jemma knew that now Mark wanted to thrust once more, to push more roughly than she would let him. But this lesson was about self-control; that's what she was teaching him here, and she could see that he appreciated it.

Eyes closed, he rocked gently, endlessly, concentrating on the rhythm and, when Jemma cried out and he felt the wild clenching of the muscles around his cock, he knew he'd done it – passed his first and most important test.

He opened his eyes. Jemma was leaning back against the pillows, almost swooning with pleasure. Her eyes flickered open and stared into his. She was panting. The circles around her nipples looked swollen, and bigger. He put his hands over her breasts, feeling their sponginess, their softness, and her nipples, so rigid now.

'I really have to push now,' he said apologetically, and moved back down the bed a fraction.

He started to thrust, enjoying himself, but he hadn't enough control yet to delay for too long, and soon his climax came. To his obvious surprise and delight, Jemma came again, too. Soon they slept just like that, still linked together, and awoke later to make love again.

Or, as Jemma put it, to start on the second lesson.

At four o'clock, as promised, Jemma kept her appointment with Dominic. She was always punctual about work. She arrived at the door of his cabin freshly showered and perfumed with her camera make-up in place and her hair brushed until it gleamed. She wore an ice-blue silk wrap, and white leather mules.

'Dead on time,' he said in appreciation as he swung the door open at her knock and let her in. He then

locked the door firmly behind her so that they would
be undisturbed. He smelt, she noted, of apple shampoo
and shower gel.

Jemma's heart started to beat faster as she looked
Dominic over. From a boy to a man in a single bound,
she thought in faint amusement. In contrast to Mark's
body, Dominic's was bigger, more solid, more robust.
At the moment she could see a great deal of it. He was
obviously freshly emerged from the shower, just like
her, and he was wearing a brief white towel around his
waist and nothing else.

'Sorry,' he said in explanation, pulling his hair free
of its tail as he walked over to the dressing table. He
snatched up a brush and started to untangle the knots.
'I fell asleep earlier. Too much wine with lunch, I think.'

'Annalise certainly had too much wine with lunch,'
Jemma said wryly.

He gave her a questioning glance in the mirror. 'Is
she still . . .' he asked delicately.

'Sleeping it off?' Jemma nodded. 'She passed out
as soon as we came below, so Mark and I nipped next
door to my cabin. When I passed the stateroom on the
way here, I thought I'd better check on her. She's still
draped across a chair, snoring away like a hog.'

Dominic laughed. 'She'd love your description of
her,' he said, putting the brush down and taking up a
bottle of cologne.

'Well she isn't likely to hear it,' said Jemma, smiling,
and sauntering over to the bed.

This cabin, while sporting a lot of the walnut

panelling that was a feature of the whole boat, was furnished in cool, refreshing white. Texture seemed important here, from the nubby cotton coverlet on the bed to the watered silk of the chaise longue and the thick fake-fur rugs on the floor. She saw with interest that Dominic had set up his camera and lights by the chaise, and draped one of the furry rugs across it.

'This white's useful,' he pointed out, seeing her curiosity. 'Kicks back a lot of light, and cuts down the need for too many reflectors.'

'So we're shooting in here?'

'Yep.' He turned back to her. 'Something different.'

'How different?' queried Jemma, intrigued.

'You'll see.' He went over to the camera and switched on the lights, activating the master and slave flashes. They whirred noisily as they took up the charge, then settled down to a comfortable bleeping that signalled they were ready to go to work.

Dominic loaded the film while Jemma watched him covertly. He was such a beautiful man. Right now, tanned from their time in the sun and with his wild mane of black hair, he looked more like a renegade Native American than a world-renowned photographer. She had never seen Dominic lift weights, but his body was certainly well developed, each muscle clearly delineated beneath his healthily glowing skin.

Broad shoulders, she thought with a lustful sigh, admiring his back view. Tapering to a narrow waist, even narrower hips. His buttocks moved lightly beneath the confining towel as he bent to check the focus on the camera. His thighs, covered with black down, clenched as he moved.

Jemma longed to run her hand up over those strong legs to find what lay beneath the towel, but this was business – they were professionals. Stifling her baser desires, she said: 'So you want me on the chaise, yes?'

'Yes,' he said, not looking up.

Jemma brushed past him, restraining an urge to stroke his thigh as she passed. She sat down on the fur-draped chaise, legs together, the ice-blue silk wrap pulled decorously up about her throat.

'You look like a virgin fearing ravishment,' noted Dominic as he peered at her through the lens.

Jemma raised her eyebrows at the lens. 'Well, I just don't know what you're planning to do. And it's making me nervous.'

He nodded briefly, but was clearly disinclined to ease her discomfort by telling her what was going to happen.

'Speaking of virgins . . .' he said after a while, straightening to drape an arm over the camera and regard her with amused thoughtfulness.

'A lady never tells,' Jemma said primly.

'He's all right though? Not in need of a friendly fatherly advice session or anything like that? Something along the lines of "premature ejaculation happens to the best of us"?'

Jemma felt offended on Mark's behalf. 'He performed beautifully,' she said coldly. 'That is all I am prepared to say on the matter.'

'Oh, very frosty,' noted Dominic. 'OK, ice maiden, take the wrap off now.'

Jemma hesitated in confusion. 'But . . . aren't you going to get dressed?'

Dominic gave her a teasing half-smile. 'Do you want me to get dressed? Will it make you feel safer or something?'

'Don't be silly.'

'So take the wrap off.'

'But I thought you were going to shoot this session up on deck,' said Jemma, not prepared to let it go as she fiddled with the knot on the robe's tie-belt. 'You said the light would be good, didn't you?'

'I did. But I changed my mind. I didn't want interruptions, and on deck there might have been some.'

The knot was undone. Jemma paused to eye him suspiciously. 'Did you ply Annalise with all that drink?' she asked accusingly.

'Not at all.'

'Oh.'

'Max did.'

'Oh! But Max was complaining at lunchtime, about her drinking.'

Dominic shrugged. 'They're going through a bit of a tough time. But he knew this was the last session, the *pièce de resistance* of the entire Paris exhibition. He didn't want us disturbed while we're working on it.'

'So he got his wife drunk.'

'Well, she helped.'

'I worry about Annalise, I really do,' frowned Jemma.

'Worry about doing some work,' said Dominic, and Jemma took the hint. She opened the front of the robe.

Chapter Seventeen

'Just leave it open like that for the moment, and lean back against the furs.'

Jemma looked behind her. 'They are fake, yes?'

'Annalise may have her faults, but she would never have real fur on her person or in any of her houses,' Dominic reassured her. 'Relax.'

Jemma complied. With the silky blue robe open to display her breasts to their best advantage, but pulled together over her thighs to conceal her bush, Jemma leant back against the furs. She followed Dominic's instructions closely as he started to direct her.

'Arms above your head, that's it. Now just one arm. Let the other lie across your lap, no, your left, not your right. Look at me. Now look over there; look bored,' he rattled out as he fired busily.

Jemma lounged back and went into a half-trance while he changed films and got ready to start again. Dominic rummaged in one of his bags and tossed a long amber necklace into her lap.

'Props,' he explained. 'Put them on.'

Jemma did so. The amber glowed, sending shards of twinkling golden light across her sun-darkened skin. The effect was startlingly sexy.

Dominic carried on shooting, duplicating the poses he had just done and then moving on to some fresh ones.

'Put your legs up on the chaise now,' he ordered. 'Let the robe fall open, but bend that knee closest to the camera. Push the robe back, so we can see that bare thigh but not your bush.'

And so it went on. At least he still seems confident enough, Jemma pondered, even if he is treating me like a block of wood!

Thank goodness Mark had served her well earlier this afternoon. That had taken the sharp edge off her sexual appetite – hadn't it? As she watched him working, she found that she felt aroused. She wished he would take that silly towel off, in fact; and abandon work for the day and get on to that big, inviting bed with her.

'Dominic,' she complained mildly after an hour, 'I'm getting stiff.'

'Just changing film.'

Which meant more posing, she thought in exasperation. Well, she realised with teeth gritted in determination, she was being paid enough to do this. She watched him fasten a small attachment to the camera, then recheck the focusing. He came over to the chaise then, to give her more orders.

'Straddle the chaise,' he said quickly.

279 A PRIVATE VIEW

Jemma did so. Then she watched in amazement as he tossed the towel aside. His erect cock bobbing invitingly before her eyes, he flipped one leg over the chaise so that he sat facing her, their knees touching.

'Surprise.' He grinned and leant forward and kissed her, just as the flashes fired. 'It's a delay facility,' he explained huskily against her mouth. 'So that I can capture the artist and his muse. Do you like it?'

'I like this,' groaned Jemma, pulling him into her arms for a longer, deeper kiss.

Dominic's hands rose and enclosed her breasts. That was one of the other differences between a boy and a man, she thought in a daze of desire. Mark's hands had not fully covered her breasts, but Dominic's did. And Dominic's felt so much harder than Mark's, their touch more firm, more assured. Her nipples bloomed like spring blossom beneath his masterly caress.

'We're still working,' he reminded her, running a trail of little kisses down her throat until his mouth reached the place where his hands rested. Then he cupped a breast and brought the nipple to his questing mouth, sucking hungrily.

Jemma leant against the back of the chaise and blissfully accepted what he was doing to her.

'We don't have to be,' she said hoarsely.

Dominic's head lifted and he stared into her eyes. 'Take the robe off now,' he said. 'But leave the necklace on.'

Jemma obligingly removed the ice-blue robe, tossing it well out of shot. She leant back again, eager to see what he would do next. The furs against her back and under her bottom felt exceedingly erotic. Her eyes dipped to admire Dominic's towering penis. His balls were resting upon the fur, his legs splayed wide, like hers, by the chaise. For the moment, his hands were placed casually upon his thighs.

'Tell me what you're thinking,' he said, and his eyes were on her full, tanned breasts with the amber sparkling between them.

Jemma licked her suddenly dry lips. 'I want to touch you,' she admitted.

'Where?'

'Your cock,' she sighed. 'I want to touch your cock.'

'Do it then,' he said.

Jemma leant forward, her naked breasts swaying invitingly, and ran one finger down his sturdy stem until her finger met the dense mat of hair that covered his balls. Applying both hands now, she tucked her fingers underneath his treasures so that she could lift and caress them. Dominic's penis twitched furiously in reaction, its eye opening to sport a dewdrop of pre-come.

'That feels good,' he groaned, and the flashes fired again.

'Oh!' said Jemma in surprise.

'It works like time-lapse photography,' Dominic explained breathlessly. 'You've seen those shots of flowers opening, where the process is speeded up so that they seem to open in a huge rush?'

Jemma nodded, then bent her head and slowly tongued the tip of his penis.

'Well,' panted Dominic, 'it's the same technique.'

'Oh good,' said Jemma wryly, wondering at the male facility for being intrigued by gadgets. 'Do you like this technique?' she asked, applying her mouth to his cock's engorged stem and taking little sideways nibbles at it with her teeth.

'Mmm,' he moaned appreciatively.

'And this one?' she murmured against the hot, hard length of his penis, raising her head and moving forward a little.

Jemma leant forward and snugly enclosed his cock in the deep cleft between her breasts. The amber brushed his hot, needy flesh with a pleasing coolness before Jemma tossed it back over her shoulder, out of the way.

Using her hands to cup her breasts together, she was able to move her torso up and down so that his penis, caught in her dark valley, was caressed very thoroughly by the soft, mobile mounds that clasped it.

The flashes fired. This time Jemma didn't start with surprise, but she found to her annoyance that she had forgotten to keep her hair from falling forward over her face. That shot wouldn't be any good.

'Good?' she asked softly.

'Your hair was over your face,' Dominic pointed out shakily, intent on what she was doing to him but ever the technician.

'I know. Sorry.'

'Lean back a moment.'

Jemma released his cock and lay back against the chaise, languorously raising her hands above her head to clasp the carved and gilded rim. Her breasts lifted enticingly as she moved. Dominic watched them.

'Your nipples are very hard,' he pointed out, reaching out and running the back of one hand over them.

Jemma shuddered deliciously. 'I know. Too hard for the shot?'

He shrugged and gave a rueful grin. 'I don't see how we're going to alter the state they're in, even if they are. But they're not. Don't worry. Relax.'

Jemma needed no further encouragement. His hand dropped, slipping down over her ribcage, into the neat dip of her waist, over her navel and the slight curve of her belly, then settling on her densely furred pubic mound.

The flashes fired.

Deftly, his finger slipped lower, parting the crisply curling hairs to find her slit and unveil her waiting bud. He rubbed the slippery, erect clitoris gently with his thumb, meanwhile sliding his fingers further down, finding her hot entrance, pushing easily inside.

'You're very aroused,' he breathed, leaning close to her mouth, and kissing her lightly, teasingly.

'Are you surprised?' Jemma murmured, raising her thighs a little so that he could more easily manipulate her.

'No,' he breathed, his tongue teasing her lower lip before his teeth followed, biting so gently that there was no question of bruising.

The flashes fired again. Jemma glanced at the blank eye of the camera, curious about what was being recorded there. The artist and his muse, making love. A self-portrait of Dominic, with the woman who inspired him.

And she had thought he did not intend to touch her again.

He was touching her now, probing more deeply and more urgently with his fingers. How many were there inside her now?

Three, she thought. Enough to be wildly stimulating without causing real discomfort. She was aware of her own wetness, of the sucking sounds that were coming from her sex as his hand caressed it. When Dominic told her to slide down a bit, and then lifted her thighs so that they rested on his shoulders, she was more than ready to proceed.

His thighs were slipping under hers. His hand left her cunt, drying itself briefly upon her nest of hair, then joined its twin in lifting her up. Jemma found herself lying flat along the length of the chaise, with her buttocks resting upon Dominic's hotly pulsing cock and her knees spread apart over his wide shoulders.

'Put it inside you,' Dominic said urgently.

Jemma tried not to blink as the flashes fired again. Her gasping breaths matching his, she reached between her wide-open legs and brought his ferociously erect cock down a little so that the tip of it could be eased inside her ready depths.

She wriggled her hips down on to him, sending a shiver of sensation through them both as she impaled herself upon the lust-swollen glans.

Dominic did not wait for her to complete the process. With a needy curse he pushed forward. Jemma let out a small cry of satisfaction as he was suddenly lodged inside her.

The position she was in had facilitated very deep entry, and the feelings that shot through her as he pushed home were exquisite. She felt that she had never been fucked so completely as this. But she couldn't move an inch; all the moves would have to be his.

Within seconds, he was making them – moving gently and steadily in and out of her. First in, pushing, pushing at her, and then out almost completely so that her outer lips received more than their usual share of sensations. Then in again, pushing so hard, filling her so completely. Out again, leaving her empty, waiting, wanting.

'Oh God, Dominic,' she moaned, trying to move, but unable to.

He pushed in, almost brutally this time. The gentleness was gone now, but she was too aroused, far too ready, to need it. He pulled out almost to the hilt. Her breaths were coming in desperate little sobs as she watched him leaning over her, having her exactly as he chose.

Dominic rammed home inside her again. His head went back as his cock lodged deep inside her and a gasp escaped him, but his control was very good. He drew it back again, until only the hotly aroused helmet of his penis was still inside her. Looking down, Jemma could see the gleaming length of his cock outside her body, slick with her juices. She could feel the head inside her, big but not big enough.

Dominic leant forward, placing his palms flat on the chaise to balance their panting bodies. The flashes fired again and it came home to Jemma then that this was being recorded, that this, Dominic fucking her in this thorough yet maddeningly titillating way, would be hung upon a wall in an art gallery in Paris. A select few would go to see the private view, and then the doors would be thrown open to the general public.

If this was art, it was certainly enhancing her appreciation of the creative process. It quietly amused her to think of someone purchasing one of Dominic's portraits of her. She would hang on someone's wall, a beautiful icon, the new muse of the world-famous photographer, Dominic Vane.

'Tell me what you want,' said Dominic, refusing to come back inside her this time until she begged for it.

'Do it to me,' she whimpered.

'Do what?' he teased, pushing just a little, enough to give a taster, a mere miserly glimpse of the paradise she wanted.

'Fuck me,' she groaned, and his whole huge length surged into her.

'Like that?' panted Dominic. He pulled out again, out until he almost slid free, and this time, furiously, Jemma thrust her hips at him and reclaimed his cock with a deep-throated moan of victory.

The flashes fired.

Recorded for posterity, Jemma thought dazedly.

Dominic Vane fucking his muse. Or is his muse fucking him?

Dominic's balls were a hard, hot and furry cushion under her naked, soft-skinned buttocks. When he pushed hard, they slapped against her anus, an additional titillation for her. Dominic pulled back again – but this time, instead of the awaited jolt of his penis slamming back into her, he withdrew completely!

'Just slowing things down a bit,' he panted, encircling the sturdy base of his wet and reddened cock with thumb and forefinger, and squeezing firmly.

It was the same manoeuvre she had practised earlier on the boy, Mark. Jemma watched as he did it, thinking that he was much bigger than Mark, and that she wanted him back inside her this instant.

'Patience,' Dominic smiled, correctly reading her expression. 'That'll be better.'

Freeing his cock from his tight grasp, he guided it once more to the ready opening of her sex. Smoothly, watching her face as he did it, he slipped the whole length of his cock deep inside her.

This time, when he started to move; there were no teasing half-withdrawals; this was fucking, glorious full-blooded fucking, at its very best. His hips rocked steadily on the chaise, propelling his mighty organ in and out of Jemma's cunt at a fast and satisfying pace, setting up a marvellous friction that aroused her almost beyond bearing.

Her full naked breasts quivered deliciously at every thrust Dominic delivered. He could not take his eyes off them. They were acutely aroused, the nipples very swollen, the soft flesh delicately flushed with the pleasure he was giving her.

When the flash fired again, they were both oblivious to it.

The whole of Jemma's being seemed centred upon that big thrusting cock intruding into her sex, dividing it, filling it, making its juices flow, making it suck and clutch avidly at this horny male intruder.

Dominic felt his penis being constantly enclosed in the tight, wet sheath that clenched and released, clenched and released. The sensation of her cunt opening for his maleness and then enfolding him, swallowing him up to the hilt, was one of the sweetest and most stimulating he had ever experienced.

Uncaring of the watching camera, he pushed Jemma's legs down until they locked about his waist, then he slid his arms under her and scooped her up so that the front of her body was in close contact with his.

Now, as he thrust up into her, Dominic could feel Jemma's tits bouncing arousingly against his hard-muscled chest with every jolt. Her breath fluttered in his ear as she moaned and clawed at his back, encouraging him to do it, do it now.

The pace of his thrusts increased, and so did their ferocity. He penetrated Jemma harder and deeper, plunging again and again into her soft eager sex that pulled and sucked at his penis so desperately. His buttocks had risen from the chaise, he was supporting her full weight now against him, holding her, ramming his cock hard into her, feeling her soft breasts wobbling against the furious pounding of his heart.

It was too much. The wild charges of electricity that had been building in Jemma's loins for some while now possessed her totally. Her back arched hopelessly as she pressed her clitoris down against his bony pubic mound. Her orgasm brought a scream of satisfaction from her as it pulsed and flowed and filled her with sublime feelings.

Hurriedly Dominic clamped a hand over her mouth, but it was too late. If Jemma's ecstatic scream had woken the drunkenly slumbering Annalise, it was just too bad now, he decided. He took his hand away and kissed her briefly, intent now on his own pleasure as he thrust ever more vigorously.

He bit into the soft flesh of her shoulder to stifle his own bellow of satisfaction as his cock spasmed and released its seed. It throbbed heavily inside Jemma, renewing her own pleasure so that her clitoris answered, pulsing afresh into new orgasm. She groaned her pleasure this time, burying her face in the sweet clean scent of his thick black hair.

The flashes fired.

They both raised their heads, looked into each other's eyes, and smiled. A light film of sweat covered them both. Dominic relaxed on to the chaise, holding Jemma against him.

'I think that's a wrap,' he murmured against the skin of her throat. 'For now, anyway.'

'Hmm?' asked Jemma dreamily, floating in some

nirvana a thousand miles away and only vaguely aware that everyday life was still going on around her.

'We'll finish the session later, at the villa.' He smiled against her hair, kissing it lightly.

And then it will be over, thought Jemma, returning to earth with an unpleasant bump. If the centrepiece was nearly done, and all the other work they had done together was at the lab, then this whole episode was drawing to a close. She thought gloomily of cold, grey London – and of cool, grey Steven.

'What's up?' asked Dominic, his hand smoothing over the nape of her neck.

'Nothing,' said Jemma, keeping her tone as light as possible.

He lifted her head with his fingers. She could smell the scent of her own sex on his hand. Piercing green eyes looked deep into hers.

'Really nothing?' he queried.

And then the flash fired, and they both blinked, and laughed.

'Come on,' said Dominic, patting her behind companionably. 'Let's go and find Max, and cheer the old bugger up.'

Chapter Eighteen

Max, languishing below in the reading room and leafing through *L'Histoire d'O*, was more than ready to be cheered. They decided to take a picnic in the inflatable dinghy and paddle over to the very small private beach which belonged to Dominic's villa.

Jemma told Mark to get a basket ready with wine and food, then she changed into a new white bikini which emphasised her tan, and set off in the dinghy with Dominic and Max.

As the *Annalise* was anchored so close to shore, the journey to their pretty destination took only a matter of minutes. Laughing with almost adolescent high spirits, they hauled the dinghy up on to the beach and flopped down on to the sands together to admire the beauty of the day.

Apart from anyone who might care to watch them from the sea – and there were very few boats out there today – the beach was truly private. It formed a perfect protective crescent in the small bay, and was covered in soft white sand. At its back, foliage-covered cliffs rose, and a path was cut out of the cliffside – the path leading to the villa.

'It's lovely here,' Jemma said ecstatically, leaning back on her elbows and throwing her head back to the sun's hot caress. 'Isn't it Max?'

'Certainly is,' agreed Max, although his eyes were lingering not on the curves of the coastline but on Jemma's own curves, so stunningly emphasised by the skimpy white bikini.

Dominic went down to the dinghy while she and Max reclined there. He brought back the picnic hamper and a bag with sunscreen and bits and pieces in it, then went back to the dinghy. Jemma watched, admiring his superbly toned body in its brief black trunks, as he fastened a rope around the necks of several bottles of champagne, attached one end to the dinghy, then lay them in the sea to chill.

'I'm very pleased for both of you,' said Max, who was also watching Dominic.

'In what way?' Jemma looked at him in surprise.

Max turned over on to his stomach and gazed at her. 'Because you're lovers, aren't you? The curse of the muse has departed at last.'

Jemma returned his dark-eyed glance warily. 'How did you know?'

Max gave a short laugh. 'I have my sources. Celestine, for one, and she's no fool whatever anyone might think. Also, you seem to find it impossible to keep your hands off one another.'

'Well, I'm pleased that you're pleased,' said Jemma with a wry smile. 'But I'm worried about Annalise. She seems to be taking it badly.'

Max shrugged, his eyes hardening. 'She'll live. She's burying her head in a bottle for now, but she'll snap out of it when she sees it doesn't change anything. She's lost her hold over him, and that's a fact. She's going to have to accept it.'

'That sounds a bit hard,' said Jemma.

'My darling girl, live with Annalise for long enough and you realise it's the only way to be.'

'You two look serious,' said Dominic, rejoining them and flopping down in the sand beside Jemma. 'What's up?'

Jemma and Max exchanged glances. Then Jemma said: 'We were talking about Annalise. She suspects we're lovers. Max knows we are, by the way.'

'So what?' Dominic looked hard at Max. 'Is she going to raise hell if you tell her?'

Max rolled over on to his back and closed his eyes, clasping his hands elegantly across his tanned stomach. 'She already knows, dear boy. In her heart, that is. The way you two behave together, one would have to be a fool or blind not to know what was going on. And, as I told Jemma, she'll get used to the idea.'

'But do you think she will?' Jemma eyed him doubt-fully. 'Really?'

'Look, her pride's hurt, that's all. She thought after Vena there'd never be another muse for Dominic, and that eventually he would turn to her in that way. She thought that if she gave Dom all this if-you-sleep-with-your-muse-you'll-lose-your-talents malarkey, she would keep him firmly in her pocket. Then you came along, my angel. And I think I've indulged her enough over this matter. She'll come around.'

'Max is right,' Dominic told her. He stood up and held out a hand. 'Come on, let's swim.'

Puffing aside her misgivings, Jemma rose and, with a laugh, ran down to the water's edge with Dominic while Max looked on. The first shock of the water as they splashed in up to the thigh was delicious. It was not too cold; it was just right.

Dominic struck out powerfully and swam a relaxed length of the beach while she floated lazily on her back and gazed up at the perfect blue bowl of the sky. She heard him come splashing back towards her, then felt his arms go around her; she straightened quickly, her feet touching the sandy bottom just as his hard body came up close to hers.

Pushing back the hair from his eyes, he caught her close to him and kissed her deeply, pulling her body in tight against the front of his until she felt the first heavy stirrings of his erection against her thighs.

Then, when she laughed playfully and pushed him away, splashing water over him, he retaliated in kind, finally sweeping her up into his arms and wading back to the shore with her clinging to his neck. He dropped her lightly on to the sand beside Max, then sat down and rummaged in the bag for towels. He passed one to Jemma, and rubbed at his own chest and hair with another.

'Oh, hello,' said Max, opening his eyes with a yawn. 'Back so soon, you two?'

'We've been back for ages,' Dominic teased him, his eyes running admiringly over Jemma's body. 'Jemma, that bikini's turned transparent in the water.'

Jemma looked down. Max woke properly and struggled up on to his elbows before this vision was snatched away from him. 'Wow,' he said. 'Very nice, too.'

'It's not supposed to do that,' said Jemma, amazed to see that her dark nipples and her even darker bush were fully visible through the sodden fabric.

'White always seems to,' Dominic said sagely.

Jemma turned to him in amazement. 'So why didn't you tell me that when you saw me come out in a white bikini?'

'Children, children,' interjected Max. 'Must we squabble over this?' He gave Jemma a friendly leer. 'Look, it's transparent anyway and it must be uncomfortable, so you might as well take it off. It's so much nicer swimming nude, anyway. Look, I'll demonstrate.'

Max stood up, stretched, and in one swift movement pushed his bathing trunks down and stepped out of them. 'Look,' he said to the reclining pair. 'Doesn't this look more relaxed?'

Jemma and Dominic looked up at Max's compact body in admiration. The only thing that ruined the smooth lines of it was his cock, which was getting very excited by all that business with the white bikini and was standing erect, ready for action.

'You don't look terribly relaxed, Max,' joked Jemma.

'What, this?' Max gave his naked looming penis a couple of hearty pumps with his hand. It stood up harder still. So did his balls, rising robustly in their forest of hair between his thighs. 'That's just looking at your heavenly body, Jemma. The water'll cool it down.'

And he stomped off down the beach and into the waves, his hard heavy buttocks jiggling most attractively.

'Well, he's right. What's the point of wearing this if I look undressed anyway?' Jemma sighed, reaching back to unfasten the bikini top. Her nipples were as hard as walnuts from the coolness of the sea-breeze. And looking at Max's erection hadn't helped.

'Here, let me,' offered Dominic, and he reached over and unclasped the insubstantial garment, pulled it down her arms and tossed it aside. He turned back, gazing at her naked and unfettered breasts. 'They're so beautiful, it's a crime to keep them covered.'

'Oh yes.' Jemma smiled. 'Just the thing for shopping in Oxford Street in the rush-hour, the new bare-breasted look. With these bobbing about all over the place, that'd stop the traffic.'

Dominic leant closer and scooped one tit luxuriously up into his hand, weighing it as if it were a particularly luscious fruit. 'Gorgeous,' he breathed, watching closely as her nipples became even more engorged. He smoothed his thumb over the nub, back and forth, back and forth.

'Oh, that feels good,' sighed Jemma, watching Max cutting vigorously through the water, seabirds shrieking and wheeling high above him. Further out to sea, she saw the launch leave the *Annalise* and speed away around the far point of the bay, toward Nice.

'Pull your pants down,' said Dominic. 'I want to see your bush.'

'You saw it earlier,' she teased.

'I want to see it again.'

'You can see it anyway, as these are transparent.'

'Jemma,' he growled on a laugh, lightly pinching her teat.

Jemma happily complied. The wet little garment felt uncomfortable now, anyway. Max was right. Swimming naked was far better. She pulled the pants down, and kicked them off.

'Satisfied?' she asked archly, gazing deep into Dominic's green eyes.

'Such thick fur,' mused Dominic, dropping his hand from her breast to touch this new point of interest, stroking it as though it were a cuddly animal. Jemma opened her legs a little, letting the stroking develop into a deeper massage. Dominic's fingers were opening out her petals and searching for her moist and ready centre when Jemma saw Max emerging from the waves.

'Max is coming,' she said to Dominic, feeling suddenly shy.

'So?' Dominic's finger found her, pushed, was suddenly in. It felt amazingly good, but she pulled his hand away with a pang of regret and closed her legs primly, turning on to her front.

'Will you rub some cream into my back?' she asked sweetly.

'If it means I get to touch you,' said Dominic, reaching for the bag, 'yes.'

'Good swim, Max?' she asked, propping herself up on to her elbows. The hot sand pressed against her recently stimulated pudenda, making her feel distinctly horny. Trying to quell the feeling, she pressed her buttocks together.

Max saw the clenching of the muscles on her naked bottom and thought that it was a very delectable little bottom, like a peach, and how he would like to split that peach with his cock right now.

Once aroused, Jemma always found it particularly hard to regain her equilibrium. Today, even the sand conspired against her, feeling so sexy-smooth against her belly, and so teasingly abrasive against her nipples. Propped up on her elbows as she was, talking to Max, her tits barely grazed the sand, it was like being intermittently lapped by a cat's rough tongue.

And Max wasn't helping. As they talked, his eyes remained glued to her naked breasts, which were hanging so enticingly between her arms. Jemma didn't dare look down his body. She was sure he was becoming erect again, and the way she felt at the moment, it would probably tip her over the edge into orgasm if she saw a tumescent cock.

Now Dominic was stroking the cream into the skin of her back. She pulled her hair forward over her shoulder to keep it out of the way while Dominic attended to her with long, soothing strokes of his hand. He worked his way down slowly from her shoulders to her waist and then, avoiding her ultra-sensitive buttocks, he went on to her thighs and the backs of her calves.

'You've missed the best bit, Dom,' Max pointed out merrily, grabbing the tube of cream and squidging a good dollop on to his hand.

He knows very well that Dominic hasn't missed my bottom, thought Jemma, amused. Dominic's just teasing, thinking avoidance of my most sensitive parts will make me become more aroused. And he's right.

Max, however, plunged straight in, rubbing her naked globes so briskly that she almost cried out in delight. Each stroke seemed to pull at her anus and her vagina, and each movement of her flesh as he rubbed the cream in drove her hot little clitoris deeper into the wildly stimulating caress of the sand.

'Turn over and I'll do your front,' he suggested, when he had finished.

'I'll fetch the wine,' said Dominic, feeling surplus to requirements for the moment.

Jemma turned over and sat up, snatching the cream off Max.

'If you keep doing that to me, Max, I'm going to come like crazy,' she pointed out, and started to anoint her own skin with the cream.

'And why not?' Max grinned rakishly.

'Why not indeed. But let's eat first. I'm famished.'

'And for afters?' prompted Max.

'We'll see,' Jemma said.

Jemma covered the front of her legs with the protective cream. Getting up on her knees, she stroked cream into her belly, over her ribcage, then took her time in thoroughly covering her breasts, arms, throat and face.

'This is torture,' Max complained.

Jemma glanced down his body as she refastened the tube. His lovely penis was up again, she noted with interest. She tossed the tube into the bag as Dominic rejoined them with the wine. Soon they had the picnic set out ready upon the rug: baguettes split and stuffed with cheese and salads; barbecued, honey-dipped chicken legs; ripe, fragrant fruit; and they were clinking their glasses of wine together, and wishing each other good health.

In companionable silence they ate and drank. Jemma dropped some salad down on to her breast and, to her surprise, Max leant over and licked it off her.

'That looks like fun,' observed Dominic, taking a mouthful of wine before leaning over, too, and taking her nipple into his mouth.

Jemma gasped in delight as she felt the alcohol tingle and titillate her budding flesh. Dominic sucked her hard, letting the wine stay in his mouth to add to the sensations she experienced.

'Let me try that,' said Max. He took a gulp of the wine, keeping it in his mouth, then took her other nipple between his lips.

Jemma looked down at the two dark heads fastened to her breasts and felt her world cartwheeling into

sensuality again. The petals between her legs unfolded
and softened as her juices began to flow. She leant back
on her hands and threw her head back to the sun's caress.

'It's more fun eating Jemma,' chuckled Max as he
drew back. 'So much more interesting than a boring
old baguette.'

'Stay like that,' Dominic said to her, and he found
a ripe pear in the bowl and peeled it, and sliced it in
half. Reaching down between her legs, he slotted the
pear into her dewy slit so that its widest part was held
by the muscles over her vagina, and the stem tickled
her clitoris. It felt warm and sticky there, and not
unpleasant.

Dominic then knelt between her thighs and pushed
them apart, grasping them firmly in his hands. His head
dipped and she felt his mouth moving against her outer
lips; felt the scratch of his chin against the much softer
and ravishingly sensitive skin around her anus.

Dominic drew back with a mouthful of ripe pear,
swallowed, and then vanished again between her legs.
Jemma lay back on the sand, enjoying the harsh touch
of his beard and tongue, relishing the pear's dripping
wetness that almost seemed a part of her own juicy
secretions.

'God, that's sexy,' murmured Max, watching him
feed on her. His eyes met Jemma's. 'Look at what it's
doing to me, watching the pair of you.'

Jemma looked down his body and saw that his penis
was almost painfully erect, pushing hard up against
his belly.

'Poor Max,' sighed Jemma, her own bliss making her more sympathetic of his obvious discomfort.

She looked down her body at Dominic's dark head, buried deep between her legs. As he finished feasting on the pear, he began to devour her willing flesh instead. His tongue was lapping lazily over her erect bud now, and his chin's friction against her eager opening was becoming a delicious torture.

'What do you mean, look at what it's doing to you?' Dominic asked Max blithely, lifting his head for a moment. 'Look what it's doing to me.'

He indicated the mighty bulge trapped beneath his brief black swimming trunks. The pink tip of his cock was questing at the waistband, trying to peep over, trying to join in the fun.

'Take the trunks off, then,' said Jemma, panting a little from the emotions he had stirred up in her with his feasting. 'That'll feel better.'

Jemma watched avidly as Dominic did as she suggested, pushing the trunks down and kicking them off so that his penis swayed like a metronome against his belly. Then he knelt up between her wide-open thighs.

'It does feel better,' he admitted. He looked down between her spreadeagled legs. 'But too tempting, in this position.'

'If you can't stand the heat, change places,' suggested Max in some discomfort.

'Poor Max,' cooed Jemma sympathetically.

She reached down and enclosed his penis in her hand. It seemed the kindest thing to do. Max groaned and pushed his hips toward her, encouraging her to caress him more firmly. Tightening her grip on the hot shaft, she began to pump it energetically.

Dominic gave a muttered curse, overcome by watching this stimulating loveplay. Nudging Jemma's thighs wider with his own, he pushed the turgid head of his cock down between her legs and found the opening he sought, thrusting in with extreme eagerness and little finesse.

But Jemma was ready for him; more than ready.

They formed a perfect triangle: Dominic busily pushing between her thighs, Jemma receiving his attentions with delight while she brought relief to Max with her hand.

She was doubly stimulated and pleased by the fact that Dominic was no longer bothering to hide the sexual nature of their relationship from Max. It all seemed so open here, with the three of them, and it felt indescribably relaxed, being away from the haste and tumult of the real world.

Max was pumping madly now against the pressure of Jemma's hand. In delicious excitement she watched the gleaming head of his penis appear over the edge of her fist and then retreat, and then reappear, in a frenzied series of thrusts. Such bliss could not be long continued and, suddenly, Max shouted his pleasure as his seed spurted from his cock like cannon-fire, arcing away into the sand.

Dominic saw his friend's tribute being delivered and quickened his own pace, too aroused by this three-way sex game to do otherwise. Raptly he watched the bounce and judder of Jemma's breasts, and the quivering of the muscles under the silky skin of her stomach, as he pushed relentlessly into her.

Her head was thrown back, her arms akimbo, her hands clawing at the sand now in the frenzy of her lust for him. Arching her back, Jemma thrust down furiously on to his big, eagerly pumping member, feeling his balls banging against her flesh as he skewered her up to the hilt again and again.

Dominic, panting hotly now, reached down and placed the heel of his hand over her yearning clitoris, pushing gently but firmly, resting his palm most stimulatingly over her pubis and spreading his fingers over her fluttering belly.

Max watched Dominic, who was as magnificent as a mating stallion in this wild elemental dance of sex, his muscles rippling and straining, his head thrown back in ecstasy, eyes closed, every atom concentrated into the needy shaft between his legs, as he took his pleasure inside Jemma.

When he came, he roared his delight to the wide blue sky above them, then slowly his pumping subsided and, gasping for breath, he grew still. Jemma moved restlessly, seeking her own pleasure. Dominic exchanged a glance with Max, and looked fondly down at Max's cock, which had rapidly reasserted itself while he watched their joining.

Withdrawing smoothly from Jemma, Dominic changed places with Max and, as Jemma watched in a daze of joy, Max entered her with a huge thrust. His cock felt shorter than Dominic's, but it was sturdy and thick, very pleasing as it started to move inside her.

Watching the happy pair, Dominic found one of the chicken legs on the picnic rug and smeared the grease from it liberally on to his cock, which was rising again as he watched Max covering Jemma. Moving behind Max, he watched the hearty pumping of his robust buttocks. Reaching out, he spread them a little with his greasy fingers and saw what he was searching for immediately.

Max's anus was winking saucily at him, contracting and expanding in pleasure as his phallus was warmly clenched in the tight grip of Jemma's vagina. Max glanced back with a grin, knowing what was planned for him, but he did not stop his thrusting; he was so aroused that he couldn't.

Dominic's admiring eyes rested on the heavily shadowed balls that bounced so engagingly between Max's legs with each push of his sturdy cock. Then, making sure that he was well lubricated so as to cause his friend no discomfort, he gently nudged the head of his cock into the inviting little hole that beckoned to him. Max's sphincter tightened rapturously for one moment around his glans, inhibiting further progress, but then, as Max paused in his thrusting and relaxed, Dominic was able to gain full entry.

He sighed his pleasure as he began to move inside his friend, who returned to the serious business of pleasuring Jemma. They were a perfect threesome, completely joined and interacting beautifully, each of them reaching dizzily for the heights of pleasure.

Jemma came first, stimulated beyond bearing by Max's heavy thrusting, and then Max succeeded in reaching his own final goal, falling across her with a hoarse cry as he was pleasured from both sides. Finally, Dominic, pumping vigorously into Max now, let out a triumphant groan as he too came really hard.

They fell upon the sand and lay for long moments, the three friends, legs and arms and torsos all linked together. Sweat dried on their lean, damp bodies. And then, inevitably, because the sun had gone behind a cloud and a brisk breeze was now whisking in off the water, Jemma began to feel cold.

'Let's play beachball,' she suggested, disentangling herself.

Max and Dominic willingly fell in with this plan to warm up. Jemma bounced to her feet and hauled the ball out of the bag, blowing it up with mighty puffs. Then she put the stopper in and tossed it to the recumbent Max.

'Come on, Max, no slouching,' she laughed, and he jumped up, hauling Dominic after him.

They ran and played and kicked the ball back and forth along the beach like carefree children while the wind constantly seized it and threatened to drag it out to sea. Running into the surf to retrieve it, Jemma tripped and came up drenched and laughing, her breasts gleaming wet and bobbing invitingly as she ran back up the beach.

Seeing both men were growing erect again at this

stirring sight, she knelt down in the sand and cheerfully tongued Max's quiveringly upright cock while caressing Dominic's penis with her hand. But these enjoyable games were soon abandoned, because now they felt hard spatters of rain beginning to fall, and the breeze had turned chilly.

'We can continue this back on the boat,' Jemma assured them both, with a wink at Max.

Grumbling but agreeable, the two men packed up the hamper. Jemma gathered up their wet bathing clothes, smiling to see that neither of them lost their erections as they walked with her back down to the dinghy. Max shoved the little craft away from the shore while Dominic picked up the oars and started rowing strongly. Max jumped in beside Jemma, cuddling her close to warm her up. Her nipples were standing out with the cold, and solicitously Max rubbed his hands over them to generate a little heat.

His touch generated quite the wrong kind of heat, though, thought Jemma. She was suddenly anxious to get back aboard the boat so that Max could continue his caresses in a snug cabin under a cosy duvet.

But when they boarded the *Annalise*, the crew met them with shouts and waves. Something was wrong. As they gained the deck, shivering, young Mark dashed forward thoughtfully with three thick towelling robes, and gratefully they slipped them on. His eyes dwelt hungrily on Jemma's naked breasts and thighs before she vanished beneath her robe, pulling it close around her. He was holding an envelope, she saw.

'What's this?' asked Max, reaching for it.

'From Mrs Klein,' said Mark as the other members of the crew stood around in silent gloom. 'She said to give it to you immediately you came back on board. She left, sir. Took a suitcase of clothes and her jewels, and went. She had Tony take her into Nice on the launch, sir.'

Max looked at the envelope as if it might bite him. He looked up at Jemma and Dominic. 'Come on, both of you. Let's go down to my stateroom and get warmed up, and I'll see what Annalise has to say down there. Mark, bring us some hot coffee, will you?'

'Yes, sir,' said Mark, and Jemma gave him a smile that brought a blush to his cheeks.

She squeezed the cheek of his bottom as she passed by, then followed Max and Dominic below. As soon as they were in Max's big red and gold stateroom, Max opened the envelope and unfolded the note inside. He read it, and went pale beneath his tan. He passed it to Dominic, who scanned it swiftly.

'Has she left you?' asked Jemma gently. 'Oh Max –'

Max shook his head vehemently. 'It's worse than that. Dominic!' he cried desperately as Dominic brushed past him, heading for his own cabin.

'She's taken the films,' said Max dazedly. 'And she's collected the rest of Dominic's work from the laboratory in Nice. She's destroyed all the work he's done with you; every last bit of it.'

Dominic came back in, breathing hard with rage. 'She's taken the film out of the camera. Max, I'll phone the lab. Perhaps she hasn't reached there yet.'

'You can try,' said Max morosely, and Dominic hared off again. 'I knew she was jealous of your relationship with Dominic, but this is utter lunacy. Really, she's gone too far. The exhibition. What will happen about the exhibition?'

Jemma could say nothing to comfort him. They waited in silence until Dominic returned, his face stricken.

'They said Mrs Klein collected all the work – all of it – half an hour ago,' he told them, sinking down on to the bed. 'Annalise has collected work for me before, so they had no reason to suspect anything was wrong. You've collected stuff for me too, haven't you, Max? They know both of you. They trust you. Why shouldn't they? And now all the work Jemma and I have done together, it's gone. Destroyed. We all know that Annalise doesn't make empty threats.'

Jemma thought of Annalise's constant warnings to her. Keep clear of Dominic, or there'll be repercussions. And Jemma had blithely called her bluff, not once but several times. She had played to beat Annalise, but, in the end, Annalise had won.

Or had she?

'My boy, I'm so sorry,' said Max, feeling miserably responsible for his wife's misdemeanour.

'Where will she go?' asked Jemma when Dominic was silent.

Max heaved a sigh. 'Probably to our flat in Paris. Look, I'd better get packed up and go after her. Do you mind? Of course you can stay on board as long as you like. That goes without saying.'

'Of course we don't mind, Max. You go ahead.' Jemma went to the door. 'Come on, Dominic,' she said to the shattered man sitting on the bed. 'We'd better go to your room.'

Dominic looked up at Jemma, his green eyes tragic. 'It's all destroyed,' he said numbly.

'Well, the work we've already done is,' corrected Jemma, feeling her spirits lighten inexplicably as she went to the bed, took his arm, and escorted him to the door.

''Bye, Max,' she said, looking back at him with real affection. 'I hope it goes all right.'

Max nodded, and since there was nothing more any of them could say, she closed the door upon his unhappy face and led Dominic along the corridor to his own room.

Later, when they had each taken a soberly separate shower and put on warmer clothes, they sat in the enclosed lounge at deck level and looked out at the rain running down the panes of the big sliding glass doors while drinking comforting cups of strong black coffee. Max had gone. The crew were on the flybridge. They were alone.

Dominic looked across at Jemma, wondering at her apparent imperturbability. She looked not a bit upset. In fact, her lack of concern over this disastrous development filled him with what he knew was an unreasonable rage. Didn't she care that his work, his priceless work, was destroyed? Wasn't she supposed to be his muse, his inspiration, the person closest to him in the entire damned world?

Brimming with tense, miserable energy he stood up, hooked his thumbs aggressively into the waistband of his jeans, and glared down at her.

'Listen, doesn't any of this affect you?' he demanded in irritation, sweeping a hand through his thick dark hair. 'All our work's wasted, or haven't you noticed that yet?'

Jemma stared up at him coolly, and raised an eyebrow, but her coolness was faked. She was thinking how magnificent he looked in the heat of his anger, green eyes flashing, every muscle clearly delineated with the tension of the moment. He wore only a thin V-necked black sweater and sand-coloured desert boots with his jeans, and she thought that never had she found him quite so desirable, quite so lusciously tempting, as she did now. She felt quite wet, looking at him towering so threateningly over her.

'I've noticed,' she said calmly, 'that Annalise has given up trying to dominate you.'

Dominic sat back down with a thump.

'I've also noticed something else,' she added, putting her empty cup on to the side table.

She sank back cosily into the deep leather couch which was the exact colour of the richest Cornish cream. In fact, she looked like a cat that had got the cream, thought Dominic in grudging admiration. But she was right. Annalise had retreated.

'Well?' he asked gruffly.

'You've made love to me – your muse – and contrary to everything Annalise has tried to make you believe in the past, our lovemaking hasn't had any sort of adverse effect on your talents. Quite the reverse, I'd say.'

Dominic thought about that.

'All right, I'll concede that point,' he shrugged, then stabbed a finger at her. 'But the work's gone, Jemma. All gone. And the exhibition's very soon.'

'Then we shall have to work very hard together,' said Jemma.

'What?'

'To make it up. To rebuild the body of work, and meet the deadline for the exhibition.' Jemma stood up, and settled herself down beside Dominic. 'Celestine will help,' she assured him. 'So will Armand.'

Dominic mulled all this over for a moment, then leant back, visibly relaxing, linking his hands behind his head as he gazed at her.

'Do you think I need a new agent? I like Max very much, but Annalise . . .'

'Some distance between you seems like a very good idea,' said Jemma cautiously. 'But it would be a shame to lose Max.'

'I think they'll probably divorce, anyway,' said Dominic with a sigh.

'Then that would solve the problem.' Jemma placed a caressing hand on his thigh. 'No more Annalise.'

Dominic looked down at her hand, then up at her face. 'I feel like a weight's been lifted from my shoulders.

And you did it; you lifted it from me. I was trapped, and you set me free.'

'We can start rebuilding the collection from the centrepiece down,' said Jemma, growing excited at the thought of the work they had to do. She stroked upward along his thigh until her hand rested lightly over the bulge of his sex. 'We could start right now, down in your cabin, with that clever delayed-action device you have on your camera. Those shots we did together on the chaise longue must have been very good, don't you think? Well, let's reshoot them.'

Dominic placed a warm enfolding hand over her hand and pressed down, lifting his hips a little, relishing the contact. 'You'll stay on, then?' he asked.

'For as long as it takes,' Jemma said happily. London, Steven, everything else could go hang. She had been dreading going back to all that, anyway. This was where she wanted to be, beneath the hot Mediterranean sun, working and loving with Dominic.

Dominic grinned and stood up, pulling her up with him. Running his hand possessively down her flank, he kissed her lips lightly. Suddenly the kiss deepened. Their tongues met, caressing and playing. Dominic's hand snaked beneath her shirt and squeezed her naked breast lustfully.

'I'll put the film in,' he murmured against her mouth, 'while you're getting undressed.'

As they went below, Jemma could not resist asking the question that had been intriguing her for some time. 'What are you actually going to call this collection when it's finished, Dominic?' she said as she followed him along the corridor leading to the sleeping accommodation.

Dominic paused outside the door to his cabin and gave her a rakish grin. 'I'm going to call it *A Private View*,' he told her, and ushered her inside so they could start work.